# THE FALLEN CHILDREN

## DAVID OWEN

ATOM

First published in Great Britain in 2017 by Atom

1 3 5 7 9 10 8 6 4 2

A CIP catalogue record for this book is
available from the British Library.

ISBN 978-0-349-00269-9

Printed and bound in Great Britain by Clays Ltd, St Ives plc

Papers used by Atom are from well-managed forests
and other responsible sources.

Atom
An imprint of
Little, Brown Book Group
Carmelite House
50 Victoria Embankment
London EC4Y 0DZ

An Hachette UK Company
www.hachette.co.uk

www.atombooks.co.uk

*For Mum*

# Foreword

*The Fallen Children* owes a tremendous debt to John Wyndham's essential 1957 novel *The Midwich Cuckoos*. As an eleven-year-old I saw the (quite terrible) 1995 film adaptation *Village of the Damned*, fell in love with it, and sought out the book. Its central idea stayed with me, and when I reread it as an adult I realised that, despite being in many ways decidedly old-fashioned, it held the seed of a story fiercely relevant to young people today.

Young people are not properly nurtured in the UK. The bar for entry to education and training has been raised out of reach for many; English universities charge the highest tuition fees in the developed world,[1] and student grants have been replaced with loans.[2] Those who do make it face a scarcity of opportunity; youth unemployment is the worst it's been for twenty years[3]

---

1 see http://www.telegraph.co.uk/education/universityeducation/ 12013303/University-students-in-England-pay-the-highest-tuition-fees-in-the-world.html

2 see http://www.bbc.co.uk/news/education-36940172

3 see https://www.theguardian.com/society/2015/feb/22/youth-unemployment-jobless-figure

and access to benefits is increasingly restricted. The UK faces a youth mental health crisis; a third of teenage girls in England suffer with depression and anxiety, and more young people than ever don't believe they control their destiny.[4]

It has not been this hard for young people to make their way in the world for generations, and yet they are saddled with the blame, widely written off as lazy, entitled, and self-obsessed; the so-called 'selfie-generation'.

It really sucks.

*The Fallen Children* reflects this by borrowing the core concept of *The Midwich Cuckoos* and inflicting it upon contemporary teenagers. These young people face impossible circumstances outside of their control and fight them regardless, even as the world around them assumes the worst and does everything it can to drag them down.

That's the amazing thing about young people; even when so many have given up on them, they will never give up on themselves.

It will be hard, and they will make mistakes, and sometimes they will want to give up – nobody gets an easy ride in *The Fallen Children*. I hope this story – of children with unlimited potential and their struggle to find a place in the world – shows that the world must believe in young people, as they are the key to a better, kinder future.

David Owen, August 2016

---

4 see https://www.theguardian.com/society/2016/aug/22/third-teenage-girls-depression-anxiety-survey-trend-truant

# THE
# FALLEN
# CHILDREN

# A Livestream

The screen is divided into three boxes: a video game, a chat room, and a livestream of a girl in her bedroom. She is sitting on the bed, hunched forward over the desk, a video game poster tacked on the wall behind her.

There is no warning before the girl folds into a slump. Just a crackle of static – like a ghost yearning to speak – and she's asleep.

Her virtual adversaries make the most of the unexpected lull.

Game Over. KillerKeisha has fallen in battle.

Messages of confusion and annoyance fill the chat room. One-by-one her spectators exit the game.

Text continues to crawl across the bottom of the screen.

Playing my way to uni! Click the button to donate.

A menu pops up in-game. Two options: *Respawn* or *Quit*.

The livestream image flickers. Then the sound of her bedroom door opening, creaking shyly wide: the girl has company.

She does not stir.

The bed covers shift. They are being tugged toward the foot of the bed, dragging the girl beyond the webcam's field of vision.

*Tug.* A careless gesture offers the briefest glimpse of the intruder.

*Tug.* Fingers, long and gnarled.

*Tug.* Grabbing at her thighs.

A low, resonant hum rises inside the speakers. After a moment only the side of the girl's face remains in view. The sound fuzzes, fizzles. Dies.

The girl in the screen does not wake.

# PART ONE

# PART ONE

# Chapter One

**Morris**

It's a weird feeling, literally running for your life.

Their footsteps behind me boom off the walls of the grubby brick houses that line the road. Closer every second.

Months sitting around indoors has not done great things for my cardio. The cold rakes at my lungs as I heave another desperate breath and a stitch bites at my side, but I force myself to ignore it all and keep running. My best hope of cheating death is knowing the estate better than my three pursuers. This is the last place I want to die. So much blood has been spilled on these streets already that no one would notice a few pints more.

I kick off the kerb and leap through a narrow gap in the bushes at the edge of the industrial park. I used to head this way after school to meet Keisha for a smoke and some make-out time. Before she put an end to all that.

The road is slick with rain. My battered old trainers struggle for grip. I risk a glance back just in time to see them burst through the bushes. There are two smaller guys I don't recognise, but I know the guy leading them all too well. Me and Tyrone used to be mates – or I thought we were – until he changed from friend to thug; as soon as he realised he could flick my head off my shoulders with his little finger, we were finished.

I slide between a parked car and a skip piled high with bricks. Being small has its downside – see above – but it also has advantages sometimes. A layer of fog has settled and the air feels thick and heavy. Reflected streetlights bleed through to the tarmac, which glows eerily underfoot. It's late, the streets as empty as always at this time, especially on a Sunday full of rain.

A row of squat council houses hides a sharp corner. I skid around it and Midwich Tower looms into view. In the hazy air it looks like a stack of dull light bulbs teetering into the sky.

The problem is, I've forgotten my key. *Again.* I'll have to press the entry buzzer and pray. Mum left for work ages ago so there's no point ringing our flat, but Keisha might still be awake. They're gaining on me. No choice but to try. I whip my phone out my back pocket and call her as I run.

No answer.

I'd avoided Tyrone successfully for weeks, not going out at night, ignoring text messages and calls, but tonight I caved. I just had to get out of the tower.

It's sod's law that I practically walked right into him.

It all kicked off.

I should have guessed this would happen. Three grand borrowed from Tyrone. Drug money, every penny, but I tried not to think about that. I'd hoped the loan might make something of me – hoped I could spin it into profit. It turns out that being fresh out of school with no exams and crashing out of an apprenticeship isn't the best way to make your fortune.

All it's going to make me at this rate is dead.

I round a corner into the car park and the shadow of the tower. I cut close to the low perimeter fence and vault over into a scrubby back garden, tripping over kids' toys before I reach the next fence. I land in the bin enclosure just as I hear them reach the corner.

The stink of the bins lingers on the air and I hold my breath against it. The tower-side gate into my enclosure is shut, so they won't see me if they don't come looking. I push myself into a narrow space between the big wheelie bins. The freezing metal feels like it scorches my skin.

Straight away the footsteps slow down. A lifetime of nights hanging out here means I know the car park better than anywhere else in the world. Which is a bit sad, really. There's the crappiest collection of cars ever, some of which haven't moved for years, as well as a fresh pile of fly-tipped junk around the already balding tree. A lot of places for someone to hide. They don't know it like I do, and now they're not so confident.

'You see him?' says one voice.

'Nah,' says Tyrone. 'Watch yourselves.'

They move across the car park like police combing a crime scene. I listen to the scrape of their feet. The metal bins make me shiver. Yeah, all right, I'm shaking. Something doesn't feel right, and it's not just the guys sniffing me out for a beating.

It's *too* quiet. There's usually sirens or a plane roaring

11

over or some waster with their TV cranked up too loud. The only thing I hear now is a sort of low-level hum, barely loud enough to break through the *thud-thud-thud* of my heart in my ears.

'Morris!' shouts Tyrone. 'Come out, come out!'

My heart shudders like a goldfish shaken in its bowl. I tense my legs, ready to spring over the fence. I know all the best routes of escape.

'Remember what I said,' he says. 'There are other ways to pay up, Mo.'

That's how it starts. A favour. Then it becomes a regular phone call. I'd be working for him before I knew it.

I can't go down that road. Not yet.

Their footsteps move away from me towards the tower. There's a gap in the enclosure fence just wide enough for me to see through. The small playing green, grass sodden and slippery, lies between me and the tower entrance. A single orange light suspended over the heavy door lights up a dirty metal plaque engraved with the words: *Midwich Tower*.

Home, sweet home.

Me and Keisha used to play a game. We would go up to the roof of the block and imagine what we'd buy for our friends and family if we won the lottery. It made me feel good, that generosity, even if it was just imaginary. That was the first time I noticed Keisha was changing. Instead of saying she'd buy her dad a Beamer and her mum a personal shopping day at Westfield, she said she'd just buy the tower and blow it into gravel.

I can see my bedroom window, as blank as all the

others at this time of night. I glance higher to Siobhan's window, hoping she might still be awake. It's dark. She'll be snoring like a warthog in a gas mask by now. The only lights are in the corridors, and even those look dimmer than usual, like they've been smothered.

'What was that?' says one of the guys as they walk into my narrow field of vision. They've rounded the peeling red railings that separate the grass from the path. The smaller guys are staring up at the tower.

'You think he climbed away?' says Tyrone, and kisses his teeth.

When I was a kid I used to be able to climb up the side of the block like a spider, though I was always too scared to go higher than the third floor. It was supposed to impress Keisha. Maybe it did, for a little while.

'Swear down, I saw something up there.'

Tyrone ignores him and glances around like I might jump him any second. Like that would be a good idea.

If I stay here long enough they'll go away. It won't get me off the hook for long, but it's enough for now. It gives me one more chance to try and sort everything out. I'm going to start by always remembering my bloody key.

Tyrone creeps towards the door. It'll only open if they tap an electronic fob or if someone buzzes them inside. Luckily most of the locals are too paranoid to let strangers in the building this late.

He curses in frustration as he walks for the locked door. 'Forget this. We'll get him when—'

He collapses on the spot before he can finish the threat.

The other two shrink back like he's been hit by a sniper's bullet. Tyrone lies completely still, the side of his face against the pavement like he's listening for vibrations. The other two overcome their shock and run forwards. As soon as they reach him their legs switch off and they hit the ground too.

## Keisha

I don't remember falling asleep. I don't even remember feeling tired.

The first thing I register is a damp patch against my cheek where my dribble has soaked into the bed sheets. My headphones are still plugged in, but the wires are tight around my neck. I sit up straight to slacken the noose and a sharp pain pierces my stomach, making me wince.

Then I notice the desktop screen and realise the stream is still live, beaming my face onto the internet.

To add insult to injury, I've been kicked from the game due to inactivity.

Well, this isn't embarrassing at all.

The chat feed is revealing:

Keisha, u all right?

WAKE UP.

She's getting some black beauty sleep.

Now she's dead . . . in the game I mean.

After that the comments slowly degenerated into abuse, only some of it racist, before even the haters got bored and the chat emptied out. The timestamp on what must have been the first comment after I fell asleep was twenty minutes ago. How is it gone midnight?

'Sorry, everyone,' I mutter, as if there's anyone left to listen.

I exit the game and shut off the webcam.

I've never fallen asleep during a livestream before. It can't be good for viewer numbers. Usually I'm too busy owning fools to even think about napping but now it feels like a cat is scrambling to climb up behind my eyes. There's no reason I should be this groggy.

Something else doesn't feel right, something I hadn't noticed before, something that slowly creeps up on me now. I woke up at the bottom of the bed, where the covers are scrunched into a ball. The door is ajar . . . My revision notes are strewn across the floor . . . My cup of water has been spilled . . .

*Someone was in here while I was sleeping.*

The notification light blinks on my phone. I swipe the screen awake and find a missed call from Morris, about five minutes ago. Like I want to deal with him right now. Thank god it didn't wake me up.

I'm clearing up the mess when a noise in the living room makes me jump.

'Mum?'

I open my door, peer out before crossing the hallway. A table lamp's been knocked onto the floor. It's rocking rhythmically back and forth, throwing shadows across the walls. Mum's lying on her side on the sofa, her head lolling back against the cushions and her mouth open like she's trying to catch something. It's pretty common for her to fall asleep in front of her programmes. But this time the TV screen is blank except for the short message: *You are not currently receiving any signal.* She usually

15

wakes up the second the TV's switched off – it's the only way Dad can get her to bed.

'Mum,' I say again, gently taking her hand.

I look around the sitting room and through to the kitchen. There's no sign of Dad. I squeeze her hand but she doesn't even stir.

'Come on,' I say, shaking her shoulder, panic rising in my chest.

The unsteady light makes it difficult to see her face clearly. I have to lean in close to see that her chest is rising and sinking. Air whines from her nose every time she breathes out. At least the excitement of her late shows hasn't finally killed her. But that doesn't explain why she won't wake up. A tendril of dread reaches down my throat into my stomach and makes me feel like a little kid.

'What's going on?' I say.

Without warning a voice booms from the TV behind me, making me jump. The signal is back.

*'They mostly come at night. Mostly.'*

*Christ!* Mum always has it way too loud, no matter how many times the neighbours complain. She's not even old. It started when she cranked it up to block out the arguments from upstairs, and it just ended up staying that way. I find the remote and switch it off.

That's when I notice the sound outside the front door. A throaty purr, almost electronic. I hurry across to make sure it's locked. It's not. In fact, it's open. Only a crack, but in Midwich Tower anyone with half a brain keeps their front door locked at night.

I put my eye to the peephole. The fisheye view shows

the grey corridor is empty, the orange bulb overhead glowing less brightly than normal. It must be on its way out. It'll take them months to replace it.

I pull the door wider and peer into the hallway. It's freezing out there and quieter than usual. I wrap my arms around myself.

The noise starts again. A purr that vibrates along the hallway from the stairwell and then grows distant, as if it's moving up the building. Gritting my teeth against the pain in my stomach, I follow it up the cold concrete steps.

On the seventh floor, one floor up, someone lurches into my path and we collide. Automatically my hands come up to fight, but then I see it's just Maida, the girl who lives in the flat above me. She's barefoot and trembling in baby blue pyjamas.

'You heard it too?' she says.

I nod. 'I couldn't wake up my mum.' It surprises me how much I sound like a frightened child.

'My whole family,' says Maida.

She lives with her parents and shares a room with a younger brother. She's a year younger than me. If I even look at her in the halls her dad frowns at me, like I'm going to corrupt her with a glance. They're pretty strict Muslims. She watches my livestreams. That's all I know about her.

Except now I know she's involved in whatever the hell is going on here.

'There's blood on you,' I say, noticing a spatter of red marking the inside leg of her pyjama bottoms, already hardening into a dark crust.

17

She points back at me. 'You too.'

I look down at my jeans. My crotch is spotted with blood. I press my fingers to it. There isn't any pain, but my fingertips come away startling and wet with too-bright red.

## Morris

Silence settles, disturbed only by that low hum. I stare through the fence at their bodies. A breath of wind ruffles their clothes but they don't move an inch. I stay crouched between the bins. It could be a trap. A really weird trap.

When I can't bear it any longer and my knees start quivering with cold I get up and push open the gate. It creaks with rust. All the windows in the tower are still unlit, which means no one has noticed what's going on outside. As I near the block the humming gets louder. I take another step forwards and address the heap.

'Hey,' I say quietly, then louder, 'Hey! You okay?'

In reply, one of the guys *snores*. They're asleep!

This doesn't make sense. They went from homicidal to nap time in seconds flat, with nothing in between. I step away.

Looking around, I notice something on the path just beyond the tower entrance, where it narrows between the block on one side and a long wooden fence on the other: lying flat on its stomach, chin against the pavement, is Mr Hillier's cat, its legs splayed at odd angles like it fell asleep mid-strut.

The humming swells in my ears and makes my skin tingle. I look up at the tower again and shudder.

18

If I try to reach the door, I could wind up joining the slumber party on the pavement. But if something's going on inside, Keisha needs my help.

I grab my phone and dial her number again. It rings until it switches to generic voicemail. She hates it when I leave a message so I hang up.

Another grumbling snore draws my attention back to the guys on the path. I pull my thin coat tighter around me. Then I point the phone at them and start to record.

## Keisha

Something has happened to us. I grab Maida and pull her close to me.

'Are you okay?' says Maida, like I'm crazy.

It should be me asking the question. I nod, trying not to think about the blood.

We stare hard at each other for a long moment. Then together we turn towards the stairs and begin to climb.

The purring has stopped now, but the hum that's been hanging in the background gets louder the higher we go. We climb all the way to the top. Floor thirteen. Up here it feels like there's an electric current on the air, a pulse that tingles on my skin and chases away the cold.

We shuffle side-by-side along the bare concrete corridor. The floor is damp and gritty under my feet. The air smells like wet dog. The lights aren't even strong enough for us to see the end of the corridor. It looks endlessly dark. At the far end is a hatch in the ceiling that leads out to the roof. It's supposed to be sealed but Morris bust the padlock ages ago so we could sunbathe and stuff. It's a miracle none of us ever fell over the side.

I don't know what does it – maybe the false happiness of those days with Morris, or just remembering the warmth of the sun – but something in me snaps, and all the fear and anger I've been holding back washes over me. I *have* to know what happened here; what happened to me.

I accidently kick an empty and discarded Relentless can, and it clatters along the floor. Ahead of us we hear the *thunk* of the hatch slamming shut – so there *is* someone there. I run towards it, but before I reach the hatch I trip over something in the darkness and fall flat on my face. Groping around to feel my way, I touch something warm and soft and I cry out. It's a body, sprawled across the corridor.

Maida helps me to my knees. In the dim light I see the face.

'Dad?' I push my fingers clumsily against his neck to feel for a pulse.

A small pool of blood has clogged the dust around his nose where it hit the concrete. It must be broken. Before I can find a pulse he snores loudly, the same hippo-snort that barges through my wall every night and keeps me awake. I shake him hard but it doesn't interrupt the noise.

'My dad snores like the apocalypse too,' says Maida.

I try a reassuring smile, as much for me as for her, but it comes off more like a grimace. I glance up. Dad has collapsed outside old Mr Hillier's flat. He's lived in the building longer than anyone. The block doesn't have a working lift, so he hardly goes out anymore, and nobody visits him. We have a spare key so we can bring him

20

shopping a few times a week and make sure he's okay. There's no reason Dad should be up here in the middle of the night.

A heavy clacking noise starts up overhead – it must be on the roof – and the humming intensifies alongside it. Bright white light flares in the dirty safety glass of the windows, and the orange bulbs along the corridor blaze so brightly I think they're going to burst. I pull Maida close as the floor starts to shake, making every door knocker along the hall rattle.

There's a *whoosh*, like an airlock opening; the corridor seems to drain of oxygen and for a moment I can't breathe. Then the humming stops abruptly. The white light vanishes, taking the rattling with it. Oxygen rushes back. Overhead the orange bulbs fade to their usual candle glow.

My body feels carved hollow. I can barely describe it. When I look at Maida I know she feels it too.

Abandoned.

# Chapter Two

**Keisha**

Dad jerks awake, sucking in air like he hasn't breathed for days. He lifts his face from the concrete with a moan of pain.

'You don't want to move too quickly,' I tell him.

We help him to his feet. He winces as he dabs at his nose. 'What the hell happened?'

I look at Maida and she shrugs. There's too much to explain, too much I don't understand . . . All I know for sure is fear.

Dad draws us away towards the stairs. 'I must have tripped or something. You okay, love?' he says to me as we start down. I nod and he turns to Maida. 'Does your dad know you're out at . . . what time is it, anyway?'

Maida looks sheepish. 'If he'd been awake he wouldn't have been too happy about it.'

'Maybe we'll keep it between us, eh?'

It doesn't work out that way.

As soon as we reach the seventh floor her dad appears in the stairwell entrance sporting a frown and some serious bed head. A white vest clings tightly to the boulder of his stomach.

'What are you doing out here?' he hisses at Maida.

He's fuming, of course. No surprise there; we've heard through the ceiling how he bellows at his daughter for the slightest thing.

'It's my fault,' says Dad, before Maida can speak. 'I had an accident and she came to help.'

It's hardly a fool-proof explanation, but going by the state of Dad's bloodied nose alone it's plausible. We all wait for Mr Masood's reaction. His eyes fix me with a warning, and he ushers Maida away towards their flat without another word.

'Close one,' says Dad.

We head back down to the flat, Dad mumbling about his nose, but I barely hear him. I'm replaying the evening, still trying to piece it together. The strangeness of finding Mum, then Maida, then Dad. The blood on my jeans. The fact that someone was in my room.

When we get back, the front door's still hanging open like I'd left it, and inside Mum is on the sofa watching the end of a movie as if nothing out of the ordinary has happened. When she sees the state of Dad she shrieks and makes such a fuss it's like he's returning home from war or something. Above us, we can hear Maida's dad shouting his disapproval at his miserable daughter. That's the last thing she needs, and I want to go up there and tell him so. I stop myself at the door, knowing that I wouldn't know what to say to make any of this better. I wait to hear Maida's voice, silently plead for her to fight back, to do what I can't. Mr Masood doesn't give her a chance.

I'm just about to shut the door when I hear a familiar voice call from down the corridor.

'Wait up!'

## Morris

She tries to shut the door in my face – like I'm a debt collector or something – but I'm fast enough to jam my foot against the frame. Yeah, I'd risk my toes for this girl.

'Your mum buzzed me in,' I say, breathing hard. 'Just give me a minute, yeah?'

She steps into the corridor and pulls the door to behind her. I can tell she's rattled. Usually she looks at me with disgust – disgust I know I don't deserve – but now she's pale and distracted.

'I'm really not in the mood for another row,' she says.

'This isn't about me and you,' I say.

She moves her hands to cover the top of her jeans, but not before I see a stain there. I probably shouldn't be looking, but I swear it's blood. I can't ignore that.

'You okay?'

'It's not your job to worry about me.'

'I do, though. And something really weird is going on.'

'Yeah,' she says, and she glances down at her jeans. 'I noticed.'

# Chapter Three

**Siobhan**

The supply teacher keeps us at arm's length on the way to the front office, like she thinks we might chuck up on her or something.

'I'm going to be sick *all over* the floor, miss,' I say, just to watch her squirm.

Keisha rolls her eyes so hard I can practically hear them. When Keish put her hand up to say she was feeling sick, the whole class stared at her like she'd started singing the YMCA in Swahili (these days she's teacher's pet – the one nobody likes); when *my* hand went up, they all just laughed (my reputation as a chancer hasn't wavered). Only this time, I'm not faking.

Unsurprisingly, the supply teacher couldn't care less.

Somebody is already parked on the sick bench in the reception area. It's Maida, that Pakistani girl from the block, holding her stomach like it's trying to escape.

'You feel sick too?' Keisha asks.

Maida nods. 'But it's worth it to get out of maths.'

I snort-laugh. 'I'd high five you,' I say, 'but I might spew.'

Miss leaves us without a word. She's already been gone too long. Her classroom is probably on fire by now.

I drop onto the wooden bench. There's nothing like a hard seat to remind you how much your arse and thighs have spread. Keisha stares reluctantly at the tiny space that isn't being taken up by my body fat. I'm basically a disease to her these days. While she weighs up her options, I remind myself not to care what she thinks.

I take out my phone and check my eyeliner flicks in the camera. I tried getting it just like the video showed. My eyes look a bit wonky, but it's not too bad.

'You both deserve to feel sick,' I say, adjusting my fringe. 'Neither of you liked my cupcake business on Facebook yet.'

'Are your cupcakes Halal?' says Maida.

'I do chocolate and strawberry swirl.'

She hisses through her teeth. 'I'm afraid your cupcakes are against my religion.'

She catches Keisha's eye, and I see them both fight off a smile. Right, so they're laughing at me. Classy bitches.

Whatevs.

'What's your excuse, Keish?' I look her straight in the eye because I know it makes her uncomfortable.

'I don't think we're friends on Facebook.'

'Oh,' I say, smiling tightly. 'That's right.'

She can pretend all she likes but I know she gives a shit. I *know* she feels guilty for ending our friendship, cutting me off like I meant nothing to her.

Keisha finally sits down, but talks across me like I'm not even there. 'You okay after last night?'

Maida sighs. 'I didn't get much sleep.'

'Your dad seemed pretty pissed off.'

I only know two things about Maida:

1. Her dad always seems pretty pissed off.
2. When she smiles it looks strained, like she's a lot older than her age.

To be honest, I've never been bothered to get to know her.

'All he cares about is getting me into medical school. He'd go mental if he knew I was missing maths right now,' she shrugs. 'Far as I'm concerned that's the one upside to feeling this rubbish. I couldn't give a toss about maths, or medicine.'

'What's wrong with wanting to be a doctor?' Keisha says.

'Nothing. Not for you, anyway. You'll kick the crap out of your exams; the rest of us are just hoping we can scrape through.'

Keisha opens her mouth to argue but Maida doesn't give her the chance.

'Anyway, this doctor thing is my dad's dream, not mine,' she says. 'I don't want to deal with all that blood.'

Their eyes meet for a second, like they know something I don't, before they both look at their laps.

'If I was smart enough to be a doctor I wouldn't think twice,' I say.

School's never been my thing. If I had a choice between school and a crappy job, I'd take the job. At least then I could save. But getting a job is easier said than done –

there was a web design apprenticeship I wanted, but I couldn't get a place.

Maida's lip twitches. 'I don't know. With my surname people expect doctor, IT helpdesk, or corner shop owner. Anything else and my CV goes right to the bottom of the pile. I always hoped I'd discover I have some kind of amazing natural talent, you know, like playing the piano or plate-spinning or something. But it's looking more and more like I was born nothing special.'

'Shut up,' I say. 'None of us can expect that stuff to just *happen*, as if life owes us; but we're all born with *something*. Believing in yourself is what counts.'

Keisha rolls her eyes again. Of course *she* doesn't get it. She's the one who made me realise the only person I can really trust is myself.

'What does your dad do that's so great, anyway?' I ask.

Maida smiles wryly. 'IT helpdesk.'

The receptionist emerges from the office with a clip-board wedged against her gut. She looks at us through glasses slung low on her nose.

'All of you feeling unwell?' she says.

We nod like synchronised swimmers.

The secretary makes a note on her clipboard. 'What's wrong with you?'

'Stomach ache,' we all say at once.

She hoists a roughly plucked eyebrow, then works her way down the page.

'Okay, any unusual food eaten recently? Any allergies?'

'I'm allergic to this interrogation,' I say.

Maida's the only one who laughs.

28

The secretary ignores me. 'Any undisclosed medication? Any bleeding?'

My stomach does a back flip. I'd almost forgotten. 'I—' I begin, stopping when I sense both Keisha and Maida stiffen beside me.

The secretary looks at me over her glasses.

'I, uh . . . noticed you haven't liked my cupcake business yet, miss.'

'No,' she says, slashing a biro across the clipboard. 'And I've told you before not to add me on Facebook. You three stay here until you feel well enough to go back to your lessons.'

She slouches back into the office and shuts the door.

A wave of nausea washes over me. Bile rises in my throat. Keisha watches like she's trying to decide if I'm faking it or not.

'I woke up with blood on me last night. I just thought I was early or something,' I say. 'Why did you two act like you're hiding stigmata or something?'

Keisha and Maida exchange an uncertain look. It makes me want to smack them both.

'Did you notice anything strange in the block last night?' Keisha says.

'Strange like what?'

She takes out her phone and goes into her videos. 'Morris sent me this.'

I palm the screen away. 'I don't wanna see no video Mo's sending you late at night.'

Keisha almost laughs. Almost. 'He knows what would happen if he even tried.'

She holds the phone so we can all see the screen.

The video is dark and blurry, with streaks of orange streetlight trailing across the picture. The block is on the right, the playing green opposite, the pavement cutting through the middle. Slumped across it is a small heap of bodies in front of the tower entrance.

'Offing people now, is he?' I say. 'Getting dumped by you really did mess him up.'

A snore fuzzes through the speaker to prove me wrong. They're not dead. They're fast asleep.

Maida's eyes widen. 'Outside, too?'

Keisha nods.

'Who are they?'

'Morris said they were just some guys hanging around the block.'

The sleepers are face down, so there's no way to recognise them. Still, I'd bet anything Morris knows exactly who they are. I wonder what he's got himself into.

Behind the camera we can hear him breathing hard. There's a scraping noise, and then something long and thin pushes into the frame. It's a stick, wavering forward to poke at the bodies. They don't move a muscle, not even when Morris jabs one of them in the ear.

'He really is an idiot,' I say.

'He says they fell asleep when they got too close to the block,' Keisha says. 'Like there was a force field around it or something.'

I can't help but laugh. 'What are you chatting about?'

While Morris continues the prodding on the screen, Keisha tells me a story about falling asleep, somebody being in her room, following a weird noise up to the top floor. She shakes her head at every detail, like they might

30

not be true, even with Maida jumping in occasionally to back her up.

'So what actually happened?' I say.

Neither of them can answer.

Before I can tell them they've both gone batshit crazy, the phone speaker fills up with a steady humming noise. A flash of white light floods the screen. Morris swears – loudly – and the camera swings around to face the tower.

The humming drops away to silence. On the screen I can just make out the roof of the block. Above it a streak of light is etched into the sky. It could just be camera glare. After a few seconds it fades away. Morris is swearing like there's prize money. He must have seen *something*. He lets out a long breath. Then there's the sound of a groan.

The camera view returns to earth and focuses on the collapsed bodies. All three are beginning to stir and stretch. Morris swears again and runs for the tower entrance before the video cuts off.

Yeah, like he didn't know *exactly* who they were.

## Keisha

'Do I need to confiscate that?'

Automatically I shove the phone into my pocket. Mr Arnopp, my head of year, is standing over us with a mischievous smile. He's not wearing his glasses, so the bright blue eyes that make all the girls (and a few of the boys) go weak at the knees are on full display. We were too busy watching the video to even notice him.

'Just because it's better than yours, sir,' I say.

'You know me, I'm still quite reliant on carrier pigeon.' He puts his hands in his pockets and rocks on his heels. There's something sharp in his gaze when he looks at Siobhan beside me. 'What seems to be the problem, ladies? Typhus? Perhaps a startlingly localised outbreak of Ebola virus?'

I try to smile but I can't quite pull it off. There seems to be a scarily localised outbreak of something much worse. The possibilities mount up at the back of my mind. I hold them firmly at a distance.

'Ladies troubles, sir,' says Maida.

I think of the blood on my jeans and my stomach lurches.

Mr Arnopp grins. 'You won't get rid of me that easily. One day in the future, Keisha, my dear, I want you to be curing such terrible plights. The last time I found you sitting here you were on the brink of expulsion.'

My teacher had confiscated my phone; I had called her a bitch; and after years of being late, skipping days and getting detention, the headteacher had been ready to kick me out – would have, too, if it weren't for Mr Arnopp.

'You've come a long way since then. Don't screw it up now.' He smiles. 'Your studies are what count.'

It feels like I might be sick all over my shoes.

'Dick,' Siobhan mutters under her breath.

'Can I talk to you for a minute, sir?' I say.

We go around the corner into a corridor that always smells like armpits because it leads into the gym. As soon as we're alone he's less good-natured.

'I thought you didn't see Siobhan anymore,' he says.

32

I nod, struggling to meet his eye. 'Sir, I think something might have happened.'

'You know I'm looking after your best interests,' he says, like he didn't hear me. 'Tell me you know that?'

'I know, sir.'

'You think people like that are going to help you get to university?'

I shake my head.

University. I have to make it happen. Grades. Money. Everything I need to get out of this place. The thought is overwhelming: my future feels so close and yet so far away. I could escape, or I could be trapped here forever. I can't let anything push me off-track – but I can't hold my feelings back any longer.

Without warning, all the terrible things I've been trying to ignore rush at me. The blood on my jeans. The pain in my stomach and between my legs. Until now I've stopped my mind from sliding toward the worst case scenario: someone getting into the flat, drugging me. Coming inside my room while I can't defend myself.

A sob sticks in my throat. Mr Arnopp notices, and puts a hand on my arm. Usually I wouldn't mind. Today my instinct is to flinch. But I know he doesn't like that.

'Get back to class, okay?' he says. 'Don't waste your time with her.'

I nod, and go back to the others without another word.

'He's such a knob,' says Siobhan. 'A fit knob, but still a knob.'

I stand by the bench, sick and sad. These days I find it difficult even to look at Siobhan. It's not fair, but ever since I made the decision to shut her out I can't help but see her less as 'Siobhan' and more as 'What I could have become': fat and stupid. Going nowhere.

I start to gather my bag. I don't want to think about the last proper conversation we had. After I told her I didn't want to be friends anymore. After I accused her of leading me down a dead end in life.

Only now it seems like something has happened to us – something my body knows but my mind doesn't understand – and no matter how hard I try to ignore it, that something links us together again.

My chest tightens. I need to get back to class.

'Let's meet by the green after school,' I say, slinging my bag over my shoulder. 'We need to talk about this properly. The sooner we work this out the sooner we can forget about it.'

I hurry into the corridor, ignoring a fresh stab of pain in my guts. Before I get far Siobhan is at my shoulder.

'What?' I say.

Her face hardens for a moment, like she might just walk away again. Instead I see her make the decision to speak.

'Watch yourself with Mr Arnopp, yeah?' she says.

'What's that supposed to mean?'

'Don't you think the way he behaves with you is a bit—'

I cut her off. 'He's the only one who believes in me. He's trying to help me make something of my life.'

'You don't need him for that, Keish. I just want you to be careful.'

I feel an irrational urge to hit her. I dig my fingernails into my palms.

'We're not friends anymore,' I say. 'I don't need your help.'

I turn and march away down the corridor. Judging by the look on her face, my words hit her harder than any punch ever could.

# Chapter Four

**Morris**

A group of kids chase a football around the green. It bobbles over the uneven turf like fists below ground are punching it along. It was always a nightmare playing there. I remember when the 'No Ball Games' sign first appeared a few years ago. It took less than an hour to get vandalised. Now it just says 'Balls' and someone has drawn a proper hairy pair.

Everyone assumes it was me. I guess I can't blame them.

'The Nightout was the whole building,' I tell the girls, waving an arm at the block over our heads. 'I had a word with a few people and they all fell asleep in weird places and didn't remember. Tubs was on the toilet.'

'Tubs is *always* on the toilet,' says Siobhan.

'Yeah, but he doesn't sleep there, does he?'

'Wouldn't surprise me,' she mutters.

Next to her, Keisha leans on the fence and stares at the shopping bags around her feet while Maida glances nervously up at her seventh floor window. It's almost like the old days when we'd hang out here all night after

36

school, except Maida wasn't part of the group back then.

The parakeets chitter in the trees on the other side of the green. If you look hard enough you can see their bright emerald bodies skipping between the leaves. They don't belong here, but over the years they've bred and bred and now they're everywhere. It doesn't hurt to have a bit of colour around the place.

Keisha watches the parakeets. *The ones that got away*, she used to call them. She invented a whole origin story about their bid for freedom against the odds. I grin at her even though she isn't looking.

'What did you just call what happened last night?' she says.

'The Nightout. Catchy, right?'

She doesn't reply. Instead she grimaces and runs a hand over her stomach like she's checking for damage. She's proper pale, and I think about putting an arm around her shoulder, but don't: she'd snap it right off, no matter how ill she is.

'We still have no idea what happened,' says Maida. 'Maybe it was just a gas leak.'

I can tell from her face she doesn't believe it. She's looking pale too, and so is Siobhan.

We all go quiet because Mrs Earle comes round the corner and shuffles past, making sure she doesn't lock eyes with anyone, instead using a hand to adjust her perfect perm. She's lived on the tenth floor for years, and seems to think the tower is some kind of upper class apartment block. A few years ago she started a Neighbourhood Watch, which is how we got the 'No Ball Games' sign. We just call her the Hag.

'It wasn't a gas leak,' I say when the Hag's gone. There's no way I can let it get dismissed that easy. 'I went to the library and looked it up online.'

'*You* went to the library?' scoffs Siobhan. 'Did an alarm go off at the door?'

Sometimes it's best just to ignore her. 'I couldn't find anything. There's this thing called narco-leppy where—'

'Narcolepsy,' corrects Maida.

'All right, Einstein, *narcolepsy*, where you fall asleep like, *snap*, but it's really rare and it's just individual cases, not everyone at once.'

'You guys are well paranoid,' says Siobhan. 'You're probably just messing with me. It's normal to fall asleep at night, you know.'

'What if it's something worse?' says Keisha. 'It's not normal to wake up with blood all over you.'

'Like what?'

Keisha drops her eyes back to the shopping bags. 'Someone might have done something to us.'

Siobhan sprays a laugh into the cold air. 'You mean like we were abused or something?'

The word 'abused' hangs like a dagger. No one manages to look at anyone else.

'Come on, don't get carried away,' I say.

All she does is look at her shoes. It seems like I should keep talking.

'You saw the video! That's all the evidence we have.' I feel myself start to heat up with anger. I was lucky not to be inside the block when it happened. Now it feels like my duty to get to the bottom of this. This is an opportunity for me to do something good. To get Keisha's attention again.

The parakeets flutter in the trees. Behind us a couple of the kids break out into a scuffle and immediately start insulting each other's mums.

'Remember when I stole that kid's bike seat?' says Siobhan. 'What was his name? He weren't from round here.'

The memory makes me smile. 'He was two years older and you made him cry.'

'Then his dad came round to find out who nicked it and he thought it was you. I swear he was gonna kill you, Mo, even when I told him it was a joke! Then Keisha gets up in his face and cusses him out, saying how that waste man had it coming. It was amazing.'

Keisha sighs. 'Let's not do this.'

'What? It was jokes.'

'I'm not here to reminisce and watch you get all mushy. I feel sick enough already. I want to work out what happened last night.'

Siobhan straightens up and steps to Keisha. I get behind her, ready to protect her if Siobhan makes a move. The girl's got some bulk.

'You think you're better than us now, is that it?' says Siobhan.

Keisha doesn't move from the fence. 'You know it wasn't like that.'

I catch Keisha's eye. The last thing I want to talk about in front of everybody is why she broke up with me.

Maida moves away from us. 'And to think I used to get jealous of you guys hanging around out here.'

39

'Whatever,' spits Siobhan, striding off towards the tower door.

Keisha's voice is rising, like she's about to flip the switch. 'I hope last night was nothing, so I don't ever have to speak to you again!'

Siobhan whips around to shout back but stops dead on the spot. For a second I think the instant naps are back. She gropes at the air like she's trying to open an invisible fridge. The colour drains out of her face.

'You feel that?' she says.

My ears pop, like something in the air has shifted. Then I see how pale the other girls have gone. They scrunch their faces up and moan. At the same moment they double over and start heaving.

## Keisha

I've never felt anything like it. I'm powerless to resist. The children on the green chorus *eewww!* and leg it, one of them stopping just long enough to take a picture on his phone.

After a couple of body-breaking convulsions I feel my stomach empty out. My head spins as I spit my mouth clean and wipe at my face. When I straighten up I see Siobhan and Maida doing the same thing, puddles of sick around their feet. We stare at each other like someone has told us a terrible secret.

Morris steps over the mess and puts a hand on my back. 'You all right?'

I shift away from his arm and look at the mess around us. The liquid that's slowly carving a path between the paving stones is bright blue, almost glowing, and it's littered with dark chunks.

'What the hell did you all eat for lunch?' says Morris.

Siobhan flaps at her face like she's going to faint. Beside her, Maida stares down at the contents of her body like it's the most fascinating thing she's ever seen.

'We all felt it, right?' I say.

The other girls nod.

'Felt what?' says Morris.

What was it? I'm not sure, but for a moment, just before we all doubled over, it was like we were all connected somehow. Like I was inside their minds and they were inside mine. I could feel their sickness as well as my own, the tightening of their throats, the spike of fear as they lost control. As *we* lost control. Everything we felt was tripled – we shared it.

I hand Maida a tissue to wipe her shoes and skirt but the blue has already stained.

'Thanks for giving *me* a tissue,' says Siobhan.

'You don't have a dad who'll go crazy if he sees this.'

'This is disgusting. I can't deal right now.' Siobhan fumbles in her pocket for her fob, swipes it against the pad and slips inside the tower door.

'And I'm late for prayers,' says Maida.

'Wash your things in the sink before your dad gets home,' I say. 'I'll clean up out here.'

It sounds like we're covering up a murder. Relieved, Maida escapes through the door before it bangs shut.

Morris looks at me and smiles. Except for last night this is the first time we've been alone in months.

I take a half-empty bottle of water out of my school

bag and start trying to wash away the mess. All it does is dilute it; pale blue grossness swills around our feet.

'What the hell was that?' he says.

'It doesn't concern you, Morris.'

'You can't shut me out of this. I saw what happened last night. I'm part of it too.'

'You weren't inside,' I say. 'Nothing *happened* to you.'

Someone in my room. Unable to defend myself. The blood on my jeans. Once again I force myself to shove the thoughts away.

'Please, Keish. Let me help you.'

His voice sounds whiny and desperate. All I want is to get away from him. I fish out my keys and pick up the shopping bags.

'I have to take these up to Mr Hillier,' I say.

'Look, my mum's doing overtime,' says Morris. 'You could come over. We'll get a takeaway, talk about what's going on.'

My fob beeps against the pad. I yank the heavy door open. 'And who would pay for that takeaway?'

It's like I've slapped him. 'That's not fair.'

'Remember what we talked about before?'

Before I can disappear inside he grabs my arm and squeezes my wrist. There's a flare of pain and I drop the bags. I try to pull away but he won't let go.

'Give me another chance,' he says.

I grit my teeth. 'Let me go.'

My voice shakes unexpectedly. I want to fight him off, but his grip seems to drain my strength. It's *Morris*. I can't be frightened of Morris.

'Please,' I say.

A pulse seems to move through me, emanating from my stomach. At first I think I'm going to be sick again. It travels towards Morris's hand on my skin, and his eyes go blank – just for a second – before his hand pings open, letting me pull my arm free.

I willed him to let me go . . . and he did.

There isn't time to think about it. I grab my bags and slam the door, leaving Morris on the doorstep staring at his hand in disbelief.

# Chapter Five

**Keisha**

I can't concentrate. Schoolwork. Streaming. The second I try and focus my head starts to swim. So instead I'm here, sitting with Mum, watching a bunch of Americans bidding on storage bins that have not at all been filled up with antiques for the cameras. We used to watch the reality shows together but after a while the desperation of it all – the contestants, the way we'd laugh at them when they failed – put me off the whole thing.

If Mr Arnopp could see me now he'd never speak to me again.

He texted me earlier. Good seeing you today. Teachers aren't supposed to give pupils their numbers, but he said that didn't apply to us. Siobhan doesn't trust him, but she's the last person I should be listening to. You can't read anything into a text like that.

'I can't believe someone would just leave behind a military helicopter,' says Mum, as the show cuts dramatically to the adverts.

Most people would find her naivety charming.

She checks her phone and tuts. 'Your dad's doing overtime again.'

It's the same almost every day now. His office is digitising files – or something equally boring – and Dad's taken charge. I know he's doing the extra work to help with my university funds, but it feels like he hardly lives here anymore.

'You all right, love? You look pale.'

'I've felt better.'

Mum smiles. 'I knew there had to be a reason you were out here with me.'

'We hang out sometimes.'

'Not for a long while.' She mutes the adverts. 'You need your mum?'

I roll my eyes at her. Only for show. I do need her. Maybe more than I ever have before. I just don't know how to tell her. What can I say? None of it quite seems real. I'm frightened to even try and explain; just the thought makes it harder to keep the tears away.

'Last night . . .' I realise I don't know what to say next.

I try again. 'Last night, something . . .' I pause to squash the croak in my voice.

There's a thud on the ceiling from Maida's flat. It sounds like something being thrown onto the floor. Heavy footsteps move across the room, and we hear her dad shout so loudly he could be inside our flat.

'*Get back here!*'

'Not again,' Mum sighs.

Maida's voice isn't loud enough for us to make out the words, but we hear her shouting back. She always shouts back.

*'This isn't good enough!'*

'When is he going to let that poor girl live her life?'

The adverts are over. Mum unmutes the volume on the TV to drown out the noise above us.

'Mum,' I say, trying to take back her attention.

The shouting doesn't stop. Mum stands up to grab Dad's barbell and bashes the end of it against the ceiling.

'He's too proud to keep shouting if he knows we can hear him.'

Sure enough, when she lowers the barbell everything's quiet upstairs. I'm worried about Maida, but it's anger I feel, nagging at me to set it loose. It could almost belong to somebody else; it could almost belong to Maida herself.

I stand up and head for my room.

'Don't you want to see how much the helicopter's worth?' Mum calls after me.

'I'm going to bed,' I call back. 'Let's talk about it later.'

## Siobhan

I'm watching a YouTube video when I notice it again, this feeling inside my mind that I can't quite read – it's like I'm detached from myself, but still connected to something bigger. Something I can't quite figure out. It's doing my head in, whatever it is.

I turn the volume up to try and drown it out. Forget it. *Forget it.*

The video's supposed to be teaching me the kind of JavaScript that could get me working on Angular. I'm only half sure what that means. Tonight more than ever the code looks like an alien language.

Keisha got me into coding, actually, though she gave it up to focus on her schoolwork. At first I thought it was stupid – I still think it's a bit stupid to be honest – but after she showed me a few things I realised I could actually do it and I began to think that maybe, just maybe, I'm not the thickest person in the world after all. I don't know, maybe it's even something I can use in the future.

Whatever. I'm just not feeling it tonight.

I sink the last cupcake. Experimental flavour. Peanut butter and orange. It tastes like I injected it with bin juice. Definitely not something I'll be offering to my customers. Not that I have any. Except for Mum.

I switch to a make-up tutorial. The YouTuber, Tinker, is probably the hottest girl I've ever seen. She's only my age, but she has her shit together. Her eyebrow game is always on point.

Having 300,000 subscribers and companies sending you free stuff all the time probably helps.

I open my webcam in a different window. Try to copy what she's doing with her blusher – I'm always looking for a new way to apply my mask – but it's hard to focus on Tinker's familiar sunny voice. I squeeze my eyes shut. The strangeness inside my head won't bugger off. I know I'm in there, but so are Keisha and Maida, the faint echo of their emotions. There might even be a third person, but it's all too unclear and unsettling to focus on. Part of me wants to follow them; part of me just wishes they'd leave me alone.

'Siobhan, Cupcake?' My bedroom door opens. Mum leans into the room. 'Do you want . . .?'

She stops mid-sentence. Frowns. Like she's caught a whiff of a nasty fart. It's almost like she feels it too.

'What's wrong?'

She shakes her head and smiles uncertainly. 'Nothing, never mind. Gary and me are going to Netflix and chill if you fancy it?'

'I don't think you know what that means, Mum.'

'Oh. Well, come out if you change your mind, Cupcake.'

She came up with the nickname when I started making cupcakes. It's imaginative, for her. Gary, my step-dad, thinks it's hilarious, but only after I told him what having a 'muffin top' means.

The make-up tutorial finishes. I start another one. Tinker's been pretty much my only friend for the last year.

*Sad.*

I nod to myself. It's proper sad, but I'm glad she's been there.

I close my eyes and reach out for Keisha, just to see if I can push my way into her head. After all this time, there's a connection between us again.

After all this time, I'm not sure I want it.

## Morris

It used to be a lot easier pulling myself up through the hatch. Even though I got older and taller I stayed just as scrawny as ever. It doesn't matter how many press ups I do in my room when Mum isn't around. It would take some serious workout plan to put meat on these bones.

The roof is bloody freezing – winter seems to be in a

hurry this year. A sharp breeze scuds across and slices through my jacket. I hurry into the shelter of the little hut in the middle where all the electrics and stuff are kept, TV aerials piled on top like a bad hair style.

Ever since Mum left for her night shift I've been watching the video over and over. Not the bit where Tyrone and his crew are out cold on the ground, the bit that comes after. The streak of light that blurs away from the top of the block. Something was going on up here during the Nightout. I've watched the video a hundred times and each time I'm left with the same, single, batshit crazy thought in my mind: ALIENS.

Rows of streetlights surround the tower like an army coming to conquer us. I drop to my knees in the gravel that covers the entire roof. It's too dark to see anything properly. My hands scuff against crisp packets and empty beer cans, cigarette butts and nondescript lumps that are probably bird crap.

I don't know what I'm looking for. What do aliens leave behind? Ectoplasm or whatever. That might be ghosts. I'm not an expert on things that aren't supposed to exist.

I want to laugh at myself. This is stupid on pretty much every level, but then so is everything that's happened since I decided to leave Midwich Tower that night.

I don't just want to find something up here – I *need* to.

The screen on my phone is bright enough to illuminate the gravel. Nothing unusual shows up. I swipe a hand across the ground, sending grit skittering across the roof, and my fingers come away charred with something dusty, like soot. I get to my feet and hold my phone up high to widen the beam and open out my view. The moment I do, everything comes together.

I'm standing in the middle of a perfect scorched-black circle, darkest in patches spread out around the rim.

Christ on a bike. Something took off from here.

## Keisha

They're staring at me when I come to my senses.

I cry out and stagger backwards. This isn't my room. The walls are stripped bare, flakes of rotten wallpaper peeling away like scabs. It should be a nightmare but the pain of the splinters from the exposed floorboards in my feet is too real. A film of cold sweat covers my skin.

I'm standing in a muted halo of light that pushes in from the street through the dirty glass of the uncovered window. Three other girls stand with me. Maida and Siobhan stand opposite each other, dressed in pyjamas and a tattered T-shirt respectively, their arms straight at their sides. Their eyes are open but unseeing. In the gloom I can just make out the face of the fourth visitor. It's Olivia, an older woman, maybe late twenties, who lives on the top floor of the block. She looks blankly ahead, her curly hair half shrouding her face.

I wrap my arms around myself against the cold. I could slip away back to bed before any of them see me and pretend this never happened. I start to move but a whispering noise inside my skull urges me back into place. It should frighten me, but the sensation is oddly comforting. When I stand beside the girls again it feels like I complete a perfect circle.

I rest a hand on Maida's shoulder. 'Hey.'

She snaps awake and teeters on her heels like she might fall over. Once she's steadied herself she shakes her head and looks at me like she's caught me leering over her bed.

'I was dreaming about you,' she says, before looking at the others standing around us. 'I was dreaming about all of you.'

The others wake up suddenly, their eyes focusing and jerking immediately towards me. They look expectant, like I'm supposed to say something that explains what the hell is going on. A brief pang of horror blossoms into a pleasing warmth inside my chest. I smile at them. As we stand together in this room, in the middle of the night, I feel an unexplainable *fondness* for them all. It's like I've been programmed to love them.

'It's okay,' I say. And they nod as if this is enough.

'Where are we?' says Siobhan, her voice stripped of its usual attitude.

This is the first time in a year I've seen her without make-up. It makes her look so young, so vulnerable, and her fear seems to shine on her skin. It's like looking at someone I knew a long time ago.

I look around the room again and see it properly for the first time. We're still in Midwich Tower. We haven't sleepwalked too far. I recognise the shape of the living room, the door that leads away to the bedrooms and bathroom, the empty space for the kitchen behind me. It looks so barren without furniture.

'The vacant flat on the eighth floor,' says Olivia, like she's read my mind. 'It's the only unoccupied unit in the building.'

She regards us suspiciously, like we might be playing a prank. I don't know her. I've spoken to her a handful of times around the block. She had a boyfriend for a while, but I guess it didn't last. I remember that she's a nurse. We asked her to check on Mr Hillier once when he cut his hand chopping vegetables. She might be someone I could ask for help figuring out what happened to me during the Nightout . . . but not yet. First I need to know how she fits into this.

'Olivia, were you sick yesterday?'

She looks at me like I've just asked her bra size. She nods and turns away, making it clear she doesn't want to say any more about it.

'I don't know what's going on,' I say. 'But it looks like we're in it together.'

Their expressions shift. They're trying to deny it. They're trying to tell themselves that I've lost it, that everything has been a big, bizarre coincidence, but they're scared. The connection we share means that I can hear Olivia's knotted thoughts as she tries to come up with a rational explanation, and sense Maida's misplaced relief that she hasn't been left out of something important. It's faint, like a weak phone signal, but it's definite and real.

'Worst squad goals ever,' whispers Maida.

'Do you all feel it too?' I say.

All eyes are on me. It feels like an invisible wire has been strung between our brains. I felt it yesterday, just before we were sick, and it's already stronger. We have to find out what it means.

I remember what happened with Morris. As soon as I felt like I was in danger something powerful took over –

a force that came from me but was also greater than me. I can't help but feel like it's not going to be the last time I'll need it.

'We have to look after each other now,' I say.

'That's rich, coming from you,' says Siobhan. She shoves past me toward the door. 'Forget this, I'm going back to bed.'

She storms out into the hallway. Olivia follows her sheepishly, but looks back over her shoulder when she reaches the door. 'I have your number, right?'

I nod. I gave it to her when she was checking on Mr Hillier, just to be friendly.

I'm left alone with Maida. 'You okay?'

'You're always asking me that.'

'Sorry. But right now I think it's a fair question.'

'I'm all right,' says Maida, and she looks surprised by how confident she sounds. 'I'm kind of used to everybody thinking I'm weird and ignoring me. At least I'm not by myself in this particular weirdness.'

'We don't know what *this* is yet,' I say.

Being a part of anything in Midwich Tower can't be a good thing.

'I better get home before somebody notices.'

We walk to the door together and find the lock is shattered, like one of us kicked it through to gain entry. Must have made a racket. And nobody came to investigate? For some reason, this chills me more profoundly than anything – you can't so much as open a can of beans in Midwich without drawing a crowd of spectators. I pull the door closed behind us and, in the darkness at least, no one should be able to tell that it's damaged.

The corridor feels like a constricted throat. We descend the stairs in silence until we reach Maida's floor.

'Don't get too carried away with this,' I say.

'I think it's too late for that.'

'Just let me know if you need anything. You don't have a phone, right?'

Maida taps the side of her head and smiles. 'I don't think we'll be needing it.'

Even when she's out of sight I can feel her smouldering satisfaction inside my head.

# Chapter Six

**Keisha**

The toilet water glows blue. It looks like cheap energy drink. My stomach is empty, but I can still feel it churning. I feel bloated, the waistband of my pyjamas digging into my skin. I spit into the mess.

I drop back and lean my head against the cool stem of the sink. Around the building I can feel the others suffering along with me. The rawness of their throats is also in mine. The hardness of the bathroom floors against their knees leaves dents in my skin. Our hearts are pounding together.

It feels terrible. It feels wonderful.

It drives me crazy.

A knock on the door. 'Everything okay in there, Keisha, love?'

Definitely not. 'Yes,' I shout.

It's been just over twenty-four hours since the Nightout and this bond between us is stronger than ever. I clench my eyes shut. I don't want to be connected to them. Not when I've spent the last year doing everything I can to disconnect.

I climb to my feet and flush the toilet. The disgusting blue gunk swirls away, but it's marked the inside of the bowl and takes five minutes of hard scrubbing to clean.

'I'm not all right,' I say when I unlock the door and face my mother.

She pouts with exaggerated sympathy. 'Stay home today.'

I move past her and cross the sitting room into the kitchen, where I drop into a seat at the table. The usual selection of supermarket brand cereal is on offer, but my stomach is too delicate to even think about it. No one can eat feeling like this, not even Siobhan, I think, and instantly I feel her flash of annoyance, like she actually heard me.

I always eat breakfast. I always go to school. It's all I've done for the last year. I made it my routine. If I take a day off I might miss something important. Something that comes up on an exam. It shouldn't matter that I'm exhausted enough to use a box of cornflakes as a pillow right here on the table. Last time I stayed home from school it was because I was suspended.

'You can get any work you miss off Mr Arnopp,' says Mum, zipping up her Tesco fleece. 'You know he'd never let you fall behind.'

Mr Arnopp would sooner kill me than let me fall off the rails. The other week he described me as his 'only hope'. So no pressure or anything.

I fill a bowl with a cocktail of cereals and drown it in milk, trying to revive my appetite. The mixture crackles as it settles, and for a second time I'm sure I'm about to hurl. I close my eyes and will the feeling to pass.

My parents never made it this far in school. They already had each other. As soon as they could they dropped out, got jobs, and got married. I came along soon after. I've never met someone with parents as young as mine.

University was well out of reach for them and they never expected me to get anywhere near. They haven't said it, but I know it's true. No matter how much they support me I know they're both surprised.

Neither of them have any idea how much it actually takes for someone like me. One day off school could easily lead to two days, five, then a fortnight. Then before I know it I'm stuck in this block with three kids, Morris pestering me for sex every night like he has something to prove, no prospects, no hope of escape.

I push the bowl of cereal away from me. Whatever has happened could push me off course. I won't let it. I can't panic.

'That's it. If you lost your appetite something must be wrong,' says Mum, grabbing her handbag from the counter. 'I have to go. It's your choice – just don't overdo it. If you don't go in send me a text and I'll phone school on my break.'

When she's gone I chuck away the cereal and stand in the middle of the flat. Dad left for work before I got up, and he won't be back until late. The idea of having the flat to myself for the day *is* tempting. I could get schoolwork done without being disturbed. I could livestream without feeling embarrassed about talking loudly into the microphone. It might even pull in a few donations.

I lock the front door and make sure it's secure.

It'll also give me some time to think. I walk slowly through to my bedroom and try to focus on what I can feel from the other girls. It's like our brains are networked on dodgy Wi-Fi. All of us are feeling sick. I guess Maida and Siobhan aren't going anywhere near school either. All I can feel from Olivia is worry, mounting by the second.

I pick up my phone from my desk. There's only one message. Morris, again.

Sorry about yesterday. Can we talk?

I can't let him know I'm home for the day, or there goes my peace and quiet; but at some point I'm going to have to deal with him properly. He still acts like I owe him something.

I tap out a message to Mum and try to ignore the guilt I feel for staying home. It never used to be like this. I used to do anything to get out of school. Morris and I would bunk off together and spend the day in the park, or hide out in his flat. His mum never cared if he went to school or not. As soon as Siobhan was free we'd grab her and spend the night hanging around outside, doing nothing.

When I was suspended I stayed indoors with a hell of a lot to think about. The headmaster had wanted to expel me but Mr Arnopp said I had a future. He said he would help me live up to my potential.

He made me feel special.

The price was that I had to leave my friends behind. Whenever I felt the urge to join them outside I sat at my computer and livestreamed instead. I tried to explain it to Siobhan. I even tried to get her to work harder, too. It just ended in an argument, and that was that.

My phone vibrates. It's a text from Mr Arnopp.

It had better be serious lol.

I smile, hoping it really is a joke. Sometimes it's hard to tell with him. It vibrates with a follow up.

Let me know if you need anything x

He's concerned about me. There's nothing wrong with that. I can't believe I almost let Siobhan poison my mind against him.

No matter what people say at school, I'm not a slag. They always assumed a popular black girl from the block must be sleeping around. I never did. I never have.

It was a way to defy their expectations.

The Nightout might have taken that away from me.

I open a new tab and search: *date rape symptoms*.

Just typing the word 'rape' makes me want to laugh and cry at the same time. My hypothesis boils down to, 'Someone drugged the whole building and assaulted me while I slept.' Clearly I'm being paranoid ... but something happened, and I have to at least try and rule it out. I click on a link and read a list of what women experience afterwards, expecting none of it to apply.

*A sense of having been violated.*

*Nausea.*

*Lingering shame and guilt.*

*Lower abdominal pain.*

*Strong self-doubt.*

It could be a list of everything I've felt since the Nightout. As soon as I woke up I knew something had happened to me, even if the blackout had taken my memory of it. It was more than just the blood; my body and my mind knew that something was wrong.

I Google that. *Blacked out. Blood. Vomiting. Mystery.*

Predictably, it shows me a list of gross diseases illustrated with images straight out of a horror movie. But in amongst the gore are some local news stories – a couple about drunken teenagers out of control and, buried *way* down the search results, some nonsense about a village in Cornwall and aliens.

I feel terrible – my stomach is disintegrating. I want to cry. I close the Google tab and go into the kitchen. All the medicine is kept on the top shelf of the cupboard over the sink. I scrape a chair across the floor and climb up. The shelf is strewn with packets and bottles that have faded and leaked over the many years since they were shoved up there. There are expired painkillers, solidified cough syrup, a range of over-promising hay fever treatments (Mum's nemesis every single summer), and something to do with bowels that I don't even want to understand. Any of this lot looks like it would kill me rather than settle my stomach.

While I'm searching I feel a flare of panic from one of the other girls. My elbow accidentally knocks an ancient-looking tin of golden syrup. It tumbles past me and bounces off the sink before it hits the floor. The 'medicine cupboard' is basically a death trap best ignored. I glance down.

The lid has gone flying off the tin, and money has spilled all over the kitchen floor. I jump down and scrabble to collect the bank notes. There must be hundreds of pounds here. I retrieve the tin and look inside. More notes are rolled up tightly and crammed into it. There must be *thousands*. The tin is sticky in my hands. There's a small dent where it hit the edge of the sink but nothing too obvious. The money feels dangerous, like I'm holding a live grenade. We've never had much money. That's not unusual for anyone living in the block. Something tells me that I wouldn't like where this has come from. I shove the notes I'm holding back into the tin and push the lid into place, suddenly nervous, like someone's watching.

I climb back onto the chair, return the tin to the top shelf. I'm replacing all the other stuff around it when the panic that has been lingering at the back of my brain surges forward and hits me like a punch. I almost lose my balance. It isn't just the money. My hands start to shake.

When I take the chair back to the table I spot a stray twenty-pound note sticking out from under the fridge. I snatch and pocket it quickly just as another torrent of fear smashes into my head, blurring my vision and making my chest squeeze tight.

I lean against the counter and try to push it away. I close my eyes and without trying to, I open myself up to the others: fear pours off Olivia in waves. My phone vibrates in my pocket and I know it's her. I have to hold onto the doorframe as I read to keep from falling over.

The text from Olivia is only four words.

*I'm pregnant. It's impossible.*

My panic surges to meet hers. Everything I feared.
It's come true.

# Chapter Seven

**Siobhan**

We sneak into the empty flat like we're robbing the place. It's the middle of the day.

I hurry inside with Keisha. Mo stakes out the corridor to make sure nobody sees.

Morris is the only person she hurt more than me, yet we both jump when she calls for us. If I could have ignored her, believe me, I would have – but she's literally in my head, her panic bashing at my skull; I don't know what his excuse is.

The lock is still broken from last night so Morris wedges the door shut with a pile of junk mail.

Daylight streams into the empty living room. The air is mostly dust. I swear it's colder in here than outside.

'Why here?' I say, hugging myself for warmth.

'It's the only place in the block that feels safe,' says Keisha.

She sounds paranoid. Her hands are shaking. I raise an eyebrow at Morris but he shakes his head for me to stop.

'You get them?' she asks him.

Mo hands over a plain blue carrier bag. 'Guy in the chemist gave me a well funny look.'

Keisha tips out three small boxes. Identical. A brand I recognise from TV. Three tests. One for her. One for Maida.

And one for me.

This whole thing is crazy.

'I think Mo has more chance of being preggers than me,' I say, trying to break the tension.

It mostly works. Mo laughs then tries to stifle it when Keisha glares daggers. After all this time, she's still got him whipped.

'You can laugh all you want,' Keisha says to me, 'but I know you can sense what Olivia's going through. She took a test and it said she's four weeks pregnant. She hasn't slept with anyone in months.'

'Like I'm surprised,' I say. 'You seen her?'

She's right though – Olivia's freaking out like a little tornado inside my skull and her panic is contagious. My heart is starting to race.

'What are you two on about?' says Morris.

Keisha ignores him. 'Think about it: ever since the Nightout we've been getting sick, especially this morning. We've all felt something weird in our stomachs. And the blood . . .'

She trails off. My heartbeat gets faster and faster.

'Look. I know it doesn't make sense,' she says. 'At least this way we can be sure.'

The best I can do is shrug, like all I'm doing is playing along. But the fear has its claws in me now.

Morris makes the mistake of smiling. He's got a

proper cute smile, like it's turned on by a switch. Right now Keisha looks like she wants to slap it off his face. He's humouring her, and she knows it.

'Come on,' she says, taking my elbow and pulling me into the bathroom.

'Anything I can do?' says Morris.

She shuts the door without replying. 'Best thing he could do is leave,' she mutters.

'He's just trying to help. You know he'd do anything for you.'

She studies the back of one of the boxes. 'I know.'

The bathroom window is plastered with newspaper, so the light is faint. It's all cracked tiles, floorboards black with rot. The air's so musty we cough and cover our noses.

'If we do have a little problem, this stink might be enough to flush them out,' I say.

No laugh. Tough crowd.

*What if she's right?*

If she's right, I'll deal with it. That's my decision to make.

Keisha hands me one of the boxes. Fear digs a toothpick into my lungs. I tip the test out onto my palm. It's a baby blue plastic stick with a circular panel at one end.

'What do I do with it?'

'Pee on it, I think.'

'Thought maybe that was just films.' I turn the test over in my hands. 'Can't believe I'm doing this. What about Maida?'

Keisha shakes her head. 'I couldn't get hold of her.'

We look at each other. We both know that isn't quite

true. Maida is tuned into us right now. Bracing herself. The invisible wire between us is pulled tight as it'll go.

'I'll try and get a test to her soon,' Keisha says.

'So. Two of us, one toilet,' I say. 'How we doing this?'

'I guess we take it in turns. Who's going first?'

I want her to see that I'm brave, so I drop onto the loo. It's like sitting on a block of ice. Keisha turns her back while I push the stick between my legs. The sooner all this is over the sooner she can go back to avoiding me.

I wish I knew if that's what I really want.

## Keisha

This all feels just a bit too intimate. We never went as far as peeing together, but we used to be close. I suppose you'd say we were best friends. I made the decision to change that, and now it feels like I really shouldn't be here as the sound of trickling fills the bathroom.

I stare at a spider web of cracks on the wall. A sudden urge to laugh forces its way up my throat. Pregnant? The only boyfriend I've ever had was Morris, and thankfully we never made it that far. Almost, but not quite.

*Impossible.* That's the word Olivia used in her text.

I'm acting like a frightened child and I hate it.

When Siobhan's finished she rests the wet stick on the edge of the sink and glares at it like it's her worst enemy.

'I'll pay you a tenner to put it in your mouth,' she says.

'You're disgusting.'

She sticks out her tongue at me.

I take my test from its box. The stick feels cool and rubbery against my fingers. I try not to think about what

I'm doing but it's difficult to disconnect with three other girls hanging on your every feeling. The cold porcelain of the toilet bowl nips at the back of my legs and I jump, almost dropping the test into the yellow water.

'I've lost three phones from dropping them in the loo,' says Siobhan.

'You're not supposed to be looking.'

Once she's turned away I push the stick between my legs. It makes my stomach lurch. It's something I didn't think I'd have to do for a long time yet.

I need to take my mind off it or I won't be able to go. 'Is that why your texts were always so potty-mouthed?'

'Ha-bloody-ha.'

When I'm finished I perch the stick next to hers on the sink. I flush the toilet and put the lid down to make a seat, but I end up standing anyway.

'What we looking for?' says Siobhan.

I flip one of the boxes and scan the instructions again. 'It should just say "Pregnant" or "Not Pregnant", and how many weeks we are. You know, *if* we are.'

I feel even more stupid now that I'm staring at our pee-soaked tests. It's only been a day and a half since the Nightout. Olivia said she was four weeks pregnant. It doesn't even come close to adding up, but I have to know for sure.

There's too much at stake to risk it. A single word on this horrible little stick could change everything.

We watch the panels like we might miss something if we dare look away.

Siobhan clears her throat. 'So did you and Mo ever . . . ?'

'No,' I say firmly, keeping my eyes on the test. 'It didn't work out that way.'

'You didn't want to? I know you're a goodie-goodie now, but not so much back then.'

I purse my lips. The truth is too messy. Even back then I wasn't sure. My virginity was like a private badge of honour. But I was willing to make an exception for Morris. I promised him I would never tell anybody what happened, and despite how he's behaved since then it's a promise I intend to keep. It's the least I can do for him.

'It just didn't work out.'

Siobhan sucks her teeth. 'I respect that. Shame my libido usually overrides my brain.'

She turns to me and grins, and we both burst out laughing, forgetting for a second why we're here before her laughter dies in her throat.

'Seriously though, I can't be pregnant,' she says. 'It's been months since I did anything naughty, and we were careful. I'm stupid, but I'm not that stupid.'

'Remember that guy you almost shagged behind the bins?'

She waves her hands in protest. 'Him touching me up until I slapped him is not almost shagging him. I do have a bit of class.'

'He was fit, though.'

'Seriously fit.'

Siobhan kicks at a loose tile. 'I miss this.'

I don't know what to say. The silence feels heavy enough to make the floor collapse.

Before I have to answer the panels on the tests begin

to change colour. Siobhan's changes first and she grabs it without hesitation.

'Shit,' she says. 'Shit!'

She flaps the stick like that might change what it says. I feel my stomach drop. My whole body goes numb, like I'm floating above the rotten floorboards.

Slowly I reach for my test. A single word of text has appeared across the panel.

*Pregnant.*

The world seems to fall away from me until I'm floating in empty space. There has to be a mistake. The tests must be faulty or something. Anything.

Siobhan's still shouting. 'What do I do? What do we do?'

I look at the panel and beg it to change. I wipe my thumb across its surface to make sure the 'Not' isn't hidden away.

Our distress and panic seem to collide in the air, like tectonic plates crashing against each other, and it echoes back and forth between us – me, Siobhan, Olivia, Maida – spiralling. I imagine Olivia walking down a hospital hallway and ducking into an empty room to catch her breath. A floor below us I can feel Maida too. She's the only one now who doesn't know for sure, but she's part of the connection so surely . . . The thought makes me shudder. She's too young.

Maida's horror doesn't match mine. Although I can feel her fear, there's a stronger emotion coming from her. If I didn't know better I would swear it was excitement.

I look at the test again. I think about the Nightout. The blood on my jeans, on Maida's pyjamas. The pain between my legs. Something happened to us. Something was *done* to us.

Morris bangs on the door. 'Everything okay in there?'

Siobhan wheels away and shoves her way out of the bathroom. The door hits Morris in the face and he staggers back with a whine.

'It's positive!' she shouts, waving the stick in his face.

Morris wipes his nose and looks at the blood on his fingers. The words take a moment to register. He recovers just in time to look at me as I step from the bathroom.

'Keisha?'

I feel shell-shocked. There's ringing in my ears and my feet don't seem to be touching the floorboards. I stare at the circular panel, where there's some smaller text under the verdict. I was too stunned to notice it before.

'Keisha!' shouts Morris, snatching the test from my grasp. He looks at it as blood streams down over his lips. 'How could you do this to me?'

'To *you*?'

'Who was it?' he says. 'After everything you said to me, you run straight to somebody else?'

Numbness spreads across every inch of my body. 'I didn't . . . I haven't . . .'

Siobhan's panic has collapsed into shock. She stands against the crumbling wall, mascara running down her face.

'Listen to me,' I say to Morris, fear doing just enough to squash my temper. 'This isn't our fault. We haven't done anything. *I* haven't done anything. Someone has done this to us.'

He starts to shake his head so I keep talking. 'You

know something weird is going on. You know it more than anyone. This isn't our fault.'

I don't know why I'm so desperate to convince him. I just need him to know that I haven't done anything wrong.

Morris throws the test against the wall. 'I don't know what to think.'

He opens the front door hard enough for it to *bang* against the wall and storms away along the corridor. I hurry across to close us inside. It feels safer that way.

I retrieve my test from the floor and stare at the impossible words. *Pregnant.* And underneath that: *4 Weeks.*

I grab Siobhan's wrist and look at the test in her grip. It says the exact same thing. Four weeks. Exactly the same as Olivia.

'I was careful, Keisha, I swear.'

'It doesn't matter,' I say.

Siobhan drops the test, wipes her nose on the back of her hand. 'What are we going to do?'

I grab her shoulders and look square at her mascara-streaked face. 'We have to keep it quiet.'

'I'm sorry I didn't believe you,' she says, wiping away the snot on her face. 'How could this happen? How could somebody do this to us?'

'I don't know. I don't know.'

'We have to tell somebody.'

'No!' I say pinning her against the wall. The tears I've been holding back spill down my cheeks. 'We can't let anybody know.'

'Keisha, listen to me. This was rape.'

There it is. The word I've been too afraid to say out loud. Our minds thrum with the terror of it.

'I'm sorry,' I say, like somehow this is my fault.

Siobhan pulls me into a hug, crying hard into my shoulder. I wrap my arms around her waist and hold her tight. We stay there for what might be hours, until our chests hurt and our clothes are soaked with each other's tears.

## Siobhan

It's dark by the time we leave the flat. Stepping out into the corridor. Keisha pulling the door gently closed behind us. I've cried so much I feel lightheaded and spent. My hands on my belly, probing it, like I might be able to push my fingers in and scoop the problem out.

'Shit,' says Keisha.

When I look up, doors along the corridor are closing and the people who were watching us are long gone – all except for Louise Krawczyk, a girl who was loosely part of our group, back in the day. She lingers just long enough to make sure we know she's seen us before she closes her door.

'So much for keeping it secret,' I say.

Keisha doesn't answer. She just lowers her head and hurries for the stairs.

# Chapter Eight

**Morris**

I've lost track of the clock by the time I reach the house. In the last few hours I've circled the estate, moving closer and closer to this street, feeling the risk of being here race through my veins. I'm half-expecting to get jumped, to feel something heavy crack against my skull.

But the blow never comes.

I stop on the pavement opposite the house and stand in the shadow of a parked van. It's raining and the streetlights are smeared across the road in fat streaks. I'm soaked to the bone, trembling in the cold. Inside, the house pulses with blue light from the TV. Music pounds out into the night. No one round here would dare try to tell them to keep it down.

I pull my dripping jacket tight around me. I should have spent some of the cash on a decent coat. At least I'd have something to bloody show for it now.

After I took up their offer of money, they brought me here, to Tyrone's place. I hadn't seen him in almost a year, back when he was still living with his mum and had football posters on his bedroom wall.

The money was supposed to get my life back on track. The first thing I bought was some decent clothes for job interviews. Next, I passed my driving test. Then a washing machine for Mum, as well as fixing the brakes on her death-trap of a car. I sent a big chunk of it away to Dad in Nigeria too – the first time I'd managed to do that since he left. I had hoped it might get him off my back.

When he moved there to look after Granddad he told me it was time I started contributing. I scraped through school and managed to get an apprenticeship that paid. The only problem was that I was useless at it – I got kicked off after I accidentally electrocuted my boss. At least nobody died. I guess I wasn't cut out to be an electrician.

I wasn't cut out to be much of anything.

The money made me feel like a real person for a little while. It made me feel a bit like the person I always wanted to be. I thought it might help me prove to Keisha that I was worthy of her time.

When we grew too old to believe in winning the lottery, I would tell Keisha all the stuff I was going to buy her when I was raking in the notes. A new gaming PC. Driving lessons so we could go away on a long trip, taking it in turns behind the wheel. Maybe even help her rent a flat away from the block. Maybe even live together.

I wanted that future more than anything.

That future is long gone. Now there's barely any money left, and instead of hanging on to some notion that I can 'change my life' I'm more concerned with staying (a) alive and (b) out of Her Majesty's Prison Service.

You could say I'm not much of an optimist anymore.

I cup my hands together, breathe into the hollow, look down at the holes in my trainers. In the house, the music goes quiet between songs and I hear someone laughing. It does nothing to lighten my mood – if anything, it puts me even more on edge.

A car slides by at the end of the road, drizzle like sparks in its headlights. It wasn't my fault she left me. That was the worst thing about it. I did everything I could, but my body let me down when it mattered most.

We'd been getting closer for a few weeks, always stopping short of going the whole way. She was reluctant, but she wouldn't tell me why. I was aching for it. Most days I could barely walk properly. It was like I could always taste her on my tongue, feel her smooth skin against my fingers, hear the way her breathing would go heavy.

Maybe I loved her. I don't really know much about that.

It happened while she was suspended. I stayed home from school and called her over. We watched TV for a while, but all I could think of was her body. The glimpses of it I'd already seen. Every time she even twitched I filled up with heat. After a while I leaned in and kissed her. She didn't seem as keen as usual, but she didn't stop me. I got my hands up her top. Felt her breath in my mouth. Every inch of me was buzzing.

Into my bedroom. My bed's a bit small but I thought it was up to the job. We started taking our clothes off. I was a bit embarrassed by my scrawny chest, but I kept going. When I dropped my T-shirt to the floor I automatically wrapped my arms around myself to hide.

74

She hesitated when she unhooked her bra. But she kept going.

I saw parts of her body I'd never seen before. I put my hands where they had never been before.

'Do you have something?' she said.

I'd bought some rubbers a few months before. I got them at Tesco, went to the self-checkout so no one would catch me. As soon as I scanned the box (extra safe, just in case) the machine blared AUTHORISATION NEEDED. The old lady assistant had to twiddle with a fob and scan them through again and I ran out of there like I was a shoplifter.

I fumbled around under the bed and then spilled the rubbers on the sheet. I kissed her harder than ever and pushed my hips against her.

She turned away from my mouth. 'You okay?'

'Yeah, why?' My forehead was sweating.

She glanced down at my body. 'You're not . . .'

I followed her eyes. It must have been the first time in weeks that it wasn't ready to go. Everything had been happening so quickly that I hadn't even thought about it. I'd never even thought it might be a problem.

I kissed her again. It would turn up in a second. It had to. But after a couple of minutes nothing happened – even when she put her hand on it. It just hung there like it had somewhere better to be.

'I don't know what's wrong,' I said about a million times. My face was burning. I couldn't look at her.

'Don't worry,' she said. 'It doesn't matter.'

I got dressed. I told her to leave.

A week later, after we'd hardly talked, she came to my

room and told me she didn't want to see me anymore. Just like that.

'Is it because of what happened?' I said. 'I swear it'll be all right next time. I was just tired, or nervous or something.'

'It's nothing to do with that. Please believe me.' But she wouldn't look me in the eye. 'I think it might have been a sign. I don't think I want this.'

'What about me?' I shouted. I wish I hadn't shouted.

I regret it every single day.

And now she's *pregnant*?

A plane passes somewhere overhead. I step off the kerb. The music throbs louder and as I near the fence I see a group of them through the window, standing around the TV swinging their arms. They're playing Wii Tennis! After all their gangster posturing, they're playing bloody Wii Tennis.

The Nightout nags at my brain. It saved me from Tyrone and his thugs . . . but it put Keisha and the other girls at risk. I remember the fear in her eyes. I want to believe her when she says she hasn't done it with someone else. I don't want to feel so left behind.

Something happened to her that night.

It's time to make a choice.

Maybe this is the chance I've been waiting for. The chance to be there for her; for the baby.

The front door of the house clicks open. I duck away behind a car as the music pours out into the night. Someone steps into the cold. They fumble to light a cigarette and the flame illuminates his face. It's Tyrone. It's hard not to notice how much of him is muscle.

He doesn't see me. I want to keep it that way. So I slip away along the row of parked cars. When I'm a safe distance away I begin to run.

## Keisha

The last pregnancy test catches against the door as Maida pushes it back at me. It slips out of my hand and drops to the concrete floor.

'You need to know for sure,' I say, picking it back up.

'If anyone finds it I'm screwed.'

'We need to know exactly who's involved,' I say, trying to keep my voice level. Maida peers back into the darkness of her flat. It's well after midnight. This was the only time I could be sure her dad would be asleep. If her family caught me there would be too many questions. If they saw me handing their Muslim daughter a pregnancy test there'd be a shitstorm.

'You know I don't need to take it,' says Maida. 'You can feel it.'

Even though it was late, I had sensed Maida was still awake. As if any of us could sleep. I focused my mind on the connection between us, imagined a finger twitching the invisible wire. I tried to shove aside all the fear, all the panic, to tell her I was coming up to see her. There was no way to know if it would work.

When I'd reached the door she was waiting right behind it.

'If we just knew—'

She cuts me off. '*Knowing* isn't going to change anything. You don't need to babysit me. I can handle it as well as all of you. Maybe better.'

I think of the mascara streaking down Siobhan's cheeks. The way we clung to each other like it could freeze time. The fear that radiated from her all night until sleep finally silenced it. Olivia has calmed down, but she still feels jagged with worry.

And me. I'm barely holding myself together.

'Please, keep hold of it,' I say, holding out the test. 'Hide it somewhere in case you change your mind.'

She looks at the box in my shaking hand like I'm offering her a live grenade. After a moment she takes it and shoves it into the waistband of her pyjamas. I look for the blood stains, but they're gone.

'We'll speak soon.'

Somehow she manages to smile. 'I'm sure we will.'

The door clicks shut. I stand in the corridor and shiver. I swear the walls are closing in. My shadow stretches faintly ahead of me in the orange light. I don't want to go home. All I would do is sit in my room and be bombarded with thoughts.

*What happened?*

*Who did this?*

*Is this real?*

I make my way quietly to the stairs. As I reach them I hear footsteps coming up towards me. I shrink back into the shadows opposite the door.

Someone passes by and continues up the stairs but the light catches them briefly and I realise it's Dad. His footsteps echo away through the building. There's nowhere he should be going at this time of night. Teenagers are expected to sneak out on mysterious errands, not their parents.

After a few seconds I move into the stairwell, but before I can follow him a voice hisses up at me from below, startling me.

'Keisha!'

Morris pulls himself up the stairs, two at a time. Sweat glistens on his forehead, and his clothes are soaking wet.

'Where have you been?' I whisper.

'You look well tired,' he says.

I don't answer that. I glance up the stairs, aching to follow my dad, but I don't want Morris getting involved in that too.

'I'm sorry about earlier,' he says. 'I was out of order. I thought—'

'I know what you thought. I shouldn't have to defend myself. You can believe that or not. I meant what I told you before. It didn't bother me. There were other reasons—'

He puts up a hand to stop me and his eyes dart away in embarrassment.

'It was just bad timing,' I finish.

There's no way to tell him I couldn't be more thankful it didn't happen between him and me.

Morris nods and looks at the wall. 'I know you don't want to be with me. But you can let me be part of this . . . whatever the hell it is. Let me help you work out what's going on. Let me be here for you.'

'Do you believe me?' I say. 'Tell me you believe I was raped.'

He lifts a hand towards my face, but even though I don't flinch he pulls it away before his fingers find my skin. I remember what they used to feel like. I take a breath and step past him onto the stairs. My dad might come back down any second and if he finds me out here he'll make sure I never get the chance to follow him again.

Morris leans on the railing to watch me go. 'If you need me, you know where I am.'

'I always did.' My voice echoes up and around the walls.

It's not until I'm back in my room, lights out and hidden under the covers, that I let myself cry.

I crawl up to the pillow, begging sleep to come. Maybe I'll wake up and none of this will be happening.

The panic suddenly multiplies in my head. Siobhan is awake, and it's hitting her all over again. It feels like she'll break under it all.

I should go to her. I should leave my bed and try to offer the comfort she needs.

But I don't. We lie in our rooms, separate, but somehow together, crying until the morning comes.

# Chapter Nine

## Siobhan

The car belches exhaust into the Friday morning air. In the trees the parakeets are squawking their stupid squawks. I don't want to be out in public, then again I couldn't have stayed home one second longer. Mum banging on the door, asking if I'm all right, when clearly she can hear me spewing my guts up. She'd have followed me around all day, watching like a hawk.

On my way to Olivia's car, a dog appears from behind my step-dad's double glazing van and sniffs around my feet. It follows me, even when I hiss at it to *piss off*.

Someone chases it down – Tubs – making a noise that might be its name. Tanker? Trucker? Something stupid.

He's out of breath by the time he catches up. 'You stealing my dog, Shiv?'

*Shiv.* A sharp object cobbled together from fragile junk.

The dog stares at me like I'm its stupid little idol. Tubs shakes a packet of treats to distract it. The beefy smell of them makes me feel sick.

'Keep your fucking dog away from me,' I say, clicking open the car door and climbing into the back seat. Maida and Olivia are there already. Tubs tries to peer through the windows but they're all foggy with breath.

'It could have been him,' says Maida from the other back seat.

I know she's joking. Would she find it funny if I punched her in the mouth?

'Keisha's coming,' says Olivia from the driver's seat.

We all feel it. Keisha coming down the stairs. This weird connection we have is growing stronger by the day. It's not clear enough to read thoughts. It's not like I know what they sank for breakfast. It's emotional. We shared the pain and disgust of morning spewing. We shared the shock of looking down and seeing our stomachs already bloated. Already *showing*. That's the word all the blogs used when I looked it up. Like it's a secret betrayed by our bodies.

It's only been two days since the pregnancy tests revealed the truth. There should be no bump for at least a month. Either we're all getting fatter, or it's another little bit of impossible to add to the pile.

Up front Olivia wipes mist from the windscreen with her sleeve. Tubs is still out there. Watching us. I slide down in my seat. I don't want his eyes on me. I want to keep as much of my body to myself as I can.

Last night I went into the bathroom. Stared at myself in the mirror. Stomach swollen. Veins bulging in my tits. I wanted to wash, but the pipes would have been too noisy.

I took a disposable razor out of the cabinet. Snapped out the blades. Something I hadn't done for a long time, but I couldn't stop myself. Maybe I could cut the trouble out of me. It's my body. It should be my choice.

The door of the block opens. Keisha hurries out. She nods at Tubs and squeezes into the back seat beside us.

'Why don't you sit up front?'

She looks at me blankly, like she never even considered it.

Olivia pulls the car away from the kerb, out the car park and on to the road. The movement makes all three of us groan with sickness. It's like our mother is driving us to school. I should kick her seat. Pull her hair.

'Why is it just us?' says Maida.

We reach the main road and join the traffic.

'There are loads of women in the block,' she continues. 'So why only us four?'

It should have been someone else.

*Anyone but me.*

Olivia leans back against her headrest as we stop at traffic lights. 'Not every woman in the block would be suitable. Think about it,' she says. 'A lot of them are too young or too old. Half of them smoke or worse. Maybe we were the best bet.'

She makes us sound like mice in some messed up experiment. Beside me Keisha is shaking her head.

'What if we were chosen?' says Maida.

'For fuck's sake.' I say it before I can stop myself.

Maida keeps going. 'There has to be a reason they chose the four of us.'

'Who's *they*?' Keisha and me blurt at the same time. Our irritation seems to collide in the middle of the car, ricochets back at us, knocking us all into silence.

Olivia turns the wheel hard. Off the main road. The

longer route to school, through a derelict industrial estate.

'Let's think about it,' says Olivia, eyes on the road. 'Are any of you sexually active?'

'You mean, like, together?' I say it just to feel her squirm.

'No, I mean . . . with guys. The ones with the semen.'

I force myself to shrug. Like it's not a big deal. 'Yeah, I've been *sexually active* loads. But I'm always safe. And it's been a while.'

'Keisha?'

She shakes her head. I catch myself wanting to tap in and feel what she's feeling, and immediately pull back, ashamed.

No one even bothers to ask Maida. It's probably fair to say she's done nothing. We all feel the small spike of her annoyance.

'I'm sorry to be so blunt. I know you don't really know me, so I'll be honest too,' says Olivia. 'A year ago my boyfriend and I were trying for a baby. *Really* trying. I even had a blog about it.'

I remember her boyfriend. He had a serious spud head. Imagine pushing that out of you. I was glad when he left so I wouldn't have to see him round the block anymore.

'When it wasn't happening we saw a specialist. They said it was incredibly unlikely I would ever be able to conceive.'

She turns back to look at us. 'Do you girls understand what I'm saying? I *can't* – my body *can't* – that's what they told me. So now it all gets a bit biblical.'

My body has been invaded and she wants to pass it off as some kind of miracle? My chest tightens and I clench my fists in my lap.

'We can do something about it,' I say.

Olivia brakes hard. Practically throws me into the front seat. We're at the edge of the industrial estate, a few minutes from school.

They all know what I mean. All of us can make the decision. To end the pregnancy we never wanted.

I open my mouth to say it. The word that's like a bomb. But it slips away from me. My mind goes blank, and my lips just . . . shut down. I literally can't say it – the word has been snipped out of my brain.

When I look at the others, I know the same has happened to them.

My baby is protecting itself. If I can't think it, I can't do it.

When I tried to bring the razor blade to my skin last night, my hands seemed to rebel. They jerked away before I could cut. I thought it was just fear making my mind flash blank. Maybe it was something else.

It's sinister. It's impossible. And we all know it's true.

'Siobhan . . .' says Keisha.

'No! Someone did this to my body. They put something inside me, something I never wanted.' My voice shakes. I fight to hold it together. 'Now all of you are inside my brain. And whatever's growing inside me is trying to take control. I won't let it! It's my body! Nobody else has the right to it.'

Keisha speaks to me like I'm a little kid. 'If we just knew—'

'What fucking difference would it make, Keisha?' I shout. 'It's happening whether we like it or not.'

'It matters,' says Olivia. 'What you're trying to suggest . . .' She pauses. I see the word get scratched from her memory. 'It's too risky. After a little over a day the tests said the pregnancies were already four weeks along. They're growing faster than they should. If there's something . . . *not normal* about them, we don't know what the health implications would be for us.'

Maybe it would be worth it. I'd risk anything to end all this right now. To take back control.

They feel me think it. Maida and Olivia prickle with shock.

'Take yourselves out of my head!'

'This doesn't have to be a bad thing,' says Olivia.

I snort. 'Your barren self *would* say that.'

'We should tell somebody.'

A shudder of panic from Keisha. 'We're not telling anybody until we know what's going on.'

Her eyes are wide. Frightened. She's clinging to the mystery like it might save her from the truth. Like maybe she can still control all this.

Here's me thinking she was supposed to be the smart one.

## Keisha

She thinks she knows me, but she's wrong. She doesn't know anything about me anymore.

Olivia gets us moving again. We pull into traffic behind a bus full of school kids, busy drawing nasty shapes in the condensation. It's starting to rain again and Olivia sets the wipers going. Their heavy rhythm makes sickness push up my throat.

'People are going to ask questions. You know what they're like in the block,' says Olivia. 'If the babies are growing this quickly it's not long before we need hospitals and paperwork.'

'You can help us with hospital stuff,' I say. 'You work there.'

'It's not as easy as that. Why keep it quiet? If something *is* wrong we need all the help we can get. I'm trying to look out for you.'

'No, you're not!' I'm shouting before I realise it. 'You just want to show off your good luck. It's all right for you. You're old enough to be having a kid. We're just teenagers. Everybody will think we did something wrong! If we tell them we were raped they'll just want evidence. They'll say we're making it all up.'

Nobody argues with that.

The bus stops on the corner and we pull round it to take the final turn before the school. The pavement is packed with kids. I take out my phone to check the time, and my stomach plummets. There are fifty-two Facebook notifications. This morning I was too busy being sick and finding my baggiest school jumper to check it.

I open the app, and the image is at the top of my feed. Three photos spliced together. The first shows Morris storming out of the empty flat the other night. He looks so angry, blood running from his nose.

The second photo is Siobhan and I coming out into the hallway. It's like a paparazzi shot. Our faces are red and puffy from crying.

The last photo is a close-up of two pregnancy tests. *4 weeks*, they say, smeared with dirt from the floor. There's a black bar across the third photo with the words *these two are in trouble!* Both of us are tagged.

The car pulls up outside the gate, rain falling hard now.

'Fuck!' says Siobhan, seeing my screen. 'Who the fuck posted this?'

Back to the main feed, I see it was posted by Louise Krawczyk. I thumb down the feed. The image appears again and again, a different person posting it every time. We're tagged in every single one. There are reactions and emojis. Comments.

O M G.
Taking bets whos the biggest slut!!
They are fuckin rank.

Nobody even mentions Morris. All they care about is us.

'It must have come from Snapchat,' says Maida.

'I don't care where it came from!' shouts Siobhan. 'What do we do now?'

She looks at me with wild eyes, like I have all the answers. I shake my head. It's all slipping away, like sand passing through my fingers.

'Nobody's even asked what I think,' says Maida flatly.

I shove the door open and step out into the rain. I don't look at anybody crowding up the school driveway. I don't want to know if they're looking at me.

'Keisha!' shouts Siobhan, her voice breaking. My head fills with her despair, enough to make me dizzy.

I elbow my way through the throng. If the secret's out, I have to get ahead of it. There's only one person I can tell, one person who might believe the truth.

He helped me get control of my life once before. Maybe he can do it again.

# Chapter Ten

**Morris**

If you wanted to solve all the country's problems in one go, you'd tool up every Job Centre with rockets, wait until everyone's inside, and then blast it into space.

I know that's not fair. I'd be going with them.

The big security guy eyes me up as I walk past the computers, like maybe I've got a bomb strapped to my chest. I flash him my appointment card and he nods me through. It must be weird having a job in the Job Centre. If I could double my body weight I could be a security guard. You can't need many exams for that.

The lift takes me up to the third floor. My advisor is with some girl so I stroll across to the jobs board. There's not too much different from two weeks ago. What I don't understand is why every single job needs some kind of exam now. Even scrubbing floors in a factory at night needs a piece of paper to say you can do it properly. I'm pretty stupid but I know how to use a mop.

I slump into a bright green chair to wait my turn. A lady across the room has brought her kid and it's wandering around the room like it's a playground. I would never bring my kid to a place like this. Not in a million years.

It makes me think of Keisha and I can't help but smile.

I'm still smiling when I sit down opposite my advisor.

'Good news?'

'What? Oh, yeah, but nothing to do with this. I'm still a jobless bum.'

'Well, that's a shame. And you shouldn't talk about yourself that way.' She's a thin woman and her head wobbles when she talks, like her neck can barely hold it up. I see her every two weeks, and she's probably the nicest woman I've ever met, but I still hate her more than anyone. She's the only person who really knows what a total loser I am.

'Have you been filling in your job search?' she says.

I unfold the thick book of paper where I have to list everything I do to try and find work. You're supposed to do it online, but not having a computer at home and the nearest library being two bus rides away after all the closures makes that a bit difficult. I look at my messy handwriting. Every entry from the last month resulted in nothing. Not even a single rejection letter.

'I know it might seem hopeless right now,' she says, leaning forward on her elbows and looking at me all serious. 'But things are bound to look up soon.'

She says the same thing every time, even though just by being there to hear it I'm proving her wrong.

This time I grin at her. 'I think you might be right.'

'That's the spirit. You have something in the pipeline?'

I slouch back in my seat. I realised a couple of months ago that my Job Centre advisor is the only person I really have to talk to these days. It made me feel so pathetic

I thought about going up to the roof of the block and jumping off. I mean, not seriously. But I don't think anyone would have blamed me. I take a breath.

'I'm going to raise my ex-girlfriend's baby like it's mine. Unless the loan sharks after me break my skull first, of course. Can I get some extra benefits for that?'

She looks at me sideways, like she's not sure whether to laugh or call the security guy. In the end she sort of snorts and slides my papers back across the table.

'I'll see you in two weeks.'

## Keisha

Everybody in form is staring at us. Siobhan and I sit as far from each other as possible, and it's like the rest of the class is watching a tennis match, looking from one of us to the other like they might miss something.

They whisper. They smile, glad to have a reason to think badly of me again. Maybe they expect it of Siobhan, but it's me who's spent a year trying to be better than them – and they're glad to see me fall.

Mr Guo takes the register and then just lets us do whatever we want. Phones are out. Everybody is looking at the pictures. Louise Krawczyk smirks at me. Someone behind me cries like a baby, and a bunch of the boys suck on their thumbs.

I make sure I don't look at Siobhan. Across the room I feel her shame and anger, how she's trying to stop herself from running.

*You can handle this.*

I think it as hard as I can. Partly for myself, but I hope Siobhan hears it too.

As soon as the bell goes I rush for the door.

'Slut!' someone shouts after me.

I don't look back. My first class is English, but I elbow my way to the science block instead, ignoring the taunts and whispers that follow me. I go straight to his office door and knock.

'Please, enter.'

Mr Arnopp is sitting at his desk, sipping a steaming cup of coffee. He keeps a fresh pot on top of the filing cabinet behind him and the whole office is filled with the rich aroma. Usually I love it, but today it makes me feel sick – a recurring theme.

'There you are!' he says brightly. 'Science prodigy. Future Nobel prize winner. My girl. Are you feeling better? I was worried about you.'

I take the seat opposite him. The band of my skirt digs into my waist. 'It was only one day, sir.'

He lifts his eyebrows above the rims of his glasses. 'I know, I wasn't accusing you of anything.'

The thought of disappointing him almost makes me get up and leave without another word.

'I want to tell you why I was off yesterday.'

'I hope it was nothing too nasty.'

The back of his computer is covered with dust. There's a brown stain on the carpet near my foot. The windowless room smells like coffee and disinfectant. I focus on these things to give me courage, these constants that won't have changed after I tell him.

'Sir, I think . . .'

No, I don't think. I know.

'I was raped.'

Silence pours into the room like cement. I thought saying it would be a relief. But instead it feels like the world shifts, and my place within it becomes a little less certain.

Mr Arnopp stares at me across his desk. A breath rattles in his nose. I look at the dust on his computer. The stain on the carpet. Breathe in the stink.

After a long moment he leans forward on his elbows. 'Go on.'

Finally, I manage to meet his bright blue eyes, usually so friendly. I expect them to be full of concern. Support. Even pity. Instead they've turned hard and cold.

My mouth opens. Which words are the right ones? I wanted to tell him the truth. I wanted to tell him everything. He was the person who would believe me. Now I see that isn't true.

'Keisha, you've really caught me off-guard.'

'I'm sorry.'

He blows a breath through his lips. 'Do you want to report it to the police?'

My head shakes, almost automatically.

Mr Arnopp stands and comes round the desk, like he might offer me a hug. Instead he perches on the side of the desk and rests a hand on my arm. 'You want to talk about it?'

That's all I wanted. I didn't want him to hear about it from somebody else. Now all I manage is to shake my head.

'There's people I need to get involved,' he says. 'If you're serious about this.'

'No,' I say. 'Please.'

He nods. 'We'll keep it between us for now, all right? Because you *do* realise it would be a very serious allegation?'

I drop my head and nod.

His hand is still on my arm. 'I'm glad you came to me.'

'It won't affect my work,' I say quickly, biting back a sob.

'Hey, come on,' he says, and he pulls me up into a hug, wrapping his arms tight around my waist.

For a second I'm too shocked to react. He smells like Nescafé and aftershave.

'You know you mean more to me than that,' he says.

That's all it takes. I rest my cheek against his shoulder, and I hold back the tears as he rubs his hands up and down my back.

It's a few minutes until I step towards the door, wiping my eyes on the back of my hands, just in case.

'I'll see you soon,' he says, bending his knees so our eyes are level. 'Okay?'

'Okay.'

It's still the middle of first period. I run out of the science block and into the downstairs toilets. Only one of the stalls locks. I throw the seat down and collapse onto it, finally letting the tears out. The other girls push at my mind, probing it to find out what's happening.

The tiled wall is cool against my face. I press my cheek against it and stay there until the bell rings.

## Siobhan

It's lucky I always sit at the back of the class. Second period is Chemistry. My seat is right in the corner. It means everybody looks at me when I come into the room, but then I'm behind them and out of sight.

When they stare, I stare right back. I put on my mask. I'm not about to let them know they're bothering me.

Keisha is last into the room. She takes her usual seat down the front. Everybody ogles at her back. Sniggering. Making gestures. I should do something to defend her. But I'm just glad they're ignoring me.

Miss Robinson goes round the room and passes out equipment for today's lesson – including a flat yellow box with an analogue dial on the front, the measuring needle resting still. As its numbers go up, the display changes colour. Green to orange to warning-sign red. A circular tube like a microphone is wired to the box.

'Don't worry, it's all perfectly safe,' says Miss Robinson. She comes back around and hands out a bunch of little cardboard boxes plastered with hazard labels. A pair of surgical gloves for everyone. 'This is a Geiger counter. It measures radiation levels.'

Lastly she gives us worksheets. Always worksheets. It lists the various materials we've been given and offers spaces for us to record readings. The class chatters away. Any kind of practical experiment in science is better than reading the text book, and they don't do them as much anymore after the last one ended in a fire evacuation.

Annoyingly, the experiment means working with the person next to me. Lee is usually too busy drawing boobs and dicks on the text book pictures to pay any attention. Now he eagerly plugs in the Geiger counter and snaps on the surgical gloves. He looks at me as he does it, lifting an eyebrow.

My mask doesn't slip. 'I swear to God, you just try it.'

A deflating glove whizzes past us with a lazy fart noise.

'Do you *want* radiation to melt your skin off?' says Miss Robinson, retrieving it.

First off we hold the scanner in the air. Even when it's not pointed at anything the needle on the dial wobbles. The box emits tinny clicks like stones falling down a cliff.

'Background radiation,' says Miss Robinson. 'Write it down so you have a base level for comparing the other readings.'

Next we slide the cardboard cube marked with a blue sticker to the middle of the worktop. The counter crackles more loudly. Lee waves the scanner over the cube. The needle sways up into the green zone of the dial.

He groans. 'Boring.'

I couldn't agree more. I scribble down the reading. It's about as radioactive as old pizza.

At the front of the room, Keisha is carefully making notes. She's trying to distract herself. I sense it isn't working.

'Now take the cube with the big red warning on it. Make sure you're wearing your gloves!' says Miss Robinson, walking up the centre of the room between workbenches. 'You should get a much stronger reading.'

Lee snatches the cube, brings it under the scanner. The needle swings up into the orange. The box spits and crackles like it's cooking popcorn.

'As you can probably tell, that's the most radioactive of the bunch,' says Miss Robinson. 'It's perfectly safe in these quantities, but it would be dangerous to have anything stronger in the classroom without your parents signing a form to say it's okay to kill you.'

I scribble down the reading. Lee starts wielding the scanner like a sword and threatens the pair at the table in front of us.

'I bet your dick's radioactive!' he says, and lunges at his mate.

The wire isn't long enough. It jerks taut, making him stumble over his chair. As he reaches out to catch himself the scanner hits my stomach and the Geiger counter roars like a beehive, the needle spiking high into the red.

I back away from it, hoping nobody noticed. Lee just stares at me. He retrieves the scanner and waves it over my stomach like an airport security guard. The counter goes mental.

'You a superhero or something?' he says.

I slap his hand and everybody turns to look at us. From the front of the room I feel the rush of Keisha's fear.

Lee knows he has an audience. 'Watch this!' he shouts, coming at me again with the scanner. Before it gets too close I grab his arm and twist it. He cries out and drops the equipment.

'Leave it, yeah?'

'All right!' he moans.

Breathing hard, I let his arm go. The whole class stares at me like I'm an escaped convict.

'It must be faulty,' says Miss Robinson, picking up the counter and ignoring the violence. 'Radiation levels that high would kill everyone in the room.' She unplugs it before it can cause any more trouble.

From the front of the classroom comes the frenzy of another counter spiking high. I see Keisha holding a scanner to her stomach. The room fills up with gasps and mutters. Fear ignites inside her and slams into me. Our connection seems to have an effect on the people trapped between us – they twitch their heads and rub their ears, like something's interfering with their brains.

'I don't know what's going on,' says Miss Robinson.

I have to get out. I'm going to lose it any second. I rush for the door, mumbling about feeling sick. Nobody tries to stop me.

The cold hits me like a slap as I burst through the science block doors. I grip the metal railings in my fists. There's nobody here. Nobody to see. I let out a sob that echoes back against the building.

'You can't make a scene like that!'

It's Keisha, stopping behind me.

'I didn't – want – any of this.'

'None of us wanted this.' I hear her trying to keep her voice calm.

'You saw what that machine did in there,' I say. A tear spatters against the ground. 'This whole thing is a nightmare. Our bodies have been taken over, and we have no idea what with.'

I spin around to face her. I was expecting her to look angry. Disappointed with me. But she just seems sad. Strung out. A shared sense of dread hangs between us.

'What if they're not normal?' I say.

'I don't know.'

'What do we do if they're monsters or—'

'I don't know! That's the last thing I want.' She wraps

her arms around herself. 'This whole thing is the last thing I want.'

My legs wobble. I sink down onto the concrete. My mask is torn, and it feels like nothing is going to stop the tears from spilling out.

Keisha leans down and puts an arm around me. It isn't a hug. She picks me up, and we walk together around the main building. Onto the driveway. It's the middle of lessons, so nobody is around. We head for the road and leave school behind us.

# Chapter Eleven

**Keisha**

We were back at the tower by late morning. All the old ladies and the unemployed gawped at us from their windows – like we were both in our underwear or something. I swear they must spend all day hanging out, trading the latest gossip. As we left the car park and came up the path they all shared a knowing look, retreated back inside, shut their windows.

I told Mum I was still feeling sick. It wasn't a lie.

She looked at me for a long time, but didn't say a word. Instead she made me a cup of tea that just ended up going cold. After an hour or so she had to leave for her late shift. She knocked on my bedroom door but I pretended to be asleep.

I wish I could tell her about everything. But I couldn't take it if she didn't believe me.

The second Mum was gone I grabbed my phone and sent a text to Siobhan, asking if she wanted to come over. It's not good for her to be alone – she cried non-stop on the way home.

Maybe I don't want to be alone either.

The connection between us broods like a storm is coming, but regardless – if she sees the text she doesn't respond.

Notifications from Facebook don't stop coming. I take one more look, but they all say the same thing.

Should of kept their legs closed.
Are you really surprised tho?
kmt sluts just don't want to work!

At least they haven't found my Twitter account. It's only for games and streaming news, so nobody I actually know should follow it.

I change out of my uniform and leave it in a pile on the floor. It's never felt so good to escape my bra. My breasts look like they've been inflated and the veins are ready to burst. They're too sore to touch.

I reach for my laptop. I haven't got the energy for a livestream, so I open a new tab and begin to search. *Mysterious pregnancy.* The results are all about teenage girls doing things they're not supposed to. *Unwanted babies.* The results are too grim to click. *Escape your future.* Nothing but advertising campaigns.

A spike of shock ripples through me and I know it's Maida, upstairs. It's later than I realised. The room is dark and the screen bathes me in white light.

*Narcoleptic pregnancy.* I don't have much hope for that effort, but a headline catches my eye: ALIENS RAPED US IN OUR SLEEP, SAY CORNISH VILLAGERS.

Before I can click it an email notification pops up in the corner of the screen. It's from Maida, subject line *WATCH THIS RIGHT NOW.*

The email contains a link and a timestamp. It's one of my archived livestreams. Nothing unusual, just me setting up and greeting my audience. At first I don't understand why she'd send it. Then I notice the date.

It's from the Nightout.

My whole body seems to go numb as I click forward to the time Maida has specified.

## Morris

Dinner is macaroni and cheese that looks like baby sick and bits of breaded turkey shaped like airplanes. It really makes me feel like a man.

Me and Mum eat it on our laps in front of the TV. I should probably be worried that a sixty-year-old woman is addicted to *Hollyoaks*.

'I spoke to Dad today,' she says during the ad break.

'Yeah?'

It was months ago I last spoke to him myself. It's not easy without the internet at home. Keisha used to let me use her computer for Skype sometimes, but those days are long gone. It's probably a good thing. Last time I spoke to him he spent twenty minutes telling me I'm a sponge because Mum makes all the money to send over to them. I swear he set a world record for saying *pull your weight* in a single conversation.

As soon as I got the loan a couple of months ago I sent a chunk out to him. I hoped he might be grateful but no one has even mentioned it.

'They're all getting on fine,' says Mum.

*Hollyoaks* cuts off any chance of the conversation continuing. When it's over she switches to a crappy chat show. It's a sign I've been unemployed too long that I recognise all the bottom feeder celebrities on it.

'How was the Job Centre?' asks Mum.

I shrug. 'Yeah, all right.'

She heaves herself to her feet. 'I have to get ready for work.'

The stab of guilt is still as sharp as a samurai sword. I stack up our plates and carry them to the sink. The least I can do is take care of things at home. By the time I've finished washing up, Mum's ready in her blue-checked cleaner's smock. She kisses me on the shoulder (the highest bit of me she can reach), tells me my hair is getting too fuzzy, and grabs her door keys, leaving the car key.

'You not driving?'

'No petrol,' she says.

'You want me to walk you to the bus stop?'

'What a gentleman.' She smiles. 'Don't bother yourself, it's not far.'

When she's gone I walk to the sofa and punch the cushions as hard as I can. I hate seeing her go to work every night. *Punch.* It should be me scrubbing floors to put turkey airplanes on the table. *Punch.* I should be pulling my weight. *Punch-Punch-Jab.*

I slump back on the sofa and watch some show about houses I'll never be able to afford. My mind drifts. I take out my phone and open the text conversation with Keisha. It's a months-long streak of one way messages. My legs shift restlessly. I want to text her but anything I come up with sounds stupid, so I slip the phone back into my pocket.

I look up at the clock. Nearly 9 p.m. These are the

hours we all used to hang out, outside the block. Time never bloody dragged like this back then. Everything was better when we were together.

On the way back from the Job Centre I met Tubs coming down the path. He patted me on the back, greeting me like I was some kind of hero. When I asked him what the hell was up, he said he knew about Keisha.

I just walked away. I didn't deny it. I want him to believe it's true.

I'm heading for a piss when I hear voices out on the street. It's not unusual to hear people being loud on the estate, but I swear I recognise this lot. Dread sinks into my stomach like I've swallowed a dead cat. I mute the TV and cross to the window.

In the light of the main entrance I see three guys hanging around by the playing green fence. Tyrone is easy to spot. He's about twice the size of his crew. As I watch he peels away from the others and walks towards the door, where he's too close to the block for me to see. My phone vibrates in my pocket. At the same moment the door buzzer cuts through the flat. It makes me flinch away from the window.

Tyrone used to come here all the time to hang out and watch movies. Talk about girls. All the usual stuff. This time he means business.

The buzzer goes again. The two guys against the fence laugh. After a second next door's buzzer rings, and then the same upstairs. He must have started mashing the buttons.

I hear the familiar metal *click* and my heart tries to exit through my mouth. Someone has let them in.

The two guys don't move. Tyrone steps back into view. When he looks up at the tower I duck down, even though there's no chance he'll see me. After a second he slams the door shut, says something to the others, and they slope away together.

It was a threat. They didn't want to come inside. They just want me to know that they could.

I drop onto the sofa like my legs have melted. A choir mouths at me from the muted TV. There's no way I'll be able to pay him back. The money must be twice what I borrowed by now. I've got more chance of sprouting rocket launchers for arms than scraping together six grand.

I can't let Keisha know about any of this. She wouldn't let me anywhere near her or the kid in her belly and she'd be right not to.

There's a message waiting when I check my phone. It's her.

You need to come over. It's URGENT.

I check my reflection quickly in the bathroom mirror. There's a smear of ketchup down my front. I fill my armpits full of pound shop deodorant and change my T-shirt. This time I remember to grab my key.

When I open the front door I can't help but peer out into the hallway, just in case anybody is waiting to bash my kneecaps. It feels like cold air is leaking out of the walls. The light bulbs over my head sizzle quietly. When the door closes the noise echoes all the way along the hall. Sometimes the tower feels like an enemy. I hurry for the stairs.

At her front door I almost knock, but I remember our rule – I wouldn't knock after dark so we could keep our meetings secret. That's probably more important now than ever. So I send her a text:

Outside.

The door opens in seconds. Heat rushes into the corridor. She's wearing pyjamas, hair tied back from her face. I can see the pregnancy. Her stomach definitely looks rounder. Though there's no glow like people bang on about.

There's not much time to admire her before she yanks me inside. It feels like old times, and a spark of excitement crackles across my skin.

It fades as soon as she leads me into her bedroom. The air feels heavy, the same atmosphere as when she dumped me out of her life.

'Maida found something,' says Keisha, perching on her bed and leaning into the computer. 'You need to see it.'

I sit on the edge of the bed and look at the screen, guessing she hasn't called me over to watch YouTube videos of cats.

'She was going through my archived streams. She's been watching them ever since her dad made her delete all her own games,' says Keisha. 'The stream from the Nightout was there. It archived automatically and I forgot about it.'

A couple of clicks sets the video playing. It's the usual stuff from one of her streams. The screen is divided up into boxes, the biggest one showing the game, a bunch of characters running around and smashing enemies with lasers and stuff. In the top corner a smaller frame is filled with Keisha's face, big headphones clamped over her ears. Behind her you can just make out her bedroom.

It's been less than a week, but seeing how different Keisha looks in the video is a shock. If I didn't know better, I'd say she hasn't slept since that night.

The streams weren't something she did when we were together. They started up after we finished, like it was plugging a hole in her life. I used to go to the library so I could watch them. It wasn't just an excuse to stare at her face – there's something intimate about the videos; a glimpse of something I used to have, something I took for granted.

'What am I looking for?' I say.

Keisha is watching the video with real intensity, like she's willing it to show something different. She clicks it ahead twenty minutes.

'Quiet,' she says.

In the game there's some kind of weapon selection menu open. Nothing about it seems unusual. A noise comes through the speakers, a quiet *thud* that isn't from the game. Video Keisha doesn't hear it through her headphones.

'That must be my dad leaving, before I found him upstairs.'

I nod, but I don't know why that's important.

She clicks ahead another few minutes. The stream still looks the same as all the others. In the game Keisha is kicking arse and chatting away to her audience. She's more lively in the streams than I've seen her in real life for a long time.

Suddenly, Video Keisha drops back onto the bed. There's no yawning or eye drooping. She falls instantly unconscious mid-sentence, the headphone wire stretching out and knocking her drink onto the floor. Beside me Keisha shifts closer. Her arm against mine feels like lightning.

A low hum penetrates the speakers – the same noise I heard outside the block during the Nightout.

The character in the game freezes and is quickly offed by a gang of enemies. The menu pops up telling her to respawn.

We watch in silence as Video Keisha sleeps softly. It feels wrong to see her like this. It's *too* intimate, like something she'd usually hate for me to see. The fact that she's showing me now makes sweat prickle on my forehead.

'Watch,' says Keisha. Her voice shakes. She clenches and unclenches her hands.

The video image flickers for a split-second. Video Keisha doesn't move. There's a sharp *click*. The sound of her bedroom door opening off camera. We hear it creaking wide. Automatically I turn to look at the door-in-real-life at the end of the bed, still firmly closed. A strange purring noise vibrates inside the speakers.

'I heard that when I woke up,' whispers Keisha beside me.

In the video the duvet at the bottom of the image begins to shift. It's hard to make out in the small frame.

The game menu still takes up most of the screen. I can't help but lean forwards.

Video Keisha moves, but doesn't wake. Her soft breathing just about breaks through the low hum. She is being tugged towards the bottom of the bed. Whatever was in the room knew the camera was there but couldn't get close enough to turn it off without being seen. Papers spill over onto the carpet. Her body slides further along the bed until she's almost out of shot.

Keisha shoots forwards and pauses the video.

'There,' she says, jabbing the screen. 'You see it?'

I follow her finger. She points to the bottom corner. At first I don't see anything that wasn't there before. The frame is so small compared to the rest of the video. Then I see it. A long, dark *something* creeping up the bed covers.

'Wh—' I say, my voice sticking in my throat. 'What is it?'

'It's a hand.' Keisha turns wild eyes on me. 'Morris . . . it's – not human.'

# Chapter Twelve

**Keisha**

It isn't easy to make out. The duvet is dragged towards the bottom of the bed, my limp body sliding out of view with it. Fingers reach for me. They're long and gnarled, with swollen, arthritic lumps bulging around the joints.

'It's not human,' I say again.

It grabs my thighs, squeezing my flesh, like it's checking if I'm ripe. The sight of it, the *thought* of it, makes me want to claw my skin off.

Morris leans closer, and his voice sticks in his throat. 'Is there any more?'

The low hum swells through the speakers before the sound cuts out.

'The audio doesn't come back on until I wake up in ten minutes,' I say. 'There's nothing else to see.'

On screen, the bottom half of my body has been pulled almost completely out of view. I wish I could pretend it was somebody else, that I'm watching a movie or a stupid YouTube video. But it's my room, my face, my body. The horror of it makes me struggle to breathe.

Morris stands abruptly and turns his back on the screen. 'Is this online? Can other people see it?'

I stop playback and close the window. 'I've set it to private. You need the link to view it.'

Maida is the only other one of us who's watched. When I reach for our connection, what I sense from her isn't shock, not any more – now, it's more like *wonderment*. In comparison, Olivia, at work, is a distant beacon of permanent stress. And Siobhan feels opaque, stilted and dull.

Me, I just feel exhausted.

I sit on the edge of the bed and dig my fists into my eyes. An eerie sort of calm fills me up. I'm dimly aware that I should be screaming and kicking and crying but something holds me back from the brink. I wonder if it's the baby keeping me docile, making sure I don't get worked up and do anything to put it at risk.

'Do you believe me now?' I say.

'I always believed you.'

'No, you didn't.'

He holds up his hands like I'm attacking him. 'Keisha, this isn't the same as what you thought. I mean – that's not human.'

I stand up and push my face into his. 'It's not the same, it's *worse*, Morris. How can you not see that?'

'I mean, it's proper fucked up. But it's kind of amazing, you know?' He turns to face me and his eyes are bright. 'They put the whole building to sleep so no one notices them. Then they . . .' He gestures at the screen.

My stomach bulges against the elastic of my pyjamas. I swear it's bigger now than it was this morning. It can't be growing this quickly.

Sickness convulses through my body. Something alien is growing inside me. My lungs feel like a belt is tightening around them. I drop back to the bed.

'What were the chances?' says Morris. His hands are trembling. 'The chances of me getting back to the tower just in time to see the force field, or whatever it was?'

'What are you saying?'

He kneels in front of me, takes my hands and fucking switches on the grin like this is the best thing to happen to him in years. I'm speechless.

'Maybe I was meant to know. Maybe I'm supposed to be involved.'

I pull my hands free of his grip and find my voice with a surge of venom. 'This didn't happen to you.'

He takes my hands again. He's changing tack, pushing away his selfishness to try and make me feel better. His skin is warm against mine. I can't bring myself to pull my hands away. In spite of myself, more than anything I need to feel comforted. I need to feel like I'm not alone.

'It's still a baby,' says Morris. 'The video doesn't change that. Yes, this is all messed up, but it's happening. We have to find a way to deal with it.'

'What if I can't deal with it?' I say, gripping his hands. 'What if it's a monster?'

He smiles. 'Well, it's not burst out your chest yet.'

'That's not funny.'

He holds his smile, and something inside me breaks. I wrap my arms around his skinny shoulders and press my face against his chest. His hands cinch around my waist. Even though it's an awkward position at the edge of the bed I'm surprised by how comfortable it feels.

113

My mouth moves against his T-shirt. 'This ruins everything.'

'My hugs are that terrible?'

'Until I saw that video I thought I could still make it all okay. I was being dumb, I know; I knew it was horrible, but I thought – I'll keep going to school, take my exams, do everything like I planned.

'People would have judged me for being a black girl with a baby. It wouldn't have mattered where it came from. But now – Morris, what if the baby is a monster? What will people do? What will *I* do?'

Morris leans away from me but keeps his hands around my waist. '*Shhhhh*. You never know what's going to happen. You never *did*, not really. But whatever happens, I'm going to be here, yeah? You don't have to do this by yourself.'

I look into his eyes. He might mean it, or it might just be an opportunity for him to try and get close to me again. Maybe even he doesn't really know.

'We shouldn't tell Siobhan yet.' I disentangle myself from the hug. 'I don't know how she'll handle it.'

'You can't keep it quiet for long.'

I slump back onto the bed. 'I need to sleep for a week.'

Morris moves towards the door. 'You want something to eat? Who knows what that thing's sucking out of you.'

He's hardly the most comforting person to have around. But he's here.

'Don't leave me.'

He lingers at the door like he's not sure what to do next.

'This is where it happened,' I say. 'But I don't have anywhere else to go.'

'Okay,' says Morris. He walks across the room, lowers himself to the ground and leans his back against the wardrobe door. There's not a trace of exasperation on his face. It's like asking him to sleep on my floor is a totally reasonable request.

'Let me know if you need anything, okay?'

I nod and climb under the covers, switching off the bedside light. For a moment streetlight from the window flickers in Morris's eyes before I hear him rest his head back against the wood.

It's a long time before I fall over the edge of sleep. The last thing I see is his unmoving outline against the wardrobe.

It might be minutes or it might be hours before a flush of distress in my head kicks me awake. My phone is vibrating. As soon as I answer Olivia is screaming into my ear.

'You have to come up to the roof! Now!'

## Siobhan

It's a long way down.

The last time I came up to the roof it was with friends, blankets, and beer. It's not like it's nice up here. Most of the roof is taken up by a locked hut plastered with a big electrocution notice. There's a crop of TV aerials. A load of frozen bird crap. The floor is always littered with empty cans and cigarette butts.

But me, Keisha, and Morris made it our place. Away from all the stress. Up here we drank. Laughed. Talked about our futures. When he was younger, Mo was convinced he'd survive falling from the top of Midwich Tower as long as he rolled over when he hit the ground. I think he got it from a Bond film. He only changed his mind when we dared him to try it.

Now I stand on the edge of the wall and look down at the playing green. Nah – there's no surviving this fall. They'd find pieces of me on the main road. No way out.

The sun is coming up. The view sways. Turns out gin gets me drunker than I realised. Thanks, Mum. She left the bottle out after we finished talking. I pretty much polished it off.

It's so cold I might as well be naked.

This was supposed to be a test, to see if I can do it. If the baby will let me. Now I'm up here, I wonder if I *want* to do it.

'Get down from there.'

Her voice comes from behind me. I hold my arms up for balance. Glance over my shoulder. It's Keisha and Olivia. They must have felt my desperation. Of course. Nothing belongs to me anymore.

'Maida sent me the video,' I say, my voice all thick. 'You saw what they did to us.'

'This is not the answer,' Keisha says.

'It should be my choice,' I say.

*Drunk*, they whisper. Keisha's high horse gets a little bit taller.

'We're here for you now,' says Olivia.

'I told my parents,' I say. 'They know I'm pregnant.'

Keisha is quiet for a moment. Then she says, 'And?'

They were going to find out. Everybody at school

116

knows. All the kids in the block. Imagine Mum hearing them calling me *slut!* in the corridors. It was better they both heard it from me. At least I could make that choice.

I thought Mum would cry. Instead she went all serious and made me tell her everything. Obviously I couldn't tell her the truth so I just said it was some lad from school. Split condom. An accident.

Gary looked disappointed, but they both said they would support me. We're a family, even if he isn't my real dad. Would they say that if they knew the truth? If they saw the video?

I noticed, when I went to the bathroom, that they'd hidden all the razors.

My eyes itch, but I'm too exhausted to cry anymore.

'What else do they know?' Keisha says.

'I didn't mention you, if that's what you mean.'

'It's going to be okay.'

'I know you don't mean that,' I say, actually managing to laugh. 'I'm in your head, remember?'

'So you must know I don't want you to do this.'

All I feel is a swirl of fear, panic, anger. The usual. It's been hanging over us all for days. The only one who isn't in its grip is Maida – it's as if she's actually pleased about all this.

I stare down. All that empty air. It looks so peaceful. 'I need to know.'

I hear Keisha step closer. 'Know what?'

'If my body is still *my body*.'

And with that I pitch my weight forwards.

It should be enough to send me over . . .

Past the point of no return . . .

The world opens up underneath me . . .

At the last second, my body jerks back, my arms wheel at my sides and I rock on my heels. There's heat in my stomach, energy coursing through me.

Taking over.

Someone grabs my waist and bundles me down. We land in a heap on the rooftop. Both of them are on top of me, like I might break for it.

A sob forces its way up my throat, but somehow it comes out as a laugh. I laugh-cry, splutter and heave, sound hysterical – Keisha and Olivia look at me like I've gone completely batshit.

'It wouldn't let me,' I say, finding my breath. 'It wouldn't let me fall. It doesn't care what I want. The little monster is looking after itself.'

Keisha clocks what I mean. 'The baby wouldn't let you jump?'

'What kind of thing can *do* that?' I say, my laughter evaporating. Keish flinches at the booze on my breath. 'What the hell is inside us?'

'I had a scan,' blurts Olivia.

Keisha turns on her. 'You did *what*?'

She nods guiltily. 'Before I even saw the video, I had a scan. Just to check if everything was all right.' She gets off me and brushes herself down. 'I know this whole situation is difficult to understand. As far as I can tell the pregnancies are developing by two weeks every day, maybe a little more. I had to see what was going on in there.'

'And what did you see?' I say.

Olivia smiles. 'It was normal. Fingers and toes, everything where it should be.'

'You were supposed to keep it quiet,' says Keisha.

'A friend at the hospital helped me. Nobody else knows,' says Olivia. 'Did you know my boyfriend left me when we found out I couldn't conceive? I thought that was the end of my life. All I've wanted – literally, the only thing I've thought about since then – is to find a way. And now this has happened. Yes, it's about as far from perfect as it gets, but . . . I'm sorry, I can't just *write it off*. I have to do my best with the hand I've been dealt. I *want* to.'

A gust of wind whips through us.

'We can go to the hospital this morning,' says Olivia, 'before regular hours. You can see for yourselves. It's important to check everything's all right.'

Maybe if I knew for sure what had taken over my body I would feel better.

'Keisha?' I say. 'I can't do this alone.'

Keish stands up and looks out at the view. Eventually she nods. Just once. 'Okay, I'll go.'

We let Olivia climb down through the hatch first. Keisha grabs me before I can follow.

'That was a risky test,' she says.

'It can get inside my mind,' I say, lowering my legs through the hatch. 'That's the only reason I'm still here.'

119

# Chapter Thirteen

## Keisha

Waking Morris before he was ready used to be like trying to roll a dead horse up a hill. So it's strange when I go back downstairs, shake his shoulder, and get him on his feet within seconds.

Now he's waiting downstairs in the car with Siobhan, ready to take us to the hospital. I don't know how I feel about him being there. It should be the last thing I want, but Olivia has gone ahead to make sure the coast is clear, and there's no one else to take us. After last night, maybe he's earned some trust.

There's one more thing I have to do before we leave.

Maida's dad answers the door. He's in his dressing gown. As soon as he sees me he adjusts his grip as if he wants to slam the door in my face. In his eyes I'm the greatest threat to his daughter's innocence. Right now, knowing what I know, I'm also the greatest threat of his daughter getting punched in the mouth.

'I need to explain some schoolwork Maida missed,' I say, waving the random collection of papers I grabbed from my room.

He steps aside without a word.

I'm wearing a baggy jumper that hopefully hides my stomach. Maida's little brother, Azraf, is on the sofa eating a bowl of cereal and watching cartoons. He has a plaster on his forehead. When I pass in front of him he stares at me like I'm a burglar.

I push into Maida's bedroom without knocking. She's kneeling on a prayer mat in the tight space between two single beds. It's enough to make me hesitate, but she rises and waves me inside.

'Don't worry, I was distracted anyway.'

I make sure the door is shut behind me. 'Why did you send the video to Siobhan?'

The room is exactly the same size and shape as mine, but the two beds make it seem much smaller. The one against the far wall is surrounded by Ben 10 and Minecraft posters, the covers kicked into a ball on the floor.

Her stomach isn't as swollen as mine yet, but the change is clear to see nonetheless. She puts away the prayer mat and covers herself with a sleeved blanket.

'I thought she should know,' she says.

'What you *knew* is that she wouldn't be able to handle it.'

Maida nods. 'I could feel her, up on the roof. It was okay though. I knew the baby wouldn't let her do it.'

'How? Maida, you can't have known.'

'Haven't you noticed?' she says with a half-smile. 'If it so much as looks like I'm in trouble, let alone danger, the baby goes into defence mode. Yesterday my brother hit me and the baby made him headbutt the floor. *I* got in trouble for that one.'

I shake my head. 'Siobhan didn't know that.'

'Don't be so sure.'

Our eyes meet. Maida seems more attuned than any of us. It makes me wonder if she can read me more deeply ... maybe even more clearly than I can read myself.

She looks away first. 'I didn't think we should be hiding it from her. It's not something to be ashamed of. We were chosen.'

'You think this is something to do with your religion?'

There's a second before she shakes her head. 'No. I think this is something else.'

'If you're so proud, why don't you go out there and tell your dad all about it?' I say, pointing at the door.

She lifts her hands to try to calm me down. 'Do you know how difficult it is being treated like you're another species? When you saw me praying you acted like you'd walked in on some terrible secret,' she says. 'Yeah, sure, this whole thing is going to up my outsider status to eleven, but at least I won't be there alone. You never knew how much I wanted to be part of your group instead of stuck here with my parents.'

'You could have hung out with us if you wanted.'

She shakes her head. 'You know that's not true. I know you think something terrible has happened to us, but for me it could be everything. I'd like to see Dad force his plans on me now.'

My anger begins to simmer down, but my fists still clench, itching to knock some sense into her. 'Don't you see? This isn't an *escape* – it's just going to trap you in another future you don't want and didn't get to choose.'

Her mind is infuriatingly calm. 'Yesterday in the car we wondered why this has happened to us. Out of all the billions of women in the world they choose four girls in a shitty council block. You automatically assume it means something bad. But maybe it happened because we're special. Maybe we're meant for this.'

I turn toward the door. 'Whatever. Listen, we're going to the hospital now to get scans. Come with us. Maybe you'll change your mind when you see the thing inside you.'

She shakes her head. 'Everyone always thought you were no good and you proved them wrong.'

I leave her behind and storm across the living room, brushing past her glaring dad. A part of me wants to turn back and scream *'YOUR DAUGHTER'S PREGNANT'* and leave her to deal with the fallout.

She's right about one thing. I've spent the last year trying to show everyone they were wrong about me. As soon as news of the pregnancy reaches the adults it will all have been for nothing.

The Hag is standing out in the hallway with her old lady trolley. She curls her lip at me like I'm a bad smell. I slam the door, push past her, and hurry downstairs to the car.

## Morris

They sit in the back like I'm their chauffeur or something. Keisha sits tight up against Siobhan like she's scared she'll jump out the car while we're moving. I did consider locking all the doors, but there's no way I can do it without them noticing. I might try on the way home

123

though. God knows what state they'll be in afterwards.

'You need an escape plan,' I say.

Keisha leans forward. 'Of course we do.'

I aim the heater at her face to blast away the sarcasm. 'How do you know those scanners aren't hooked up to government computers or something? It shows ET growing inside you, yeah, and feds come smashing through the windows to take you away and stick sensors up you and stuff.'

'All right, Mulder. You're really not making this easier.'

There's a fuzzing noise in my ears, and a pain starts throbbing behind my eyes. It could be stress but I suspect not – it's not the first time it's happened when I'm around them.

I glance back at Siobhan who's staring out at the grey streets sliding past.

'I wish you'd come to me,' says Keisha.

Siobhan whips around to face her, so quick I think she's going to throw a punch. 'Why would I, Keish? Where've you been for the last year? I've had to get used to doing things by myself.'

'Things are different now—'

'Yeah, but maybe it's just not that easy for me to let you back in, you know?'

The silence that follows is so awkward I'm scared to even clear my throat. I want to put music on or something but the radio in my mum's car broke years ago.

Sometimes I wonder why Siobhan and me didn't really stay friends after Keisha ditched us both. We've known each other most of our lives. We stayed friendly, chatting a bit if we bumped into each other, but it was like Keisha was the glue and without her the friendship didn't hold together.

I check the petrol gauge. We're running on fumes.

'Shit.'

'What's up?'

Luckily we're passing a Shell garage. I pull up to one of the pumps and try swallowing down my embarrassment. 'We need petrol.'

'So?' says Siobhan.

'So I haven't got any money.'

'Oh, Mo, for fuc—'

'I have money,' says Keisha, digging into a pocket and coming out with a twenty-pound note. Taking it from her makes the last of my pride shrivel like a raisin in a microwave.

After I've filled up we spend the rest of the journey in silence. Keisha only breaks it when we're almost at the hospital. 'What did you feel when you tried to jump?'

'Really fucking scared.'

I glance in the mirror and see them looking at each other like they're trying to peer right into each other's brains.

'You know what I mean,' says Keisha. 'Did you feel some kind of energy building up inside you, something you couldn't control?'

I remember when I grabbed Keisha and it felt like some kind of force pushed itself out of her skin, shoving me away, nothing I could do about it. Afterwards I wondered if it was my conscience or something. I shouldn't have grabbed her. I regret it more than anything.

'You know what I felt,' says Siobhan.

I catch Keisha's eye in the mirror. 'You mean . . . ?'

She nods. I immediately start driving a little more gently.

'You need to tell me everything,' I say. 'You owe me that. Why do I always get a headache when I'm around you lot for too long?'

Maybe she's finally learning to trust me, or maybe she's just tired. She tells me how they can feel each other's emotions, how they all woke up together inside the empty flat right after the Nightout, how it keeps getting stronger.

'So can you read her mind, then?'

'I knew you'd ask that.'

'I think it's a fair question.'

'Maybe you should be more worried about being exposed to us.'

That's scary enough to shut me up.

The hospital is a block of windows, most of them leaking thin yellow light. It's still early enough that the streetlights are glowing, daylight failing to beat the gloom. I take us past a line of fluorescent ambulances and pull into a disabled spot, justifying it to myself by linking 'disability' with 'pregnant' in a way I instinctively know to keep quiet about.

'Can I use your change for parking?' I say.

Keisha leans between the seats again. 'Thank you for getting us here. But I think we should do this by ourselves.'

I look her in the eye and nod. I'm starting to realise that if I'm going to win her back I can't expect everything at once. My back is killing me from sleeping on her floor last night, but it showed me that I have a chance, and I can't mess it up.

'I can go visit my nan and pick you up when you're done,' I say.

'Your nan's in the hospital?'

'Nah, a care home round the corner.'

She looks at me in surprise. It's something I've never told her before. I don't think I've told anyone. It's embarrassing. I don't visit Nan enough, and I've never been able to help pay for the home.

'Text me when you're out,' I say. 'And remember, if the machine starts beeping or something, leg it.'

She smiles. It makes me want to kiss her. I watch them cross the car park before I pull away.

## Siobhan

We have to hide by a back door until Olivia lets us inside. Her nurse outfit makes her look like an ugly stripper. Curly hair dragged back into a tight ponytail.

The hospital is busy even this early. People shove trolleys along scuffed corridors and struggle under the weight of bulging sacks of rubbish. The air smells like bleach and toast. I'm starving. Suddenly I want trifle.

'Trifle would be amazing,' says Keisha.

Great. Now we share cravings.

Everyone is too busy to pay us any attention. We go up a floor and Olivia takes us to a small room with a single bed, a screen, and some other equipment that looks ripped straight from a sci-fi movie. The sight of it fills me with panic. Olivia shuts the door behind us.

'We haven't got long before the first appointment,' she says. 'Who's going first?'

We both step away from the bed.

'I can't,' I say.

It's like my fear goes toe-to-toe with Keisha's. Stand-off. In the end it's me who moves to the bed. Not because I back down – because I want to show her who's really strongest.

'When did you last pee?' says Olivia.

'Uh, last night, I think?' Now she asks, I feel like I'm going to burst.

'That's good! It's supposed to help.'

The bed is harder than I expected. 'You know what you're doing, right?'

She sort of wobbles her head in what might be a nod. 'I'm not a sonographer but I've seen it done loads of times before. Lift up your top.'

I lie back on the bed and let her hike up my jumper. My belly's got fatter and fatter over the last year. I see Keisha look at it in disgust.

I've been telling myself I don't care what she thinks. I wish it was true.

'This is going to be cold,' says Olivia.

She spreads some slime over my belly. It's like being buttered with dog slobber. When she picks up the scanner I try not to think of the Geiger counter.

Olivia swivels a blank screen so I can see. Then she glides the scanner over my belly. Presses firmly. At first the screen stays black but after a minute or so a blue cone opens up.

She increases the pressure. Makes smaller movements,

128

like she's trying to isolate a problem or find a signal.

'There it is,' says Olivia.

There's nothing inside the cone but a blur of white and blue.

A throbbing noise comes over the speakers, rhythmic and fuzzy, like rude boys blasting bass in their cars. Part of the blur becomes a round shape at the edge of the cone. Olivia points to it with her free hand.

'There's its head,' she says, adjusting the scanner slightly. 'And you can just see a hand and foot.'

The outline of a baby becomes clear. The heartbeat fills my ears. I look from the screen to my bulging stomach. And then I look at Keisha. She's staring at the screen like it has to be a hoax.

'We can't see them all, but there's two hands and two feet,' says Olivia.

'So it's normal?'

She grins. 'Told you.'

This is the bit where the mother breaks down in tears of joy, clutches her partner's hand, thanks the heavens for their blessing.

But I have no partner. And there is no heaven in this room.

All I see is the thing that has taken my body away from me.

'It looks a little bit smaller than mine, but I'd still say you're at least twelve weeks along,' says Olivia. 'Same as me.'

Keisha steps closer. 'It's only been a week since the Nightout.'

Olivia nods. 'They're growing too fast.'

'Can you tell the sex?' asks Keisha.

'Not at this stage.' She presses a button on the machine. While she cleans the slime off my belly a printer spits out a blurry picture of the baby. Olivia offers it to me as I climb off the recliner.

'I don't want that,' I say.

'You should keep it.'

I snatch the photo, scrunch it into a ball, and toss it across the room. Then I look at Keisha.

'Your turn.'

## Keisha

'They look healthy,' says Olivia, as she escorts us to the exit. 'I'd recommend a proper check-up . . .' Her words trail away, and for a moment her eyes are blank. She runs a hand over her stomach, and then seems to snap awake. 'Well, I don't think our little ones will let us.'

I feel the edge of the sonogram image in my pocket. I don't know why I kept it, except that it's evidence; cold, hard, incontrovertible.

'The rate they're growing, every day is equivalent to two weeks or so,' says Olivia. 'Pregnancies usually last around thirty-eight weeks, so I'd say we have about thirteen days until we're due.'

Thirteen days until all my plans crumble into dust. Everything has fallen apart so quickly and none of it is my fault. I don't deserve this.

'I had a blood test,' says Olivia, as we reach the back door. 'I was worried about what happened to you at school. There's no sign of radiation poisoning. The

130

vomiting has stopped. I think the babies must protect us from it.'

So my hair won't be falling out any time soon, but that doesn't change the fact that I might be carrying a nuclear bomb in my womb.

Olivia rushes off to start her shift. We push open the door and step out into the car park.

The sun has finally woken up and there are even patches of blue sky overhead. Morris hurries over to meet me like I've had surgery and need help to walk. An ambulance siren whirls past us. I let him hold onto my arm, the touch of his hand warm even through my sleeve.

'How was your nan?' I say.

He shrugs. 'Most of the time she thinks I'm somebody else.'

At the car Siobhan slumps straight into the backseat. 'I need a drink,' she says. 'And trifle. Why the fuck do I want trifle?'

I shut the door on her, then unfold the photo from my pocket and hand it to Morris. His eyes light up. Even though it only shows the blurry cone he seems to recognise the shape of the baby right away. It triggers his smile and he aims it at me.

'It doesn't have tentacles!' he says.

'We only have thirteen days left.'

Morris whistles. 'Someone's keen to get out.'

I open the back door and shift my weight down into the seat. 'That's what worries me.'

Someone has stuck the pictures on the outside of my

front door. Siobhan and me coming out of the empty flat, black and white and blurry, the words on the pregnancy tests unreadable. It doesn't matter. I tear them down, scrunch them into a ball, and hurl it down the corridor.

I hoped Mum would have left for work by the time I got home. She might have assumed I was still unwell and left me alone to sleep. But when I step inside I find her sitting at the kitchen table, still in her dressing gown, hands clasped together. It's an ambush.

'Where've you been?' she says.

I slip off my shoes and wander across to the table. 'I couldn't sleep.'

She points to one of the empty chairs. 'I think we need to talk.'

Sweat prickles on my forehead. I take the seat opposite her. Instead of looking at me she focuses on her hands, and her lips move as she tries to choose the right words.

I know what's coming. After the photos, after Siobhan told her parents she was pregnant, I knew it wouldn't be long before news spread. Nothing stays secret in the block for long. And like everything else there's nothing I can do to stop it.

'There's a rumour going around the building,' she says.

The truth is written all over my face.

'Oh, baby. Why couldn't you tell me?'

I reach into my pocket and take out the sonogram photo. It's already creased and worn along the fold. I slide it across the tabletop, and she rests a shaking hand on its surface.

After a second we both start to cry.

# Chapter Fourteen

**13 days until birth (12 weeks pregnant)**

**Siobhan**

The baby doesn't stop my fingers from typing. I might not be able to say the word myself, but luckily Google is full of desperate people with nowhere else to turn.

*How to give yourself an . . .*

And one of the Google auto-completes is *abortion*.

Nothing the baby can do about that.

As I came out of the stairs a group of boys shouted 'SHOW US YOUR MINGE!' When I ignored them they called me a frigid slut. Which totally makes sense.

Whatevs.

The search results aren't so promising. I need to get punched in the belly. Throw myself down some stairs. Stick a coat hanger up there, or wash it out with bleach. Like I could actually do that.

Could I?

Even if the baby would let me, I don't know how far I'd go.

There's a list of things that can make you have a miscarriage. Near the top is drinking and smoking.

I drank half a bottle of gin last night. The baby did nothing to stop me.

My parents aren't home yet. I go through to the kitchen and grab the gin. Unscrew the cap, take a swig and swallow.

I look at my belly. 'No cocktails on your planet?'

Another swig. No protest.

Maybe I have a chance in this fight after all.

## Keisha

The photo quivers in her hand. The expression on her face seems to swing between happy and shell-shocked, confused and angry. Eventually I can't stand the silence any more.

'It's about twelve weeks gone.'

Now she looks at me. 'You've known for that long?'

I squeeze my fists on the tabletop. 'Not that long.'

'I wish you'd told me,' she says. 'You shouldn't have had to do this alone.'

My stomach presses against the edge of the table. How to tell her I haven't been alone since it happened? Not really, not with the others always in my head like a snowstorm.

In other ways though, I've never been more alone.

'Who's the father?'

The question I've been dreading. I knew it was coming. I don't have a good answer.

I want to tell her I was raped.

I fix my eyes on her. I remember what happened when

134

I told Mr Arnopp. His disappointment. Disbelief. He was the person I trusted most.

I *need* her to believe me.

She senses my hesitation. 'Look, I've heard. About Siobhan and Olivia? It's hard to believe it's a coincidence. Did something happen to you? You can tell me.'

We've never really talked about this kind of stuff before. Even when I was going out and they knew I saw guys the most I ever got was an awkward talk from Dad about two people loving each other very much. I think Mum assumed I knew it all.

She must already think less of me. I don't want to make it worse.

I want to tell her. But in this moment I realise – I can't.

'It's Morris,' I say. 'The father.'

Now her anger is plain to see. 'I thought that was over.'

'It was.'

'I knew he was here last night,' she says. 'I'm not blind, you know. I didn't want to interfere.'

'We're not back together, if that's what you mean.' These days I don't know what the hell Morris and I are anymore.

'He needs to take responsibility!'

I take her hand across the table. 'He's been great, actually. I mean it.'

She looks at me like I might be the biggest liar in the world, but she doesn't argue. Instead she stands up and paces across the living room, shaking out her arms like she's limbering up for a fight.

'Do you want to keep it?' she says.

I think about the answer, and immediately my brain skids away to thinking about trifle. Delicious trifle.

I blink. It's not the first time that's happened. I remember what Siobhan said on the roof this morning. The baby stopped her from jumping. They're protecting themselves. Which means they can't let me think about . . .

Trifle.

Mum is peering out the window. She pushes on the door that opens onto the stubby balcony and steps out onto the puckered concrete. The breeze on my skin is a relief, and the sound of the parakeets in the trees is like a symphony after the silence inside.

'I might have expected this from Siobhan, but not you,' she says, leaning on the wall.

'That's not fair.'

'Not after the last year. You'd really turned things around.'

All my efforts are already past tense. My face fills with heat and I stifle a sob. 'I'm sorry.'

'Oh, baby,' she says, taking my hand. 'You think it was easy when I told your grandmother I was pregnant with you? Not only that, I had to tell her I was dropping out of school and getting married instead. She slapped me upside my head so hard I swear it still hurts.'

I can't help but smile. Granny died when I was still a baby, so all I have of her are photos.

'Did I ruin everything you'd planned for yourself?'

'Nothing was *ruined*. You were a surprise, I've never lied to you about that. Looks like it runs in the family.' She squeezes my hand. 'But we went with it, and we've never regretted it for a second.'

Maybe Morris is right, maybe I was stupid to think I ever really had a choice. We were born in the block, where everyone expects girls like us to get on our backs. I tried to defy them. I tried to prove that it didn't have to be true. And now it feels like I'm being punished for it. I should have known my place.

'At least if you're only twelve weeks you have plenty of time to take your January mocks,' says Mum.

I keep looking out the window. There's no way I can explain the accelerated growth. I've laid enough on her already. She'll see it for herself soon enough.

Something happens in my stomach then. At first I think it's spooling energy, our conversation doing something to anger the baby. But it's simpler than that. For the first time, it is moving inside me.

'Oh, crap.'

'What's wrong?'

It's like my internal organs are shifting. I press my hand to my stomach, hoping I can make it stop. The swell of confusion, panic, fear, and wonder is too tangled to make any sense.

'Oh, baby, it's turning over!' says Mum, grinning at me.

She places a hand on my stomach. I force myself not to flinch away. Whatever the baby was doing in there, it settles again.

'We wanted more, you know,' says Mum, leaving her hand on my belly. 'After you. But it never happened. I'll love this baby like it's my own.'

'I know you will,' I say.

Someone will have to.

And there's one person both of us have avoided mentioning.

'How are we going to tell Dad?'

Mum tips her head back and sighs.

## Morris

We make it to dinner time before she mentions it. Microwave lasagne and *Hollyoaks* are the backdrop to the most important conversation of my life.

Well, almost. She waits until the advert break.

'I'm going to have to tell your father, you know.'

I put my scraped plate on the floor and sink back into the sofa. 'I know.'

# Chapter Fifteen

**6 days until birth (26 weeks pregnant)**

**Keisha**

## SLUT

The word splays brash red across the front door, spills onto the concrete wall, the final letter slashed like an open wound.

The news has been out for a few days. It spread like nits in a classroom. Whispers and suspicious looks became leering shouts or bad-tempered insults. Sneering Facebook comments became death threats. Someone egged Olivia at the main door. Siobhan's letter box was set on fire.

We're ripening like fruit. My spine is killing me. My ankles hurt when I walk for more than a few minutes. I pee twice as often as usual, I'm afflicted by hot flushes, and all I want to eat is trifle and cheese.

Being pregnant sucks.

It's funny how, when you're young, everyone expects you to mess up your life. They even work against you to make sure it happens. And then they gloat when they prove themselves right.

'Why can't they just leave us alone?' said Siobhan, her words slurred, after she had begged her parents not to call the police.

She'd been drinking. It seems like that's all she's been doing since the scan.

I press my fingers to the paint. It's cool and tacky against my skin. I run the same hand over my swollen stomach. It's hanging out under my top. Nothing I own fits any more.

There's no way anyone else in the block can know how the babies were conceived. If they remember the Nightout at all they never talk about it.

Maybe a bunch of young women getting pregnant is enough to deserve their anger.

Only Maida has escaped it. Somehow she's managed to keep her place in all this a secret. She isn't showing as much as the rest of us, maybe because she's younger, smaller. We need to keep it that way for as long as possible.

The front door opens and I lunge to try and shove Mum back inside the flat before she can see anything, forgetting that right now I can lunge about as quickly as a dead snail.

She sees. Her mouth drops open.

'I'll clean it off,' I say quickly, as if it's my fault it's there.

She steps out into the corridor and puts her hands on her hips. 'You shouldn't have to!' Her voice bounces along the corridor.

'Quiet, please,' I beg. If anyone hears any commotion

140

they'll come out to stare like we're a tourist attraction. This week has been the most interesting in the tower's history.

'This has to stop.'

Gratitude wells in me. My belly gets bigger each day, and when the vomiting returned for a morning she rubbed my back and held my hair and waited for me to talk. She knows something isn't right.

So many times I've wanted to tell her but instead I've kept my explanations as vague as possible. I can't get away with that much longer.

The door opens again and Dad hurries out.

We told him together. It didn't go well. At first I thought he was going to disown me on the spot. Then all he would do is ask practical questions in a voice that was way too loud. *Do you know how much a baby costs? Where is it going to sleep? Why didn't you think about these things?*

He might as well have asked why I didn't keep my legs closed.

He stops in his tracks when he sees the graffiti and looks straight at me as if I'm holding the spray can.

'What the hell is this?'

'The people in this place . . .' says Mum.

Dad glances at my stomach, that familiar disappointment etched into his features. 'I'm late for work. Just make sure it's cleaned up before too many people see it.'

He heads towards the stairwell, and nearly bumps into Morris as he turns into the corridor, twirling car keys on his finger. When Morris sees me he pulls the trigger on his smile, but it misfires into a frown as soon as he sees the graffiti. He clenches the keys in his fist.

'Who the fuck did this?' He looks around the corridor like they might still be lingering.

'It's nothing, Morris.'

'It's not nothing!' he shouts at the nearest door.

I can't blame him for being angry. He's the only person who's really been here for us in the last week. Whenever we've needed to sneak around or walk somewhere, he's been there to help. He's answered his phone at any hour when I needed to talk. I've come to rely on him. Which is really weird.

Mum rests a hand on his arm. It silences him instantly. He looks down at it in confusion. She hasn't exactly been his biggest fan. That often happens when you're in the frame for knocking up someone's daughter.

'If I find who did this—'

'You'll give them a strong talking to, I get it,' I say, steering him away from the door. 'Mum, go to work. Morris, take me to school. We're already late.'

I haven't been back to school since the scan. Didn't seem much point. Mum phoned them to explain, but apparently being pregnant isn't a good enough excuse to have a week off. They threatened to 'get the authorities involved', whatever that means.

That's nothing compared to Mr Arnopp. He's bombarded me with texts and calls. At first the messages just asked what was going on and if I was okay. Then they started getting angry, demanding that I see him. I ignored all of them, until last night. If there's any way to salvage something from all of this, I need him on my side. So I replied, promised I'd go in and face him.

Morris snatches my bag off me. 'I'll clean it up when I get back.'

A month ago I would expect him to say something like that, and then come home to find it untouched. Now I know he means it.

One of our neighbours steps out of their flat as we approach the stairs. It's Frank, a guy with a huge beard who I know well enough to nod to. When I was younger I skinned my knee on the stairs, and he carried me back to my mum.

'I didn't see who did it,' he says, adjusting the cord on his dressing gown. He's been unemployed for over a year now.

'Thanks, Frank,' says Mum as we pass.

I give him a smile, but he doesn't return it. I can't help but notice the way his eyes linger on my stomach, like I'm harbouring something deadly there.

Tubs is standing on the stairs as we come through the door. He adjusts his cap and looks at me with a smirk, then winks at Morris. I grab Morris's hand in case he decides to do anything stupid.

'The Hag said it was what you deserve,' says Tubs.

We keep walking. There's no way she did the painting herself.

Tubs doesn't give up. 'I'll try and find out who did it.'

'It's not like you have anything better to do,' Morris mutters.

'I'm going to have words with that woman,' says Mum.

'Mum, please don't.'

She practically growls, and then takes a breath to calm

herself. 'You'll never get a pushchair up these stairs.' She says the same thing whenever we're on the stairs together. It makes me smile. It's something normal, a regular problem that doesn't make me feel frightened or ashamed.

'Let me know how it goes,' says Mum when we reach the car park, kissing my cheek before she hurries for her bus. A couple of girls from school saunter past us. One of them spits at my feet.

## Morris

We drive in silence for a few minutes. I'm still not sure how to be around Keisha these days, but everything I do is meant to help. And she's letting me. Maybe it doesn't mean a thing to her, and honestly, that's okay. I'm back in her life, and that's where I want to be.

'Don't let Arnopp bully you into anything,' I say.

'I won't.' She rests the side of her head against the window.

'I never trusted him, you know.'

'You would say that.'

Mr Arnopp was the reason she ditched me in the first place, so he's never been top of my Christmas card list. But it's more than that. It's not normal for a teacher to text his student like he's been doing with Keish. What worries me even more is that I'm not sure she sees it.

'Have you spoken to your dad yet?' I say.

'Mum sent him an email, but he hasn't replied.'

I shouldn't be as glad about that as I am.

'It'll be all right.'

That makes me laugh. 'I don't bloody think so.'

We turn into the school driveway. I lean on the horn to get a bunch of younger kids scurrying out of our way.

'You really are a smooth operator, Morris.'

I pull up outside the main entrance and rest an elbow on the top of my seat. 'We could go away some place,' I say. 'Get away from here.'

'Yeah, like where?'

'I don't know. We've got the car. We can go anywhere. We don't ever have to come back.'

We could go to one of the places we talked about back when we dreamed of winning the lottery. Take the car over the channel to France. Drive until we ran out of petrol and then just see what happens.

For some reason, I always wanted to take her to a boating lake. We'd take one oar each, side-by-side, and just drift across the water together. Nobody but the two of us.

It's just a stupid dream but it always made me happy.

'It's a nice idea,' she says, looking up at the school. 'But I can't run away from this anymore.'

'You've spent the last year trying to get away from here. Why not do it now?'

She looks at me for a long time.

'Can we wait here until the bell goes?' she says. 'I don't want anyone to see me.'

I nod. We wait together in comfortable silence.

## Keisha

The hordes gradually dwindle into the building until the coast looks clear enough. I wait for a hot flush to pass before I push my door open and swing my weight

145

out onto the pavement. I can practically hear my spinal column grind into every last socket.

Morris leans across the seat. 'Text me when you want picking up.'

I waddle into school. It feels like my body really isn't built for pregnancy. It hasn't had a chance to adapt. My ankles are swollen and painful. My boobs throb like they're forever expanding and even the softest clothes feel like sandpaper on my nipples. I've become an uncontrollable leaker of gassy smells.

The last few stragglers eddy around me, like I'm a boulder in a river. A boy I recognise from the block barges into me, knocking me off balance.

He turns and faces me, pacing backwards with his friends. 'You should watch yourself.'

I get my head down and hurry towards the science block.

There are no form groups here so it's mostly empty. I reach Mr Arnopp's door and stand in front of it, clenching and unclenching my hands.

'Come in,' he says as soon as I knock.

He isn't alone. The headteacher is here. Mr Arnopp is flicking at his tablet screen, tinny classical music playing through the speaker. The familiar coffee smell.

'Good to see you, Keisha,' says the headteacher, standing to greet me and offer his chair. There isn't another, so when I take it he's left standing just inside the door.

Mr Arnopp looks at me and smiles weakly. He shuts off the music and sets his glasses down on top of the tablet with a clack. His eyes linger on my stomach and he lets a long breath out through his nose.

146

'As your head of year, Mr Arnopp will be leading this meeting,' says the headteacher. 'I'm just listening in.'

I nod. It feels like I'm in trouble, like the last time we were all here, a year ago.

'Your mother informed us you are nearly four months pregnant,' says Mr Arnopp.

I don't respond. Mum has quickly had to become skilled at not seeing what she doesn't want to see. Anyone who's ever seen a pregnant woman would know that I'm much further along than that.

'I'm no expert, but I don't think that can be accurate,' he says. The headteacher opens his mouth to speak but Mr Arnopp cuts him off. 'I think it's important to establish the truth of the situation.'

He thinks I'm a liar. I suppose I am.

I can't look at him. He seems like a different person to the teacher who smiled at me, who took me under his wing, who hugged me when I was upset. There's no warmth in his eyes now.

'It's not long until your January mock exams,' he says. 'I don't see how this won't impact your ability to perform your best.'

I glance up at the headteacher. I don't want to talk about any of this with him here. He never wanted me to stay at this school in the first place.

'I wondered if I could skip them? That way I'll have time to, um, get everything sorted. These are only mocks.'

'They're *important*, Keisha. I thought you recognised that.'

I focus on the desk.

The headteacher gets a notification on his phone. He

checks the screen and lets out a long breath that wobbles his lips. 'This is something I need to handle,' he says. 'I'll be back.'

As soon as he's gone Mr Arnopp drops his hands to the desk. 'Are you really okay, Keisha?'

*Of course not.* I force myself to nod.

'When I heard the rumours, saw those photos . . .'

I wonder how he managed to see them. If he's been on my Facebook . . .

'I was really worried about you. I wish you'd responded to me sooner.'

'I'm sorry.'

He nods. 'Do you remember the first time you came to this office?'

Heat prickles in my cheeks.

'You didn't care if they kicked you out of school.'

'That was a long time ago, sir.'

'And yet here we are again.'

After I called the teacher a bitch and got kicked out of class, the headteacher threatened to expel me. Mr Arnopp talked him down to a two-week suspension after he made me promise that I wanted to make something of my life. At first I said it just so I wouldn't get kicked out, to escape that embarrassment. It was only when I got home, when I saw the way Mum looked at me, that I started to take it seriously.

'Do you remember what we talked about that day?' says Mr Arnopp.

'You said I had potential,' I say, like I'm reciting lines directly from my past. 'And you'd never seen someone so willing to throw it away.'

'I meant it,' says Mr Arnopp. 'Anyone could see you were special. Now this whole situation makes me wonder if I was mistaken.'

I grit my teeth. 'You weren't.'

He stares at me across the desk. 'You're bright, Keisha. I've tried to encourage that in you. You owe me better than this.'

My hands begin to shake, so I hide them under the desk. 'I still want to work hard,' I say, hearing the desperation in my voice. 'This doesn't have to change anything.'

'I don't know what goes through your mind,' says Mr Arnopp, his voice growing louder. He stands and turns to the steaming coffee pot on top of the filing cabinet, fills a dirty mug to the brim. 'I thought you liked me. I thought we had an understanding. After everything I've done for you.'

'Sir,' I say, welling up and biting down my anger. I know I should defend myself. I don't deserve to be treated like this. *SLUT*. That must be what he thinks.

'Say it again,' he says.

'What?'

'Call me "sir" again.'

I can hardly look at him. 'I'm sorry, sir.'

He nods, like the word gives him strength. 'I tried to give you everything. Maybe I waited too long to ask for something back.'

He takes a cautious sip of his coffee and winces at its heat. Then he lowers his free hand to rest on top of mine.

'I can still help you,' he says. 'But it's time you gave

149

me something in return.'

His skin is hot and clammy. When I try and slide my hand away he presses his weight down and pins my fingers to the desk.

'I know you want this,' he says, leaning so close that his breath brushes my forehead.

A tear rolls down my cheek. I stare blankly forward as he moves his hand up my arm to my chest. I wince at the pain of it, shudder at his touch. It's easier to let him do it. I've already been violated once, in a way that no one will ever believe. Maybe this is just how things have to be.

His hand slides over my belly. The baby fidgets like even it can't believe what's happening. I set my jaw and hold my body as rigidly as I can. He takes a sip of his coffee and breathes the heat into my ear. I do everything I can not to flinch.

Is this what he wanted all along? Every time he was telling me he could make something of me, all the texts and emails, the kind words and compliments. Maybe they were always leading to this, making it so that I would owe him something. I didn't see it, chose not to see it, because I wanted what he offered me so badly.

His hand pushes between my legs.

'No,' I say, trying to pull away from him.

He quickly grabs my wrist again and twists. Pain shoots up my arm, and in the same instance it feels like electricity starts to swirl and snap inside my stomach. It's the same feeling as a couple of weeks ago when Morris grabbed me, but so much stronger. My ears fill with a low hum like they've popped.

When I try and free my arm his coffee slops over

onto his hand, and he hisses in pain. Before he can put the mug down the energy inside me breaks loose and rushes at him. His body jerks like he's been struck, and confusion crumples his face as his arm freezes in mid-air.

The humming screams in my ears. Slowly, the hand clutching the coffee mug begins to lift upwards. Mr Arnopp grits his teeth like he's trying to fight against it, but it keeps going until the mug is directly over his head. He twists to face it.

'What are you doing?' he says.

I kick myself away from the desk and stumble to the door. 'I'm not doing anything.'

There's a final pulse from my stomach and Mr Arnopp turns his wrist. Scalding coffee splashes over his face. He roars in agony, the dark liquid running into his eyes. Steam pours from his skin and his shirt is spattered brown. He seems to regain control of his hands and claws at his face, whining in pain as he collapses to the floor.

I throw open the door and hurry for the exit. Before I reach it the lesson bell reverberates around the walls to signal the end of form. It covers Mr Arnopp's shrieks. I hurry outside and onto the path.

People mill around me as I try and push through to the main block. The humming is gone. My spine aches. My legs feel like they'll barely hold me up. The faces of the other pupils blur across my vision, staring at me, laughing at me. I can't take it anymore.

I sense Maida nearby, trying to tune into my emotions. Before I know it I'm stumbling into the toilets. The

151

cubicle against the wall is empty. I throw the seat down and drop onto it, squeezing my skull like I can pop the connection out of my brain.

It was all a lie. Everything Mr Arnopp did for me was bullshit.

As the second bell chimes around the school I slam my head against the wall and begin to cry.

# Chapter Sixteen

**5 days until birth (28 weeks pregnant)**

**Siobhan**

My bottles clank together in the carrier bag, covering the sound of voices on the stairs above me until I'm almost on top of them. I think about turning back, but the booze already inside me makes me keep climbing. The stairs sway. I rattle the bag louder so they know I'm coming. So there's no excuse to lash out in surprise.

It's like I'm a monster.

I'm the size of one. Being pregnant is a surprisingly good way to get served. I always got ID'd at the corner shop, but now I just point at my belly and say, it can't be for me, can it? Anyway, they want me out of there without any hassle – they see a kid from the estate, even a pregnant one, and get jittery like I might rob the place.

One more floor. I stop to catch my breath and stretch out my back. Tito and Devin come round the corner. They tell everyone they're roommates but they're clearly doing it. When they see me they stop dead. Tito actually takes a step back. It's Devin who gets them moving. He doesn't take his eyes off me as they pass. I can't tell if he looks scared or disgusted or some mixture of both. When they're a floor down they start whispering like schoolboys.

I don't care. I keep climbing. A pain flashes in my stomach. A stitch, maybe.

It's been a day or so since I felt the baby moving. I should be scared. I'm trying not to think anything about it at all.

There are a couple of people in the corridor. I don't stop. A mother hustles her kids away. I keep going. A guy leans out of his door to take a picture on his phone. When I hurry past him he kisses his teeth.

By the time I'm inside the empty flat I'm out of breath. I lean back against the door. There are footsteps outside, coming closer. Lingering.

'Hello?'

I swear I nearly give birth right there. Morris sticks his head out of the kitchen.

'Oh my days, Mo, don't do that!'

'Sorry,' he says. 'You all right?'

'Yeah, yeah.' I place the bottles down gently. Another flare of pain bursts in my belly. I go through into the flat, trying to make sure I walk straight.

'What you doing up here?'

'They're doing my head in at home,' I say. 'Mum and Gary won't stop following me around like I'm going to break, trying to pretend it's all okay. I actually want them to get angry. At least that would be real.'

If he notices me slurring my words, he doesn't say anything.

154

'You should be glad they're there for you.'

'They just need to . . . I know, all right? I shouldn't complain. They've bought me a bunch of maternity clothes, and they've ordered a pram and all that. But it's like they know something isn't right and they hope pretending might make it go away.'

'Bloody hell, a pram,' he says, looking at some carrier bags piled on the floor.

I glance back at the door. 'Some guy just took my picture.'

'Serious?'

Outrage clears my head for a second. 'It's like they think we belong to them now, you know? They're always watching, hanging around outside my flat, muttering at me. What makes them think they have the right?'

'You want me to say something?'

'Nah, leave it. It doesn't matter.'

That's when I notice the corner shop bags spread across the kitchen counter, bananas, squirty cream, a loaf of bread . . . There are plates and cutlery he must have brought from home.

'What's all this?'

He smiles shyly. 'I thought we'd have a feast. Sort out those weird cravings you've been having. I sent you a text.'

'My phone's off.' It has been since those pictures started to spread and people wouldn't step off.

'Stay, though. There's plenty of weird crap to eat.'

'I'm all right, honest,' I say, already backing off to the door.

'Want me to walk you home?'

'Don't worry yourself.'

I sort of squat down to grab the carrier bag. The bottles clink. Mo looks at me from inside the flat.

'Why didn't we stay friends?' he says.

I almost rest a hand on my belly, but manage to stop myself. 'It would have been too hard, just the two of us. We'd have always been looking for her, realising she was gone. It would have made me miss her even more.'

He looks at me for a long moment. 'You're okay, yeah?'

I nod, forcing myself to smile. 'I will be.'

Then I hurry off into the hall.

## Morris

Strange cravings are pretty normal. That's what Mum said. It's not because the babies are . . . whatever they are. The only shop open this late didn't have half the crap they want to eat. Tuna, croissants, pâté, this leafy stuff called kale. The last trifle was a bit past its sell-by date but hopefully they won't notice if I douse it in squirty cream and chocolate sprinkles.

I texted Keisha an invite, but I haven't heard from her since I dropped her at school yesterday morning.

It doesn't matter what the babies are and how they got here. That's what I keep telling myself. They're here now. One of them is *mine*. Nothing else matters.

Shit. I wish it was that easy to ignore.

I start dishing up.

## Keisha

The last thing I want to do is have a feast. A feast is something you do to celebrate. I don't want to sit together and pretend that everything is okay. Ever since I got home from school yesterday I've been lying low. I don't want a soul to know what happened. I feel like such an idiot.

There's a knock on my door. 'I'm going to bed.' It's Mum. 'Do you need anything?'

I don't answer. Let her think I'm already asleep.

A swipe of my thumb wakes up my phone. The text is already open. I've been staring at it since last night.

> I won't press charges for what happened today.
> You're a lucky girl. But there's nothing I can do to
> keep you from being expelled.

I can still feel his hand on my body. The clammy touch of his fingers. It makes me want to vomit. But I also remember the power that revved in my stomach, from the baby, energy stronger than anything I've ever experienced.

My body has been stolen away from my control.

Mr Arnopp tried to possess it.

The baby is using it as its vessel.

I texted back.

> I'll tell everyone what you did.

The reply arrived within seconds.

> No one will believe you.

Someone would. Someone probably *would* . . . But what about the rest of them? No one believed me at the beginning of this mess. There's no way they'll believe me now.

Don't get me wrong – I'm glad my baby hurt him. But it wasn't protecting me – it was protecting itself. And that just makes me even more frightened of it.

The number of Facebook notifications has jumped in the last few hours, enough to make me open the app. A lot of them are the same old stuff, discussions and insults, my name tagged, but a lot of the comments are arriving on something new.

I click on a link posted by Louise Krawczyk: Proof something really weird is going on, she's written.

I tap through. It's a Tumblr post with the title *The Midwich Tower Conspiracy*. I'm almost too scared to scroll down, but I know I have to see.

Okay, we all know something weird's been going on, it starts. From there it outlines the whole situation, starting with those first pictures of us outside the empty flat and the pregnancy tests.

I wanted to gather it all together, so we can look for anything we've missed. This might all seem a bit crazy, it says, but it's difficult to argue against it. Just look.

I scroll down. There are more pictures of us. Taken around corners or from cracks in doorways, zoomed in and blurry. We're never looking at the camera. Siobhan told me people were taking pictures of her, but I never imagined anything like this.

Every photo is dated. They know the dates of the pregnancies because they've seen the tests. Each picture of us is accompanied by an image of a 'normal' pregnant woman, some of them celebrity paparazzi shots or taken from Instagram. Both at 6 weeks, it says. The difference is clear.

The post then starts comparing us to pictures of women who are much further along in their pregnancies. It's only been a few weeks, but they already look ready to pop!

The baby chooses this moment to kick. It makes me jump, every time, even though it's been happening for days. I try hard not to look down at my stomach. The way my skin bulges and stretches is so . . . *alien*.

Next the post goes off on a tangent, showing pictures of Siobhan carrying bottles of alcohol, swigging at one in the corridor. It's not a great secret she's been drinking, but maybe it's worse than I realised.

The air seems to change whenever they're around. And look at this, from just before we found the tests! No way that's normal!

There's a picture of us outside, by the green, bent over with puddles of bright blue vomit at our feet.

Finally, the writer tries to reach some kind of conclusion.

I know this doesn't give any answers. Maybe they're faking the pregnancies to try and get attention. None of us would put it past them. But anybody who lives in Midwich Tower knows there's something more to it than that. They sneak about like they're planning something

There's one more picture: me, Siobhan and Olivia. No mention of Maida. It makes it look like we're wanted criminals.

Whatever's going on, it's probably going to get worse. We might have to be ready to do something about it.

And that's it. People have noticed a lot more than we thought. People in the block view us as a threat.

I go back to Facebook. It was posted an hour ago, but there's already over forty comments. I can't bear to read them. Instead I message Louise directly. Just leave us alone! I close the app.

Footsteps creep past my door. I jump up from my chair. The sound fades away across the sitting room. Then I hear the front door open.

I sneak across the sitting room just as it closes. After a few seconds I open it as quietly as I can and step out into the corridor, just in time to see Dad enter the stairwell.

The cold pushes through my socks as I hurry after him. I follow the sound of his footsteps, struggling to keep up as we climb higher and higher. I make it out of the stairwell on the top floor just in time to see him vanish into Mr Hillier's flat, the spare key jangling slightly in his fingers as the door shuts. There's no need for me to linger. I'm gasping for breath from the climb and somebody might hear. My feet are completely numb as I descend back home.

The sitting room is dark enough that I can sit on the sofa and wait like a spy in a crime drama. It's only a few minutes before Dad comes back, trying to be as quiet as he can. He heads straight into the kitchen, right past me, and opens the medicine cupboard.

I turn on the lamp.

'Keisha!'

The golden syrup tin is in his hand, lid pried loose, and he's about to stuff a twenty pound note inside.

'Where did that come from?' I say.

He shrugs like it's no big deal. 'It's just savings.'

'You shouldn't lie to a pregnant woman.'

His eyes narrow. 'Like you haven't lied to us?'

I heave myself upright. 'Why are you stealing money from Mr Hillier?'

'Stealing? I'm not stealing anything, love.'

'Then what's going on?'

Dad sighs and looks into the can. 'We've known Mr Hillier for years. He's known *you* since you were born. Now he just wants to help out.'

The cold has made it into my bones. I lean forward onto the kitchen counter. 'I didn't realise we were that skint.'

He thrusts the tin toward me. It's still packed with money, notes rolled together like fat cigars, crammed to fill every space.

'It's for you, Keisha,' Dad says. 'Mr Hillier has no family of his own, and he almost thinks of you as a daughter. He wants you to have it. For your future. Love, we want to help you through university. Truth be told, we never expected you to make it this far in school. We thought you'd be working by now.'

Nausea squirms in my gut. 'So I'm just a charity case? *That's* how I was going to have a future?'

'I don't like it either,' he says. 'I've been doing all the overtime they can give me. I just want the best for you. That's why this pregnancy . . .'

I turn away from him and walk back into the living room. Everything is built on sand. Mr Arnopp didn't really care about tutoring me. The money for my future doesn't belong to us. Every last piece of it just contributed to the greater sham.

161

'It was all me, Keisha,' he says. 'Your mother doesn't know anything about it.'

I hurry back to my room, grab my dressing gown and shoes. By the time I come back Dad has returned the golden syrup tin to the cupboard. He follows me to the front door.

'Just think about it, Keisha!' he hisses. 'We're going to need this money more than ever now.'

He tries to grab my arm but I jerk it away. The baby fidgets. I'm angry, but I don't want anything bad to happen to him that I can't control. Instead I march out into the corridor.

'Where are you going?'

'To embrace the inevitable,' I spit back at him.


## Morris

The kitchen in the empty flat is equipped with precisely zilch, so I can't even heat up the croissants before I smear chocolate spread and tuna inside to make the weirdest sandwich ever.

'That smells disgusting,' says Maida, hanging over my shoulder. 'It's making me sick. And hungry.'

I carry it through to the sitting room. 'These kids got some middle-class cravings.'

I've spread a blanket across the carpet like we're having a nice picnic. As soon as I put the plate down Maida and Olivia dive on it like sharks. Only Keisha holds back, looking at the dish with disgust.

'We still got the trifle if you want some?'

She shakes her head no. She's here, but she keeps staring at the door like she wishes she was anywhere else.

'Olivia, there's pâté in your hair.'

She barely lifts her head, just slides the curl through her mouth to clean it off.

The electricity in here doesn't work so I've lit a few candles. At least the girls haven't tried to eat them. So far. Light flickers against Keisha's skin as she reaches for a croissant. She turns it over in her hand, but her nose wrinkles as soon as it goes near her mouth.

There's something wrong. It looks like she's either going to burst into tears or beat everyone in the room to death with both fists.

'This is not my most graceful moment,' says Olivia between mouthfuls.

Maida burps loudly in response.

I try and smile across at Keisha. This should feel like old times, even without Siobhan here. I wanted this to feel like our first family meal together. It's so sad.

'These cravings shouldn't last much longer,' says Olivia, wiping her mouth. 'It's not long before we pop.'

'You really need to start using a different word,' says Maida.

I shift away some empty plates and sit at the edge of the blanket, my knee brushing against Keisha's leg. 'We need to start thinking about getting some stuff ready.'

Keisha drops her croissant. 'We're never going to be ready.'

There's still so much I haven't thought about. By now we're supposed to have stacks of nappies, a cot, *a pram*, a bunch of Disney DVDs, and whatever bloody else babies need. We haven't got so much as a dummy.

It's my responsibility. She carries the baby, I sort everything else. But I can't afford any of it. There's only a tiny bit of my money left, and – crazy as it sounds – I feel like I have to choose between a baby and buying a shotgun or guard dog or bazooka or something to defend myself against Tyrone.

I squeeze my eyes shut to chase the thought away.

I stand up and grab the carrier bags I hid behind the counter. 'I know it's a bit late, but I bought you some maternity clothes.'

It's embarrassing, tipping them out onto the floor. They're not actual maternity clothes, just seriously *big* clothes for fat people or whatever. Big enough to fit three of me inside.

Maida's first to start riffling through them. She quickly finds a blue woolly jumper with a badger (badly) knitted on the front.

'I actually love it,' she says, pulling it over her head.

Keisha doesn't look quite so happy as she looks through the pile. There's skirts with worn edges, a few faded blouses or whatever they're called, and even some shoes that might fit her swollen feet.

'Where did you get these?' she says, holding up a blue top with random Japanese letters all over it.

'Charity shop.'

Her face drops, just a little more, before she catches it. 'Thanks, Morris. This was thoughtful. I mean it.'

I glow inside.

Olivia raises her eyebrows at Maida. 'Your parents worked it out yet?'

'Dad definitely hasn't, unless he's keeping quiet,

which seems unlikely.' Maida swipes a finger around the edge of a plate and licks it clean. 'It's just annoying now.'

'They'll find out one way or another in a couple of days,' says Keisha.

'Look, I know, all right? It's not easy. At least you two are allowed to be having sex if you want.' She flashes a sarcastic look at Keisha. 'I am *lit-er-a-lly* forbidden from seeing a penis until I'm married.'

As the only person in the room with a penis, all this talk about them like they're the enemy makes me a bit uncomfortable. I flick at a bit of pâté on the blanket.

'My dad has a very clear idea what I should be.'

'And what do you want to be?'

'I have no idea! This whole thing –' Maida waves at her stomach under the badger jumper '– gives me something that's all *mine*, even if we don't know what it is yet. My whole life has been so . . . *rigid*, and this has blown it wide open.' She shakes her head. 'You should hear what he's been saying about the rest of you since the news got out. I'm not ashamed, I'm scared what might happen to me.'

'That's not right,' I say.

Keisha's voice takes a dark tone. 'The baby won't let him do anything to you.'

'He's not a bad person,' Maida says. 'He's just very traditional. And very proud. He's not really cut out for living somewhere like this.'

'There are bigger things to be afraid of,' says Keisha, one hand on her stomach.

'I'm afraid he might find a way to take this away from me,' Maida says. 'Right now feels like the first time my future has ever been in my own hands. I think my mum might know, though.'

'How come?'

'She didn't say it.' Maida wipes crumbs from her lips. 'But she was talking about taking me away somewhere.'

'Maybe that wouldn't be such a bad idea,' says Keisha.

'No way. I'm part of this.'

Keisha climbs to her feet, making the candles wobble, and walks to the window, where fog has already started gathering around the streetlights. I don't know much about the connection the girls share, but I wish I could read her thoughts right now.

'You can stay with me if you need to,' says Olivia. 'I want it to be a safe environment for all of us.'

Maida grins. 'Next you'll be telling us to do yoga.'

'I *was* considering a water birth . . .'

'Seriously though, what are we going to do when they decide they want out?'

'We have to assume, given our synchronicity, we're all going to pop at the same time,' says Olivia.

Maida groans. 'Stop saying *pop*!'

'We need to go to the hospital,' says Olivia. 'But all at the same time? It'll raise some eyebrows.'

Keisha turns back to face us. 'I don't want to go to the hospital.'

'I might be able to call in a favour, get somebody to come here and help,' says Olivia. 'You can't do this by yourself, even if you want to.'

'She won't have to,' I say, getting to my feet. 'Can I talk to you a minute?'

I lead Keisha into one of the empty bedrooms. The carpet's covered in dust and dirt. A tattered dry cleaning bag hangs from a hook on the wall. Streetlights glow through the frost on the window.

She's brought the Japanese top with her. She takes off her dressing gown and slips it on. It stretches, but it's big enough to cover her belly.

'It fits,' she says, and she sounds so sad I want to cry.

'This is going to sound weird,' I say. 'My nan was a midwife, remember?'

The way she looks at me makes it clear she doesn't remember.

'She's always told me loads about delivering babies. I think I can do it.'

'You're crazy.'

I take her hand as gently as I can. 'You trust me though. I know you do.'

She still doesn't look convinced. 'How about we both study those books, so at least we're prepared? Maybe then we won't need too much help from Olivia's friend.'

'That leads me nicely to my next point,' I say. 'I signed us up for an antenatal class.'

She looks me right in the eyes. 'You're thinking so much about the baby, it's like you've forgotten how all this started.'

'I haven't forgotten.'

'Then why do you never talk about it?'

'Because, all right . . . just because . . . it's easier.' I turn away from her and scrape tracks across the icy window with my fingernails. It reveals slivers of the estate

167

below, dark and quiet. 'I don't want to think about what happened to you.'

'I have no choice but to think about it.'

I turn back to her. 'Yeah, I know.'

She jerks her head towards the door. 'This is exactly what I was trying to avoid. Now we're just a bunch of teenagers sitting around waiting to push out kids. I didn't want this to be my life.'

My breath comes in a cloud. 'What you mean is that you didn't want anything to do with me.'

'You only want me and this baby because it benefits you,' she says.

'That's not true,' I say, lifting my hand to touch her but thinking better of it.

This isn't fair. The last week or so I've done everything she wanted me to. I've been her chauffeur, slept on her floor to protect her, bought her a slightly gone-off trifle in the middle of the night. I've been there for her when nobody else was.

Is it all just because she could give me a baby, a future? I search for the answer in her eyes. It can't be true. I can't believe that.

She throws herself against me. At first I think it's an attack. Then she pulls me into a hug and sobs against my shoulder, scrunching handfuls of my hoodie in her fists. I put my hands softly on her back, arching my spine uncomfortably to accommodate her stomach.

'I can never go back to school,' she says.

'You can't give up on it now.'

Then she tells me how the baby assaulted her teacher yesterday in his office.

'I couldn't control it,' she says. 'The baby . . . it took over as soon as it sensed the danger.'

'Why did it think you were in danger?'

She breathes unsteadily, like she's trying to suck back her tears.

'It could have been worse,' she says, her voice muffled by my hoodie. 'I could feel it. The baby could have done more.'

I pull away from her. 'But why did it need to?'

She holds her breath for a moment, looks at the floor, the walls, her hands, anything to avoid my eyes. Then she darts her head forward and kisses me on the mouth. Just a peck, like she's sampling the taste. Her lips are softer than I ever remembered.

Now she looks at me. It feels like I'm supposed to say something. My lips move, but the feeling of the kiss lingers there and I can't make any words. Just as I think of something, Keisha winces and puts her hands to her head.

'Something's wrong,' she says.

'I'm sorry,' I manage to say.

But she isn't talking about me. She whips her head back. I try to reach out to her but she flings my hand away, holding her stomach. She doubles over, moaning in pain. When she finally looks at me her eyes are wild.

'What is it?' I say.

From the living room I hear the other girls cry out. I peer around the door to see them both clutching their bellies, the blanket tangled around their feet.

'It's not the food, is it?' It would be just my bloody luck to poison them all somehow.

169

Keisha emerges from the bedroom and shakes her head. Even though her face is scrunched up with pain she manages to stagger across to Maida and Olivia. They grip each other's hands.

'Is it happening?' I say. I don't know if they're about to give birth or hatch or lay eggs or whatever the hell is going to happen with these things. I have a basic idea how to deliver a baby, but not three at once.

'It's Siobhan,' says Keisha. 'Something's wrong.'

The worst of the pain seems to pass and they hurry together for the front door. It's almost funny watching them trying to push through at the same time. I follow them to the stairwell. They can't move quickly, and sweat is pouring off them as they shuffle down the stairs.

When we reach Siobhan's floor they all let out a scream and sink to the floor in pain.

'Go and check on her!' shouts Keisha when I try to help.

The Hag is outside Siobhan's flat, wrapped in a dressing gown, frowning like someone spat in her tea. Somehow she's always around when something happens. I push past her, start banging on the door and don't stop until Siobhan's mum answers. Her eyes are wide and she pulls the door closed behind her like she's trying to hide a secret.

'I need to come in,' I say.

She shakes her head and doesn't move. I'm about to shove past her when she sees the other girls, staggering their way towards us.

'She was calling for you,' she says.

I'm first into the flat. I dash across the sitting room

170

and find Siobhan's dad blocking the doorway to her bedroom. He looks at us in terror and points into the room.

It's dark, the only light coming in from the window, the curtain thrown back. In the orange gloom I see Siobhan on the bed, her head lolling like she's barely awake. The room smells like alcohol and vomit.

'What happened?' I say.

She's crying. It's not until Keisha arrives next to me that I see why.

## Siobhan

They're here. They're all here.

I reach for them. My fingers are stained red.

Keisha falls onto her knees, howling.

Pain tears through me. The world swims in front of my eyes. I see the other girls at the door, clutching each other. We're all here together. One last time.

Another shredding inside.

The signal between us weakens. Buzzes. Flickers.

Keisha cries and cries and cries. 'What did you do?'

There's so much pain. Another wrench, and the connection is gone. Unplugged.

'I won,' I tell her, as I slip into blackness.

# Chapter Seventeen

**4 days until birth (30 weeks pregnant)**

## Keisha

The lights from the ambulance dance around the car park, skimming off the surrounding houses and spilling over the playing green. It's past midnight, but the streets are lined with people who have come to watch. The entire block sees Siobhan being wheeled into the ambulance. They shake their heads like it's a joke gone wrong. Frank is here, combing a hand through his beard. Louise Krawczyk with her family. I spot Nostrils, a woman we used to insult for her permanently snotty nose, and Stan, the miserable fat bastard who confiscated our football when it hit his car.

The Hag stands at the centre of them all, whispering as the spectators pull closer to her. I want to step to them, scream at them, hit them, but I feel too weak. I can barely stand.

A piece of me has died.

'What happened?' I ask Olivia.

'I don't know,' she says.

There isn't a chance to ask anything more. Olivia pushes through the crowd and into the back of the ambulance. Siobhan's parents finish talking to the police and climb in behind her. As the doors slam shut I catch a glimpse of Siobhan, an oxygen mask clamped to her mouth, looking at the scene in disbelief.

I close my eyes and try and stretch my mind towards her. Siobhan isn't there. *Please hang up and try again.* A part of my consciousness has been taken away and all I can feel is the lingering ache in my stomach and a profound sense of loss that I simply can't contain.

Beside me Maida glares murder at the spectators. Somehow she's taking this better than me. Morris puts his arm around me and I let him. Maybe it will bring me comfort. I lean into him. I need to feel like I'm part of something. I look down and realise I'm holding Maida's hand.

'What if it happens to us?' she says.

Fear laces her voice. The best I can manage is a shrug. I don't know how I would feel. Even a day ago I might have been glad. But after Mr Arnopp, the money in the kitchen, and now the bereavement that tugs at my insides, I'm not so sure.

The policemen return to their car and the ambulance pulls away out of sight, the flashing lights fading. The attention turns to us. People look at me like I'm a ticking time bomb. I focus on the shivers of pain in my belly and stare back at them, daring them to try anything. Maida stands with me, even though her secret is still safe.

The Hag shuffles forward. 'What have you brought on us?'

'I haven't done *anything*.'

The crowd thins out, filing back into the building. Above us the windows are full of faces. The Hag is one of the last to leave.

Only Tubs stops in front of us on his way inside. He's wearing nothing but a loose T-shirt and boxer shorts, but the cold doesn't seem to bother him.

'She did it on purpose,' he says.

'*What did you say?*' I want to claw his eyes out.

'We all saw her drinking. You don't do that if you're after a healthy baby, do you?'

Morris rounds on him. 'Fuck off, Tubs.'

He shrugs and shuffles back into the tower, but his words stick in my mind. It was hardly unusual for Siobhan to be drinking, but I can't shake the vision of her on the roof, drunk and standing on the edge. Maybe she found a way to escape it after all.

I expect to feel jealous, but what I feel is fury.

A couple of guys I don't recognise are lingering at the edge of the car park. Morris spots them too and pulls me toward the door. I want to ask who they are but Maida tugs my arm.

'My dad will be awake,' she says.

She's right. No one could have slept through this. He'll be apoplectic.

'We'll come up with you,' I say, though my legs will barely handle the stairs. Morris guides us up like he's our security detail. On every floor we can hear footsteps, the echoes of murmuring voices, the block refusing to let it lie. For the last year this place hasn't felt like home. But now it's beginning to feel like hostile territory.

Maida's floor is quieter. She inserts her key gently. All three of them – father, mother, brother – are waiting on the other side.

'I can explain,' she says.

Her dad is fully dressed, his hair combed, like he smartened up especially for this moment. He looks at me. 'Can you leave us, please?'

Something is wrong. There's no way I'm leaving her alone. I shake my head.

Maida's dad sighs. 'What is this?' he says.

He lifts a hand and wields a small baby blue box. The pregnancy test I gave her. I see Maida go tense.

'Where did you get that?' she says.

Her little brother shuffles behind her dad and clings to his leg. Obviously she hadn't hidden it as effectively as she thought.

'Is this yours?' her dad says. His voice is beginning to shake.

I step up beside her to try and help. 'We can explain all of this.'

'You,' he says, pointing the test at me. 'You gave her this. I knew I was right to try and keep her away from you.'

'This has nothing to do with her,' says Maida.

Her mother watches us with pleading eyes. I want someone to defuse the tension, but I feel determination welling up inside Maida. She wants to do this herself.

'No,' he says. 'Not my daughter.'

Maida grips the hem of the baggy badger jumper. In one swift movement she drags it upwards to reveal her belly underneath. It's the shape of a small boulder, her

175

skin stretched tight around it like it's vacuum-packed. It's easy to see how she managed to keep it hidden all this time. It only looks obvious now she's exposed. When he sees it her dad's nostrils flare and he clenches his fists, turns away from her.

A tear slips down her mother's cheek. She doesn't seem shocked. Maybe she did know it all along and kept quiet, too scared to say anything. Too scared to help.

'How could you do this to your family?' says Maida's dad.

'I didn't do anything,' Maida says quietly.

'You have let these girls corrupt you!'

I open my mouth to protest but Maida beats me to it. 'And what if I did? Maybe I'm sick of you. Maybe this is *your* fault.'

She tries to push past him, but he moves quicker than should be possible and seizes a fistful of her hair.

'You don't speak to me that way!'

He drags her back, slaps her cheek, knocking her sideways with sheer force. It's only her hair in his hand that keeps her upright. He brings his arm back again. I lurch forward to try and stop him, but before I can reach them I feel that familiar energy crackling on the air. Maida straightens up. It starts to emanate from her like a force field. For a second her dad's eyes go blank, and then he slams his cocked fist full force into his own face. Blood explodes from his nose and he staggers back, releasing his grip on her.

The feeling of pure euphoria from Maida is extraordinary.

She fixes him with her eyes and the energy surges.

A second self-inflicted punch meets his stomach, and as he doubles over he cracks his skull into the nearest doorframe. His body crumples in submission. The rest of the family scatter. He starts to crawl toward the front door.

Maida follows him, walking slowly, energy flexing around her like a shield. Weaker, but still enough to force her dad to struggle back to his feet. His face is a mask of blood.

I realise I'm standing between them. Maida looks at me. 'Step aside.'

And, like she's controlling me too, I do.

She looks into her dad's ruined face. 'You don't control me anymore.'

With one final spurt of energy, she sends her dad careening head first into the front door. He moves as fast as I've ever seen a human being move. The impact shatters the door in a spray of splinters and he lands, out for the count, sprawled in the corridor.

People scream and jump out of the way. The commotion has drawn the same crowd that was still awake after watching the ambulance, the Hag once again at the front, Nostrils and Frank with her. They stare in horror at Maida's dad, who squirms on the cold concrete like he's deflating.

Outside there are sirens drawing closer.

Morris barges through to the crowd. 'Come on, get out of here!'

Maida steps calmly out of the flat. There's a spatter of blood across the badger on her jumper, and she pulls it off over her head, leaving nothing but her thin pyjama top. She throws the jumper at one of her neighbours, then leans over her father. The energy has expended itself. She raises her arm high and brings it down hard, slapping him across the face. He makes a noise like a wet football being kicked.

'That one was just from me,' she says.

The crowd looks at her with faces full of fear and astonishment. She straightens up, looks around at them all, deliberately, carefully – and smiles.

# Chapter Eighteen

**4 days until birth (30 weeks pregnant)**

**Keisha**

It feels like we're hiding a fugitive in the empty flat. We had to bundle Maida away from the scene of the crime, and she refused to go anywhere else. She's wrapped in a cocoon of duvets in the corner of the bare living room, fast asleep, every scrap of her spent.

The second ambulance of the night slips away from the block. Its lights brush the ceiling and fade into darkness.

'It doesn't feel safe to leave her here,' I say.

No one in the block is going back to bed now. Instead they're standing in the halls, talking about everything they saw, talking about *us*, versions of the truth getting wilder and wilder until we're nothing but monsters. After what they saw, it's difficult to blame them.

I am completely drained. Part of my mind is still reaching for Siobhan, trying to calibrate my emotions with hers, and every time it comes up empty a new wave of weariness hits me.

Morris walks me home. It's like there's been a terrorist

attack. Half the doors along the corridor are open, lights blazing, voices murmuring inside. We steal past like we're the enemy, like we're prey. I pass a woman I don't recognise and she actually *hisses* at me, like I'm evil to ward off. Morris pulls me close. Conversations hush to pointed silence, people slope away until they're out of earshot.

'Freak!' someone shouts.

I wonder if their opinion of me would change if they knew the truth.

A couple of policemen are on the stairs, trying to find Maida's flat. We shrink back around the corner, Morris stepping to hide me.

By now the police will have heard ten different versions of the truth. They won't believe any of it. Men don't beat themselves half to death for no reason.

I have to remind myself I haven't done anything wrong.

The policemen make it to Maida's floor and we hurry on up past them. My floor is quieter, but my front door is open, and for a moment I'm afraid to go inside. An ambush could be waiting. Morris goes first, and the only things that mob him are my parents.

'Where have you been?' demands Mum, reaching straight for my belly as if to check nothing's damaged.

Dad lurks behind her, hair messed with sleep. 'People are saying some nasty things.' I can't tell if he's angry with them or me.

'Don't believe everything you hear,' says Morris. He flashes me a smile, and escapes further interrogation by heading back out to check on Maida.

180

'You know better than to be wandering around this place at night,' says Mum.

'Things got a bit out of hand.'

They stand together, faces screwed with concern. I can see them trying to work out what it all means.

'You should probably keep your head down,' says Mum.

'My thoughts exactly.'

At least they don't seem frightened of me. That's something I couldn't bear.

I head for my room. From the ceiling I can hear the policemen's deep, serious tones clashing with shrill panic from Maida's mother. She obviously didn't go to the hospital with her husband. I'm too tired to think about what that could mean.

Dad calls after me. 'We won't let anything happen, Keisha.'

He's trying to be reassuring, I know, but the thought of the money crammed into the tin makes me prickle.

'I'm sure you can bribe them to stay away,' I call back.

I shut myself in my room and lean against the door. The baby stirs inside me, like it's relieved to be home. *Home.* I put my hands against my belly and feel the weight shift.

'Stay in there,' I whisper to it. 'Anywhere is better than out here.'

I drop down onto the edge of my bed in front of the computer. As the screen comes to life I remember the story saved in my bookmarks. I forgot about it the night we found the video. One click and it opens.

181

ALIENS RAPED US IN OUR SLEEP, SAY CORNISH VILLAGERS.

The story is only a few lines long, from a local paper on the south coast, but suddenly I know the truth: whatever did this to us, whatever caused the Nightout, did the same thing somewhere else before here.

> A group of fishermen in the remote Cornish village of Siltoe are convinced something fishy is going on after claiming that randy aliens impregnated their wives. The cuckolded husbands claim little green men put the entire village to sleep so that they could sow their seed in private. *Six* women fell pregnant on the same night.

The picture is a stock photo of the village. It's a tiny place with the sea cutting a river directly through the middle of the houses and shops.

> According to one of the men, Richard Jacobs, all of the women gave birth on the same night, over-whelming the local doctor's surgery. The children are said to be doing well. As for Mr Jacobs, he's fighting back against the aliens by giving his son the most normal name possible: Robert.

There's a photograph of the doctor's surgery, a plain white building that could be anywhere in the world. The newspaper treated it as a joke. I check the date it was published. The story is over three years old.

Robert Jacobs. A normal name. No indication that anything was wrong with him, or any of his five siblings.

There are more of them, already out there in the world. Even without details, it's reassuring to know it happened somewhere else. This story is real. I *know* it is. We're not completely alone in this. I just wish I knew what happened to them.

I Google *Siltoe*. The best result is the council website. It looks like it was designed by a nine-year-old on a typewriter but it's enough to tell me that the village isn't now a smoking crater in the ground.

Elsewhere there are some local news stories, but nothing particularly interesting. Pub Assault Blamed on Beer, Not Racism. A little further down, Villagers Accused of Pagan Ritual.

Clearly aliens don't have the best taste in breeding grounds.

There were six of them, and now there are only three of us. We couldn't even get one of them all the way to birth. It feels like a collective failure, like we let Siobhan down. An image of her bloody hands flashes across my mind and I blink it away.

I'm glad it wasn't me. The realisation strikes me like a head butt. The baby is all I have left.

My bedroom door flies open, making me jump.

'Sorry, did I scare you?' says Morris.

'Don't worry, it's not like half the building wants to lynch me or anything.'

He stands by the door but doesn't close it yet. 'Your mum let me in. Olivia's watching Maida. I thought you might be upset.'

'What's it like out there?'

He takes my question as encouragement and shuts the

183

door. He perches on the bed beside me. His clothes are still cold from outside.

'It's quietening down,' he says. 'Everyone seems real shook up, though. They know something isn't right.'

I think of Maida smiling madly at them while her dad bled all over the concrete. That was probably a pretty clear sign that everything wasn't business as usual.

'I'm exhausted,' I say, tiredness weighing on me like a hood.

'Sleep,' says Morris, standing up. 'I'll book that antenatal class tomorrow.'

'Shit.' It feels like he made that suggestion days ago, not hours. I slump onto the bed.

'You promised.'

I'm on the brink of sleep and can barely form words. 'No, I didn't.'

Morris takes off my shoes and chucks them into a corner. 'If you don't know how to breathe properly the placenta will explode.'

A long breath trickles over my lips. 'That's not how it works.'

'I know, I know.'

My eyes are already closed. 'Do you think you could sleep—'

There's a smile in his voice when he cuts me off. 'I'm sleeping on the floor, yeah. Like I could fit in that bed with you anyway.'

A laugh tries to claw its way out of my throat but I'm asleep before it makes it.

184

# Chapter Nineteen

**2 days until birth (34 weeks pregnant)**

**Morris**

Some prick has let the tyres down on the car. Only the back two, but it still means I have to struggle with the foot pump while Keisha keeps watch over the block like someone's going to throw a grenade at us. She's wearing the top I bought her. It's pretty ugly, but it still makes me smile.

'At least they didn't slash them,' I say.

'Yeah, we're so lucky.'

It feels like there's a crack in my spine from sleeping on her floor the last few nights. I don't want Keisha to see me stretch it out, so I wait until she gets a text.

'It's from Olivia,' she says. 'She finally got Siobhan to speak to her. It wasn't a miscarriage. They think it was placenta abruption.'

I switch tyres. 'That sounds awful.'

She stares at the text for a long time. The muscle in my leg aches from working the rusty pump.

'I think she did it on purpose.'

I detach the hose with a hiss of air and screw the cap back into place. 'Wouldn't the baby have stopped her?'

Keisha shrugs. 'Maybe it didn't know it was in danger. Or maybe she got it addicted.'

'We don't know anything yet. Let's just go, we're already late.'

The tyres are still a bit spongy but they'll do the job. The class is only round the corner, at a children's centre I used to go to as a kid. Usually we'd walk it, but Keisha barely made it down the stairs without needing a rest. Plus it would take us right past Tyrone's house.

'Why are we doing this again?' says Keisha.

'Because you promised.'

'And why the hell did I promise?'

'Because whether you like it or not you're going to be squeezing a baby out of you real soon.'

She exhales and her breath fogs up the windscreen. I lean over to turn up the heater but the knob is missing.

I tried to get Maida to come along too, but she was having none of it. She's been holed up in the empty flat ever since she dented her dad. I've been bringing her food, but these days it's like she's in some kind of trance. She barely speaks to me. Only eats once I've left her alone.

'Maybe nobody there knows anything about us,' I say. 'So as far as they know everything is normal and you've been pregnant for eight months.'

'You know word spreads faster than that, Mo.'

I park in front of the centre, a yellow brick building with graffiti scrawled all over it.

'We've got no choice but to pretend,' I say.

The main room smells like a gym. Feet and armpits.

186

The heating is cranked and I start sweating like I'm going to be interrogated. Someone has laid out a bunch of squishy mats on the floor. The pregnant women are sitting awkwardly on them, their partners behind them on seats.

One couple must be young twenties, and there's a girl with her mum who can't be much older than me. It doesn't matter. Keisha is the youngest, and some of them must have heard about us, so everybody stares. I put an arm around her but she shrugs it off.

The teacher is an older woman with a grey ponytail, holding a wicker basket full of baby dolls. She smiles at us. It's like something out of a horror movie.

There's a spare mat near the radiator. We pick our way across the room. Keisha is more pregnant than any of them. We should have done this a lot sooner.

'I hate this,' hisses Keisha through her teeth as I help her down onto the mat.

'Good to see a new face.' The teacher leans towards us like she's talking to toddlers.

Keisha looks her right in the eye. 'Don't worry, you won't be seeing it again.'

The smile falters for a second. She spins away to continue talking to the people she recognises. Everyone seems to know what they're doing. I only recognise half the words. *Cramps. Tender.* Something about *tearing* that makes me shudder.

In the end I just tune out.

A few weeks ago I could never have guessed I'd be anywhere like this. Right on the edge of my future, about to topple into it head first, but this class makes it feel real. Normal. It makes it easy to forget anything weird has happened. It makes it bloody *terrifying*, which is what it's supposed to be. Right?

In front of me Keisha has her mouth open in horror. I look up to find the teacher forcing a plastic baby through a rubber vagina. It's like pushing a volleyball out of a ketchup bottle. I put a hand on Keisha's shoulder and she glares at me like she might bite it off.

This class is all about what to expect during childbirth. As far as I can tell the only real answer is 'ridiculous agony'.

When the fake baby has made its torturous escape, the teacher gets all the women to practice breathing exercises.

'Partners, get down with them for support,' she says, still smiling like we're playing a game.

When I shift down behind Keisha her whole body is tense. She looks around at the other women like she wants to kill them all with a hammer.

'You can do this,' I say.

She looks down at her bulging stomach, takes one of my hands, and begins to breathe.

## Keisha

Breathe.

I don't want to do this.

Breathe.

I don't want to be here.

Breathe.

This is not what I wanted for myself.

I see my body through the eyes of the other women

in the room: a teenage girl who isn't ready, who should have been able to do better than this, who let herself down.

Except that's not quite right and I force myself towards the truth of it: they see exactly what they expect of a girl like me.

I messed up the future I wanted.

The least I can do is get *this* version of it right.

So I breathe.

Morris squeezes my hand.

I breathe.

# Chapter Twenty

**1 day until birth (36 weeks pregnant)**

**Keisha**

It's going to happen soon. My body is bursting at the seams. If Olivia's calculations are right, it could be today. I should stay home and get ready, but I can't ignore Siobhan's text.

Putting my shoes on takes ten times longer than it should. I make it half way across the living room before Dad stops me. I didn't even know he was home. There's a letter in his hand and fury in his eyes.

'We just got a letter from the school.'

There's no way this can be good. My instinct is to run for it, but he could catch me at a walk.

'Expelled,' he says, flapping the letter. 'For violent conduct.'

My feet are killing me already. I sit down on one of the kitchen chairs. Mr Arnopp wasn't making an empty threat.

'Again? How could you?'

'You don't know what happened.'

'It says here you assaulted a teacher!'

There's a vein pulsing at his temple. A part of me wants him to get agro. Then he could see first-hand what *really* happened in that office.

'It wasn't like that.'

He slams the letter onto the table. 'Then tell me what it was like, Keisha.'

I look him right in the eye. 'My baby is an alien. They impregnated me during the Nightout. It attacked Mr Arnopp with its psychic powers.'

If he's not going to believe it, there's no harm in telling him the truth.

'Jesus, Keisha. Is that supposed to be funny?'

'Do you see me laughing?'

He turns and kicks one of the empty chairs hard. The wooden leg snaps and it topples over onto the floor.

'I just don't understand why you'd throw it all away like this.' His voice booms around the walls. 'We tried to give you everything. We were so proud. But now . . . Keisha, what are you going to do now? Tell me.'

I look away from him, worried I might cry, or scream, or try to swing my chair into his face.

There's a knock at the front door. We both stare like it's the strangest thing that ever happened. Dad only moves when the knock comes again.

'Stay there,' he says.

It's Morris. I don't think I've ever been so happy to see him. He looks at the broken chair on the floor, and then to me to make sure everything is okay.

I get to my feet and go to him as quickly as I can.

'This isn't over,' Dad hisses as I pass him.

191

The door slams behind me. Morris takes my arm like I might have been injured.

'I heard shouting,' he says.

'It doesn't matter. We're already late. Siobhan's waiting.'

He frowns, but he knows better than to push things right now.

Morris drops me at the hospital and heads over to see his nan. An orderly with a wheelchair lingers uncertainly in the hospital entrance but I wave him away. Even though this is the perfect place, I don't want to go into labour here. It's not what the baby wants. It's too public, too many people who can interfere. We don't want to be on show.

When I told Mum I wanted to have the baby at home, she looked at me like I was crazy.

'You know how much it hurts, child?' she said.

'Yes, Mum.'

'No, you have no idea. You are doing a stupid thing.'

The lift takes me up, past the floor where we had our sonograms, to the maternity ward. Somehow it seems wrong that they've been keeping Siobhan here. She isn't a mother any more.

The raised voices reach me before I'm at the double doors. It's a shared ward, but that isn't stopping her mum and step-dad from yelling. I think about turning straight around. But she asked me to come. I need to find out why.

'You'll stay away from them as long as you're under my roof,' her step-dad is saying when I turn into the room. He's shoving clothes into a holdall.

'What does it matter now?' says Siobhan.

'You weren't there,' he says, zipping up the bag. 'They're freaks, and we don't want you near anyone who could tip you over the edge again.'

They all spot me at the same time. The hostility is palpable.

'Give us a minute, yeah?' says Siobhan.

The bag slaps against the floor and they slope out of the room like sulky kids.

'Yeah, run from the freak,' I mutter after them.

Siobhan grins. 'You're mean when you're pregnant. Thanks for coming.'

'It was weird to get a text from you.' For the last week or so we haven't needed our phones. We've been inside each other's heads, whether we wanted it or not.

'I missed you,' she says, meeting my eye.

I let her take my hand. The rift that opened up when she was torn from us has started to heal. It feels good to be with her again.

She looks like she hasn't slept in days. Dark rings circle her eyes and she's thinner, not just from losing the baby. There are spots all over her cheeks and forehead.

'How are your parents taking it?'

She swings herself out of bed, wearing nothing but a hospital gown and knickers. For a second I expect her legs to still be covered in blood. They look unnaturally white.

'They're going to pretend it never happened,' she says, grabbing some jeans from the back of a chair. 'This is probably the best thing that's ever happened to them.'

193

'What about you?'

She steps into the jeans and looks surprised when they fit easily around her waist. We sit together on the edge of the hospital bed.

'I feel like I should tell you what happened,' she says.

Machinery hums in the walls like trapped insects.

'They said it was a placental abruption,' she says. 'Something went wrong. It made me go into labour.'

My stomach squeezes tight. 'You gave birth?'

'I think so. They gave me drugs. There was so much happening. I already knew . . . we all did, right?'

The smell of blood seems to fill my nostrils. I press a hand against my belly to try and calm the baby's mounting discontent.

She looks away from me. 'They don't know for sure why it happened. But . . . it can be caused by heavy drinking.'

Power sizzles inside me. I feel it creeping into my arms. She's not posing any threat, but the baby wants to see her punished.

When I speak there's a hard lump in my throat. 'Maybe they're more delicate than we realised.'

'I'm glad it's gone,' she says.

I bite my tongue until I taste blood.

'I know that sounds bad,' says Siobhan. 'But I never asked for this. It's like I have my life back.'

A sharp pain pinches at my side. 'What life do you really have?'

'One without an alien baby in it.'

'So you did it on purpose, then?'

We stare at each other for a long time. She doesn't answer, and that's all the answer I need.

'I miss having you in my head,' she says. 'I feel a bit lost now. I didn't know if I could just let you back in my life. But I'm glad I did. I missed you.'

'After this,' I say. 'I just don't know.'

I stand up and take out my phone. Siobhan watches me send a text to Morris asking him to pick me up. I need to get out of this place.

'This isn't over for you,' I say, looking her straight in the face. 'Your body will never really be yours. Not after everything that's happened.'

Her face darkens like she's going to hit me, but she knows better than that. Inside, I feel the baby's anger churn, energy waiting to be unleashed.

She turns and shouts across the ward. 'I'm ready to go now!'

Her parents bustle in. I'm about to shove past them when my phone vibrates. It's a reply from Morris.

Sorry, still with Nan. I'll be there in ten.

I don't have that long. My belly feels like a smouldering fuse reaching its end. Pain squeezes my hips. The baby was clinging on, trying to make sure it wasn't born here amid so many people, but it made a mistake. It let Siobhan make it angry, and now it can't fight back against my body.

'I need a lift home.'

Siobhan snorts. 'You serious?'

'Do I look like I'm joking?'

She looks to her parents. They aren't thrilled by

the idea but they're not about to leave a pregnant girl stranded.

It seems to take forever to make it through the hospital. We go down in the lift, and the white, scuffed walls feel never ending. When we reach the waiting room I walk right into Maida's mum.

'You,' she says, like I'm her mortal enemy. Terror fills her eyes.

Pain clamps around my hips and my legs buckle in front of her. She staggers away, and it's Siobhan who drops down beside me.

'It's happening,' I say.

A hospital orderly appears with a wheelchair, probably the same guy I saw when I arrived. Maybe his whole job is waiting with a wheelchair in case a pregnant woman goes into labour.

Somewhere in the corners of my mind I can feel the others. They're going into labour too. A singular pain resonates between us, like an electronic signal. A low hum rises in my ears. There's a shift somewhere deep inside my body.

My waters break and it runs hot down my legs. Somehow I get into the wheelchair. I look up at Maida's mum. 'Get home,' I say. 'Find her, quickly!'

They wheel me back through the corridors. It feels like I'm being taken prisoner. I manage to get my phone out of my pocket to call home.

'You have to come to the hospital,' I say.

Mum shouts something at such high pitch I can barely understand.

The muscles around my hips are white hot. I squeeze the arms of the wheelchair until it subsides.

They wheel me into the lift. Siobhan comes with me, but her parents stay behind. The metal doors start to shut, like a cell closing around me, but at the last second a hand darts between them and wrenches them back open. 'Keisha!'

Morris is getting good at showing up at just the right time.

He drops down in front of me, beads of sweat trembling on his forehead, his chest heaving.

'I guess I won't get be your midwife after all,' he says.

The lift doors close.

'I can't do this on my own.'

Breathless, he says, 'You don't have to.'

I pull him into a kiss. Lightly at first, until his body relaxes. He kisses me hungrily, like he used to, like he's been starved of it for a long time.

I don't care that people are watching. I close my eyes and wonder if this feels right. If this is a future I can accept.

A contraction almost makes me bite his lip off. He breaks away from me and wipes his mouth.

'Let's have a baby,' he says.

The lift stops and the doors slide open.

# PART TWO
## Eight weeks later

# Chapter Twenty-one

**Maida**

My forehead brushes the blank piece of paper set on the floor in front of me. The words draw shapes on my lips, as they have thousands of times before. The way Dad taught me.

'*Subhana Rabbiyal A'la.*'

I say it three times, and then sit up on my knees.

'*Allahu Akbar.*'

The second *Rakat* begins standing. Then I lower myself and sit on my left leg, right hand on my right knee, index finger pointing forward. Muscle memory, every movement automatic.

Sometimes I feel like a praying robot.

*Must. ~~Crush. Humanity.~~ Achieve. Khushoo.*

It feels like sleepwalking.

'*At-Tahiyyatu lillahi was-Salawatu wat-Tayyibatu,*'

The words have always been a beautiful mystery to me. Even Dad never bothered to learn Arabic.

That's the *Fard Rakats*, the obligatory prayers, over. I stay on my knees. I saw this movie once where these people were dying, and they started praying extra hard to make sure they got to Heaven. They prayed so hard the walls of reality began to tear.

What was it called? I snuck out of bed to watch it. It was terrible.

*Shit.* I always get distracted during prayers. It's not easy focusing on words I don't understand. Words that were drummed into me probably before I could even talk.

And I swore. I'm really nailing it.

It's not just tonight. Every prayer feels empty now. I'm going through the motions. Rinse. Repeat. Prayers have never done for me what Dad says they should. But at least I always felt like I was part of something when I was doing them. Part of the 'fucking muzza squad', as people would kindly shout at me when I went to pray at school. I don't know. They made me feel proud.

Now, nothing.

Beside me, swaddled in her nest of blankets, my baby fusses. I watch her waggle her legs like she's trying to backstroke across the floor.

My Marvel.

I leave her, just for a moment, and face forward again to say a *Rakat Sunnah*, a voluntary prayer outside my usual routine. Perhaps it'll shake some feeling loose. Perhaps I just need to *try harder*.

I scrunch the paper into a ball and hurl it across the empty flat. Touchdown. Marvel whines. I lift her in the crook of my arm and pull down my shirt. Snack time! She latches on and starts sucking. The soreness makes me wince.

In the alt-reality of the movie, it turned out that the people praying for salvation were already dead – they'd all been praying and praying, trying to lead holy lives, killing people they found sinful, all to get to Heaven. But it was impossible. The only way was down.

Apostasy! That's what it's called. I don't think that's what's happening to me. It's not like I've suddenly given up on my religion or anything. It just feels like it can't contain me anymore. I'm a protagonist instead of a bit player.

The price I'm paying for my shift in allegiance is having to live in the empty flat. Morris had to put fresh bolts on the door for my safety – the name-calling hasn't stopped. Or the threats. Or the people who linger outside at night, whispering to each other, shuffling their feet against the floor.

None of that matters now. I have my daughter. We have each other.

I'm starting to realise she could be all the protection I need.

As she suckles, I wrap one of her hands inside mine. It's so tiny, like a gremlin. When I squeeze I feel the fragile bones under her skin. She squeaks her disapproval and my nipple pops from her mouth.

The energy flows like a superpower. It burrows under my skin and my mind flashes blank. My arms move by themselves to lower her into the blankets. Then I grip my left index finger tight in my right hand.

Even if I wanted to, there's nothing I can do to stop it. I brace myself for the inevitable.

*Snap.* I wrench my finger back hard. Pain screeches up

my arm and I roar, a sound that bounces around the bare walls and recites itself back to me.

All at once she surrenders control, allowing me to cradle my hand against my chest.

The power is real. It's already getting stronger. *Way* stronger.

'Good girl,' I say, the pain expanding and contracting. 'Good girl.'

# Chapter Twenty-two

**Morris**

What I learned real quick about being a parent is that even the shortest trip anywhere becomes an epic ordeal.

You have to sort out the right clothes, which is tough when you've got no money and your kid grows at the rate of over a month a week. At least that's how it started, but now it seems to be getting faster and faster. The car needs sorting because you can't afford a kiddie seat and someone (totally not me) smeared a crappy nappy across the headrest. And you have to set the timer on your phone to make sure you're home before the kid notices he's away from his sisters and throws a fit.

Maybe that last one is just us.

All that before we go for a pint of milk.

'We could have left him with one of the others,' says Keisha, looking around the aisles like it's an alien landscape. The bags under her eyes could carry our shopping.

'Nah, it's good for him to get out of the block some-times. See the world.'

I've got the kid strapped nice and safe to my chest,

facing away from me, his legs dangling. It's been eight weeks, but he's nearly too heavy for me to carry him like this, really. My back is killing me. But I like doing it anyway.

'Oh yeah,' says Keisha. 'Lidl really broadens horizons.'

'Don't listen to grumpy Mummy.'

There's no sign that he's listening. Instead he looks around, his golden eyes watching me calmly as I grab a pack of economy bum wipes and drop it into the trolley. All three of the Children have bright gold eyes, like they're wearing novelty contact lenses. It's the only thing about them that doesn't look normal. I stroke back his tuft of black hair. He's got a proper curly quiff. When Keisha isn't around I've been trying to get him to say 'Daddy'. No luck yet.

'At least put it in the baby seat,' says Keisha.

'*Him*. And nah, I like having him in the papoose.'

She stops the trolley and gives me a look. 'The what?'

'Papoose.'

'There's no way it's actually called that.'

I think this might be the first ever time I've known a word Keisha doesn't. It's my opportunity to hold it over her for as long as possible. 'It *is*. Nan always called it that.'

An arched eyebrow means she's taken my word for it. I chalk it up in my win column. It's about time there was something in there.

She starts dragging her feet along the aisle again. 'How is your nan?'

I shrug. 'Same old.'

Keisha looks like she could fall asleep on top of the trolley. 'How much time do we have?' she says.

206

The kid lifts a pudgy hand to try and grab the phone. 'Half an hour 'til he needs to be back.'

'We better split up if we're going to get this done.'

Bad choice of words. I still have no idea if we're together – like, *together* – or not. It feels like we kind of are, but we haven't done anything to make it definite. After what happened last time, I'm way too scared to push it on that front.

'Don't get the wrong stuff,' she says, slipping around the corner.

'Like you care,' I mutter.

When they've been apart for even a few hours, the kids start to scream and wail. It only stops when we bring them back together. It's like they can't stand being separated. It means we all spend way more time together than I think anybody wants. It's not ideal, but to try to manage the situation we agreed we'd share the chores.

It's our job to shop for everyone. Even with the girls pooling their money we're way short of being flush. When I used to think about having a kid I always assumed I would have banked plenty of cash first.

Who knows what made me think I would ever have money.

Christmas is just over a month away. I have no idea how I'm going to afford that.

I scope the aisle until I find the baby formula. Keisha refuses to breastfeed, no matter how many times I tell her how much we would save. The formula costs more than all the food I eat in a week. The kids have solids so they probably shouldn't be at the breast milk as well. Is that right? Buggered if I know. Baby books are kind of useless when they're growing so quick.

Soon he'll be a toddler. Then a proper kid. His childhood is going to fly past. What do I do when he looks older than me?

We can worry about that later. Right now it's all about food. I pick up two different kinds of formula.

'What do you reckon?' I say, holding the choices in front of his golden eyes. 'What would Morris Jr like to drink?'

He doesn't have a name yet, so I had to go with something. It's fine, as long as I don't use it in front of Keisha. She refuses to give him a name, despite all my suggestions.

'I recommend the cheaper one,' says a voice behind me.

My heart faceplants my ribs. I turn around and find myself face-to-face with Tyrone. His jacket is open and he's wearing a vest underneath to show off his muscles. There's something obscene about his nipples. The kid dangles from my chest between us like a shield.

When Tyrone smiles I know it's not because he's happy to see me. He looks at the kid and puffs his cheeks into a stupid face. My boy doesn't react at all, and I love him for it.

I glance at the ceiling for security cameras.

'He's cute,' says Tyrone. 'He can't be yours?'

I draw my arms protectively round my child. Tyrone rolls his eyes.

'I'm not a child snatcher, Mo. You know me better than that.'

'I don't know you at all anymore.'

It's almost impossible to believe this is the same guy who accidentally pissed all over his tie on the first day of school when he wore it too long and used a urinal.

'I just want what you owe me,' he says. 'What you agreed to, remember?'

I force myself to hold his gaze. 'Things have changed.'

The smile drops and he takes a step closer, forcing me to back off against the shelves. He reaches inside his jacket, and for a second I think he's going to shank me. Instead he brings out a thick package wrapped up in brown tape.

'You hold this for me,' he says.

I shake my head, but he's already sliding it in between my chest and the kid. I don't recognise the address written on it.

'You've got until Christmas Day. You bring me the money, or you deliver that package. We'll count it as your first job for me.'

I try to swallow. The package feels heavy against my chest. It must be a gun.

Tyrone puts a hand on the back of my neck and leans close. 'I want to help you out, Mo.'

'Being like you isn't helping me out.' My future is dangling by a thread. The only thing holding me up is the kid.

'You became like me as soon as you asked for the money,' he says.

Keisha rounds the corner with the trolley and stops dead when she sees me, backed against the baby products, Tyrone standing over me like he's ready to rip out my throat.

'Everything all right?' she says.

'Fine,' says Tyrone, taking the time to look her up and down before he steps away from me with an appreciative nod. It makes me want to smack him. 'See you soon.' He deliberately brushes past Keisha on his way to the end of the aisle. I watch him head past the checkouts without buying anything.

'You want to tell me what that was about?' says Keisha.

'Not really.'

She grabs the cheaper tub of formula out of my hand. I'd forgotten I was still holding it. 'He didn't look too friendly. Didn't he go to our school?'

'Yeah, he was in my year.' I avoid her eyes and look at my phone instead. The package sits heavy behind the baby. 'Come on, we need to get going.'

**Keisha**

We pay for the stuff with the handful of cash we collected. In the car park Morris looks around like he's expecting a bullet. Whoever that was back there, he's got Morris rattled.

I take the back seat and put the kid between my legs, pulling the seatbelt tight across us both. We're not going to win any awards for health and safety. Right after they were born Siobhan came and offered me all the stuff her parents had bought for her baby. It would have made all of this so much easier, but I couldn't accept it – it would have felt tainted somehow.

As we drive I see Morris watching me in the mirror.

He wants to see what I'm like with the kid. It sits tucked between my legs, staring up at the side window. I should probably display some kind of motherly instinct. I put a hand on its belly and hope it's enough to keep Morris happy.

I knew it the moment they put the baby into my arms – I would never be overwhelmed with motherly love. The maternal instinct that's supposed to well up inside and rinse me clean of fear and uncertainty? No chance. Instead there's nothing but resentment.

The birth was surprisingly straightforward. Olivia had coached us for a marathon. The pain was intense. By the time I reached a bed they said it was too late to give me anything. I clung to the others inside my mind and we pulled each other through it. Like the pregnancies themselves, the birth didn't take long.

When the babies emerged the connection between the three of us sputtered and died. It was like we were trying to cling to one another with slippery hands. In the end, we just let go. I had never felt so lonely.

I'm ashamed by how much I miss it.

The road drifts by outside. I realise where we are with a start and slide down into the seat, practically pitching the kid onto the floor.

'Why are we going this way?'

'It's quickest.'

I close my eyes as the school whips past the window. There's no way anyone would see me. But I can't risk it. *He* could be there.

The school's far behind us before I sit up again. Morris frowns at me in the mirror.

'Are you ashamed to be seen with me?'

'No, it's not that.'

'Maybe no one ever expected much of me. I know I never did,' he says, gripping the steering wheel so hard it creaks. 'But I'm doing my best. I'm doing everything I can with what was given to us.'

'I'm trying to accept it,' I say.

Morris locks eyes with me. 'I want us to have a normal life.'

He doesn't say what I know he wants to say. *Together.*

Ahead of us the tower looms into sight.

'There's somewhere I want to take you,' says Morris. 'We'll go tomorrow.'

'How do they feel about screaming babies?'

Our spot is still empty. We pull up to the kerb and Morris kills the engine. The kid starts to cry.

# Chapter Twenty-three

**Maida**

The Christmas garland on the front door was supposed to make the flat feel a bit more homely. That's what Morris said, anyway. I told him it was like putting mistletoe on a turd.

He keeps talking about *our first Christmas together*. I don't think he really understands the whole Muslim thing.

Anyway, when I looked outside today, I found that someone had kindly spray-painted the holly completely black. It was more like a burnt doughnut than a Christmas decoration. I like it more this way. It blends in with all the abuse they've scrawled on the door itself.

*Whores.*

*Freaks.*

*Fuck off!*

Not exactly Banksy.

Marvel begins to cry and wriggle. The tantrum is getting earlier and earlier. She can sort of crawl – like a drunk Spider-Man – and she moves towards the door. I pick her up. They can't talk yet, but I'm sure I'm learning to read them.

'It's okay, *munni*.'

At the door I draw back the bolts and step out. Keisha's coming down the hallway. Her son writhes and wails in her arms, and I hear people shift behind their doors. It's like they wait for us. I wonder if they've been posted to keep track of our movements. Spies. Sentries.

Every day it feels more and more like something in the block is going to break. I've been thinking of it like a biscuit dunked into tea. Hold it too long, and the whole thing's going to come apart.

It's not the best analogy. Mostly I'm just hungry.

If anything *does* happen – if they decide we're a threat that needs to be removed – all I can do is wish them luck. They're going to need it.

Keisha pushes past me into the flat. Before I can close the door Olivia calls along the hallway for me to *wait!* We shut ourselves inside, sliding the bolt across.

The babies are like a squad. Lay them together in the blankets and they settle right down. They just don't like being apart.

They might be sort-of-triplets, but Marvel doesn't look like Helena, Olivia's daughter. Less hair, for one. And she's brown enough to be 'specially selected' for a pat down by airport security. SSSS. That's what will always get printed on her ticket. Helena is pale as milk. No bombs hidden in her nappy.

'What happened to your finger?'

I've wrapped it in tissues and taped it to its neighbour. It probably makes it look worse than it actually is. 'Nothing, I just whacked it on something.' Time to change the subject. 'Thought of a name yet?'

Keisha shakes her head. 'Not yet.'

'What about Morris's idea?'

She arches an eyebrow. 'Mo Junior? That's wrong on pretty much every level.'

'Oh, cheers,' says Morris.

'At least it won't get called *Marv* like yours,' says Keisha. 'Your baby is going to sound like a school caretaker.'

Such shade.

'I don't care,' I say. 'And Marvel is a *she*, not an *it*, thank you very much.'

That kills the conversation dead. Keisha and her son are like strangers. That seems to be how she wants it to stay.

'When did you last go home?' she says.

'The atmosphere down there hasn't been too friendly after I indirectly beat my dad half to death and gave birth to an illegitimate child.'

'Some people are so unreasonable.'

I shrug a shoulder. 'As far as I'm concerned this place is home now.'

The memory makes me smile. It's not that I *liked* seeing that happen to Dad, not exactly; it's just, I've never felt strong like that in my life. Nobody could have stopped that power.

And that . . . well, it was pretty satisfying.

'It worked out all right,' I say. 'Funnily enough he leaves me alone now. He's scared of me.'

'I don't think you're supposed to be happy about that,' says Olivia.

'It's not so bad having a bit of power.'

We're interrupted by a knock at the door. Not the ridiculous, three-stage secret knock Morris forced us all to learn. It almost sounds polite. Both girls freeze like it was a gunshot.

'Are you there?' comes a voice through the door. 'It's Siobhan.'

## Keisha

Siobhan – holy shit. The last time we really saw each other was at the hospital. Morris is the first to snap out of it. He goes to the door and opens it a crack. Unfortunately, Siobhan is twice his weight and easily forces it all the way open.

To be fair, she's lost a lot of weight since I last saw her. By the looks of it she's trying to compensate by wearing as much make-up as her face will carry.

'Hey, guys,' she says.

The boy begins to cry first, and the baby girls join in a moment later, their voices spiralling up like an air raid siren. They squirm in the blankets, like they're trying to inch closer to each other. Something about Siobhan gets them worked up. My skin prickles all over with the familiar sensation of energy.

'What do you want?' I say.

She looks at me like she might cry. Shortly after the birth she came to my flat looking for me and I told Mum I didn't want to see her. After everything that happened – after what she *did* – it doesn't feel right to be around her.

'This might sound a bit weird,' she says, 'but I was wondering if I could take a photo of all of you?'

She holds up her iPhone. It sounds more than weird. It sounds downright suspicious.

'Look, I know you want nothing to do with me now,' she says. 'At least let me have a photo, yeah?'

A picture of us all is the last thing I want. But Morris is already piling the babies into our arms and hustling us into a group in the middle of the flat.

'A family portrait,' he says. 'I like the sound of that.'

The Children won't stop screaming and squirming. One of the neighbours hammers on the wall. Morris just pulls us all closer together, and Siobhan points her phone.

'Smile,' says Morris.

I think I'm the only one of us who doesn't smile.

'Nice one!' says Siobhan.

She steps closer to show us.

As soon as she does the Children squeal the same short, sharp note. Power surges from them, stronger than I've ever felt before. Siobhan's eyes go blank and she staggers backwards, dropping her phone so the screen cracks.

'Get out of here!' I shout. Not just because I want her gone. I don't want anything to happen to her.

She shakes her head, eyes refocusing, and scrambles for her phone. The air buzzes. Siobhan backs away to the door.

'Go!'

Finally, she turns and runs into the corridor. She leaves the door open, and I see people standing outside, peering in for a better view. Louise Krawczyk snaps a picture. I hurry across and slam the door in their faces.

217

The energy sinks away, leaving me covered in goosebumps. Olivia looks like she might faint, but there's a ghost of a smile on Maida's lips.

Three sets of golden eyes watch the door.

This isn't the first time something like this has happened.

They almost look normal . . . but there is something wrong with the Children.

# Chapter Twenty-four

**Keisha**

The next day we leave the boy with Mum. Like everyone else she's worked out that something about the Children isn't right. Whenever she tries to talk to me about it, I just tell her I don't know what's happening. It's hardly even a lie. Dad just pretends that it's business as usual.

Being at home really isn't a lot of fun.

It's a novelty to sit up front, no timer set on my phone to warn us of the next unquenchable tantrum. I feel like a different person.

I shouldn't let myself get carried away, even if it is only for a couple of hours.

The windows are fogged up, so it's hard to tell where Morris is taking me.

I glance across at him. 'So you're taking us to the airport, right?'

He smiles, and his eyes dance. He seems to have forgiven me for yesterday. 'I thought you were scared of flying?'

'I don't know,' I say. 'I've never had the chance to try it.'

I use my sleeve to make a smudge of clear view. We're on the road that leads to the hospital and for a moment I panic that he's going to section me. To my relief we drive right past, and instead pull into a long driveway just a little farther up the road. It's attached to an old-fashioned house, three floors of it looming over us. It really does look like a mental institution, every window brandishing rusted iron bars.

Morris gets out of the car and I follow. 'It's nicer inside, trust.'

A sign beside the arched doorway identifies the house as *Shady Acres Care Home*. It certainly looks shady. The mistletoe hanging above the front door is fooling nobody.

The reception area is warm, carpeted like an old lady's house but with the smells of a school canteen. Cheap food and bleach. Morris approaches the front desk, where a young woman with her hair pulled back into a tight bun is fiddling with a plastic Christmas tree. She breaks into a smile when she sees him.

'Morris! How's it going?'

'Not too bad, cheers,' he says, drumming his hands on the desktop. 'How's she doing today?'

'She's just had lunch, so she might be tired. But you're fine to go through.' She looks over his shoulder at me. 'Who's this with you?'

Morris ushers me forward. 'This is Keisha. She's . . . a friend.'

He's not sure he's said the right thing. These days I don't think either of us knows the truth. It feels like we're tied together in a way that can't be broken.

We stay quiet as I follow Morris along a hallway and

220

up a flight of stairs. There's a lift running on a rail up its side. He catches me looking at it.

'It's not as fun as it looks.'

A gate cuts off the top of the stairs, the kind usually installed to keep toddlers from breaking their necks. Beyond that is a locked door with a keypad. Morris taps in the code like he's done it a hundred times and holds it open for me.

On the other side is a long hallway studded with doors, some hanging open. As we walk past, I see elderly people sitting in high-backed chairs in front of a television, or lying in bed, or staring out of the window. A nurse in a blue outfit smiles at Morris as she bustles past us.

'You're such a flirt,' I say.

'Yeah, right.'

'I bet you've got all the old ladies wrapped around your little finger.'

He stops outside one of the doors near the end of the hall. 'This is Nan's room. She's usually pretty chilled, but she gets confused easy. Maybe just follow my lead, yeah?'

It's like being hit in the face by a fireball. It's so hot in the small room I swear the air is shimmering. The walls are painfully floral, and every available surface is decorated with photographs in frames. Some are black and white, while others look like they could have been taken yesterday.

If someone sucked all the water out of my body, I would probably end up looking a bit like the woman who's lying in the bed in the middle of the room. Her

221

skin looks like it's been stitched together from the wings of moths, fragile and flaky, and her bones jut out at severe angles. If I touched her white hair I'm sure it would crumble. When she hears the door she looks straight at Morris.

'Christopher?' she says. Her voice is like a draft blowing down a chimney.

'No, it's your grandson. Mo,' he says, stepping up to the side of the bed and gently taking her hand.

If she hears him she doesn't show it. Her eyes find me. I'm still standing in the doorway like a frightened child.

'Is this the girl you won't shut up about?' she says.

Morris scrunches his eyes shut. 'This is Keisha.'

I join Morris at the bedside. The old woman's eyes are surprisingly clear as she studies me and smiles to herself.

'She's a beauty.' The smile crumples and she whines like she's in pain. 'I don't know her.'

'It's all right,' says Morris, stroking the back of her fingers.

'Christopher . . .' she whimpers.

'Isn't Christopher your dad?' I say.

Morris lowers his voice. 'A lot of the time she thinks I'm him, even though she hasn't seen him in years. Sometimes she doesn't know me at all. The other week she thought I was her postman from thirty years ago.'

'What's wrong with her?' I say, before flinching at how harsh the words sound.

'Alzheimer's,' says Morris. 'She started showing symptoms when she was my mum's age. Young, you know?' He looks at her with sad eyes. 'Do you remember, she lived in the block with us for a while?'

222

I shake my head. Even though I've lived in Midwich Tower my whole life I don't remember that at all.

'My dad and her never got on. I don't think he ever really forgave her for leaving my granddad in Nigeria.'

'That was brave of her.'

Morris nods. 'Nan, tell her about the time you had to deliver quintuplets. She was the bravest, smartest person in the family, I swear.'

Morris's nan smiles. 'She thought it was twins, but they kept coming.'

As she talks Morris massages cocoa butter into her hands. The sweet, familiar scent makes me feel like a child again.

'I told her five little ones in nine hours was a good rate,' she says. 'Tea towels, all over the kitchen floor. Impossible.'

'They named one after you, didn't they, Nan?'

She makes a noise that I think is supposed to be a baby crying.

I try – and fail – to imagine how it would feel to give birth to *five* Children.

Morris rubs the last of the cocoa butter into his palms. 'We had no choice but to bring her here in the end. The block wasn't safe for her, and all them stairs – it was too risky. Some days she's all right, quite lucid, really *there*, you know? Almost the same as before. Mostly though, she's all kinds of confused. We can just about afford it, though the plan was that I'd be contributing by now.' He drops his voice to a whisper. 'She wasn't supposed to last this long.'

She watches him while he talks, like she enjoys the

sound of his voice, regardless of the words. There's a slight splodge of lunch on her bottom lip. Morris notices it too, licks a finger, and wipes it away like a fussy parent.

'You haven't told me her name,' I say.

Morris blinks at me. 'Oh, sorry. I just think of her as Nan. It's Grace.'

I look at the frail old woman who barely has a name, her wits, her past, her future, snatched away and jumbled up by an illness she could never have predicted. It's impossibly unfair.

'Why did you bring me here?' I say.

Morris leans across the bed and turns on a digital radio. It's tuned to a jazz station, and the gentle slide of a saxophone makes Grace's eyes slip closed in satisfaction.

'I wanted to show you that things don't always go how you expect,' he says. 'Nan was smarter than anyone she knew and she lost everything. No one saw it coming. But you know what? You just have to carry on and deal with it best you can. Just like she's doing. I'm really trying, Keish.'

Sweat prickles on my forehead. 'Is that supposed to make me feel better?' My voice is louder than I expected. 'She ended up with nothing.'

'That's not the point,' says Morris, resting his hand on mine. 'And it's also not entirely true . . . she does have something, even though it wasn't what any of us would have wished for, even though it wasn't what she'd dreamed of. The future you wanted didn't work out because this crazy thing happened, yeah? That sucks. But it can happen to anyone. Sometimes we can't do

224

anything about it. That's life. And maybe that sucks, too. But you shouldn't give up on everything because one plan didn't work out.'

I pull my hand away from him and walk to the door. 'You're way off the mark if you thought this was a good idea.'

'Look, follow me,' he says, stepping past me into the corridor. 'I'll show you why I've been coming here so much since I left school and didn't suddenly become a millionaire.'

We walk a few doors along and into a room that's almost identical, except there are no photographs and the TV is bigger than the window. A daytime soap is playing quietly to a large old lady in an armchair. The air smells of stale perfume.

'Are we allowed to be in here?' I say.

'It's all right, I've volunteered here before. They all know me. Well, sort of.'

I don't know how I never knew he was coming to this place. I didn't think he kept anything from me. It's exactly the kind of thing I would have expected him to use to try to impress me.

He sidles around the armchair and perches on the edge of a footrest. The woman notices him, looks reluctantly away from the TV, and then breaks into a wide smile.

'Marty?' she says. 'When did you get back?'

'I came to see you.'

'It must be such a long flight.'

He takes her hand. 'It's worth it.'

The woman smiles like she's never heard anything better. Then just as quickly the giant TV snatches back

225

her attention. 'Could you go and ask the nurse for an extra blanket?' she says. 'It's getting chilly in here.'

The room is basically a sauna, but Morris nods and comes back around the chair. He starts straightening out the bed covers.

'Who does she think you are?'

'Her son is a doctor and lives in America or somewhere. He hasn't come back to see her in years.' He waves at the TV. 'He just buys her stupid presents sometimes.'

'And you just play along?'

'It doesn't do any harm. I don't think she really believes I'm her son. It just makes her feel better to think she's not been forgotten.' He walks out into the hallway and I follow him. As we pass the doors he points at all of them. 'So why shouldn't I be Marty the doctor, or Mrs Ward's husband who loved her every second right up until he died of cancer, or Mrs Okoro's brother who was so good at the javelin he almost went to the Olympics?'

Midway down the corridor there's a cupboard, and Morris grabs a fresh blanket. We take it back to the old woman in front of the massive TV and Morris drapes it across her lap. I wonder where she thought she would end up in life. I bet it wasn't in a place like this.

'It's sad,' I say.

'It *is* sad. Half the time they don't even remember me, or they wet themselves and cry until I can find a nurse. It's not pretty,' says Morris. 'But they all had a life before they ended up here. And sometimes when I'm here I can be somebody else. I can live the life of somebody who did something with it. Who *lived*. It makes me feel like there isn't just one path in life, you

226

know? Like maybe I don't have to settle for whatever was given to me.'

I study him while he watches the old woman's back. Somebody in the TV soap is hitting her partner with a lampshade and shouting about betrayal. I've never heard Morris talk like this. A year ago, when I decided I shouldn't see him anymore, it was because I believed he never thought about the future. Never had any ambition. It seemed like he was going nowhere in life and it didn't bother him.

Maybe I was wrong.

Maybe he felt just as trapped as me.

The TV programme is over, and as the titles roll the woman turns and looks at him. 'It's good to see you again, love.'

We go back to his nan's room. She's fast asleep in bed with the covers tucked around her chin. Morris kisses her forehead.

'I know what you're trying to do, Morris. But you have to understand. It wasn't just something weird or unexpected that happened to me,' I say. 'It was something horrible. It was an attack on my body. A *violence*. I can't just forget it happened.'

'I know,' says Morris, adjusting the covers. 'But you shouldn't give up because it changes your plans. You'll end up having no life at all.'

We walk along the hallway, past the doors of all these people whose fate conspired to bring them to this place. Morris says a cheerful goodbye to every nurse he sees. We don't talk until we're outside, standing in the porch. It's started to rain.

'I thought about bringing Mo Jr – sorry, the kid – to see her.'

'It's probably a good idea you didn't.'

'Why not?'

'You know there's something wrong with the Children, right?'

He pushes past me to the car. I stay on his heels.

'You've seen what they can do.'

He stops beside the car. 'Maybe it's not what you want, but you have a son now. You have to deal with that. It's your responsibility, whether you want it or not.'

'Look, I know how important this is to you. I know you want the kid to give you a future you didn't have before.' I glance back at *Shady Acres*. 'But you have to see that it isn't as simple as that. The Children are dangerous.'

He throws open the car door. 'A little weirdness isn't the end of the world.'

I block his way. 'What if that's exactly what this is?'

'What?'

'The end of the world.'

He laughs bitterly and ducks into the car. The engine fires up and for a second I think he's going without me. When he waits I have no choice but to get into the passenger seat and endure the silent journey back to the confines of the block.

## Morris

The parakeets are making loads of noise in the trees as we walk to the front entrance. It's not far off dark. I swear the days are never going to stop getting shorter.

Neither of us talks as we go up the stairs. I thought

228

taking her to see Nan might stop her from turning against the Children. It was supposed to get her on my side, make her see that the best chance we have is to do this together. Instead all I've done is driven us even further apart.

Maida is waiting for us in the flat, the kids arranged around her like she's heading up a team of superheroes. 'Have fun?' she says.

Keisha spits out a harsh laugh.

I pick up our son. 'I think I should take him tonight.'

'Fine.'

'I was trying to do a good thing, you know.'

She doesn't say anything. I've messed it up. Again. I'm trying so hard, but there's so much going on, and everything I do seems to be wrong.

Keisha leaves. I let the kid down to save my back. He balances on his feet for a second, like he might be about to stand, but when I let go of his hand he drops onto his butt.

'What are we going to do?' I say.

He looks up at me with his golden eyes, like he wishes he knew the answer.

'Everything okay between you two?' says Maida.

'Not right now. You need anything?'

She shakes her head.

'All right, I'll catch you later.'

I pick up the kid, and he moans, reaching for his sisters. He doesn't want to be with me, but he's still small enough that he's got no choice. I carry him into the corridor and head for home.

## Maida

When the coast is clear the bathroom door opens and out steps Mum.

'Did Morris say anything?'

'They had no idea.'

You can always rely on those guys to be too self-involved to notice anything going on around them.

'Will you think about what I said?' says Mum, reaching for my hands.

I whip them away before she can touch me. 'There's no way I can make you understand. I don't want to leave any of this behind.'

She gives the flat a look that says *total craphole* and then glances at the Children. They're watching us, clutching a ratty blanket between them, one I used to wrap them in during the few days they were tiny. I'm convinced they know what we're saying, or at least getting the gist.

'We could start somewhere new,' Mum says, and that's when the tears start coming. I *hate* it when she cries. It always used to unlock something inside me, no matter how much I tried to resist. I can't afford to let it get to me now.

'Dad would never let you go.'

Mum takes the frilliest handkerchief in existence from her sleeve and dabs her eyes. 'He still cares about you.'

The way a chimp cares about a kitten so much that it crushes it to death.

*Eugh*, dark.

'In nearly two months he hasn't even tried to see me, Mum.'

My voice stays neutral. I'm doing a great job of the whole calmness thing. It feels as if, with the Children right behind me, there's nothing I have to worry about.

Through the tears, Mum looks expectant. It's like she thinks *I* need to make the first move in putting all this right. Well, it's not going to happen. I'm not sorry.

'Something is happening here, Mum. Something *awesome*,' I say.

'The people here, they want to—'

'Oh, you mean the people who complained to the council about the smell of your cooking? Or maybe the guy who called us terrorists? They *never* wanted us here, Mum.'

'You think this will change that?'

'Of course not! I've always been an outsider . . . but now I'm an outsider with some powerful allies.'

Her tears are flowing faster now. 'I'm scared for you.'

'You don't have to be.' I sit down on the blankets and lift Marvel onto my lap. 'She's due a feed. You should go.'

Mum gives me that pleading *you're-breaking-your-mother's-stupid-heart* look. 'Maida, my *munni*, I don't want to lose you.'

I pull down my top right in front of her and angle Marvel's head towards lunch. It's supposed to be a grand gesture of defiance, but the girl refuses to latch and slaps my nipple.

Still, it's enough to make Mum give up and head for the door.

Instead of chowing down on my nipple, Marvel rolls out of my arms and onto the blanket. Before I can scoop

231

her back up she pushes her hands against the floor, swings back her hips, and stands.

'Whoa!' I exclaim, loud enough to make Mum spin around.

Marvel just looks at me like this is something she's been doing for ages, no big deal. Helena looks at her sister, and pushes herself upright just as easily.

'They haven't done this before?' Mum says.

'This is definitely new!'

Both of them take an unsteady step, tottering like they might fall, before catching themselves for another step. They reach each other and link hands. My ears seem to pop.

'I can't believe it,' I say, and I realise I'm crying. Actual tears of pride rolling down my cheeks.

Mum doesn't look quite so impressed. She makes it obvious by backing away to the door like the Children are waving pitchforks.

'Mum?'

She doesn't say another word. As soon as she reaches the hallway she's gone.

I rest a hand on each of their shoulders. I don't know what's going to happen next. That's what makes it exciting, isn't it? This isn't predictable. It isn't routine. It's going to be something *big*. And I'm going to be at the heart of it.

# Chapter Twenty-five

**Morris**

Days go by and I don't hear from Keisha. I spend as much of the time as possible with my phone in my hand, daring myself to send a text. That's when I'm not trying to shield Mum from noticing how tall the kid's getting, or that he's learned to walk by himself, use the toilet by himself, dress himself. Their development is accelerating, but for some reason my boy always picks things up a little bit after his sisters. I guess girls just develop faster.

His tantrums are getting worse, too; the time he'll tolerate being apart from the others shrinking until I end up just leaving him with Maida and the girls. This child will always get his way. He'll make sure of it.

The girls said their first words the other day, while Maida and Olivia were giving them a bath. *Feels good*. They said it in perfect unison – then smiled.

My boy still hasn't spoken but his eyes are alert; he listens to everything – and I swear he understands every word.

*Hollyoaks* time. Dinner is microwave curry. Like always Mum doesn't talk until the advert break.

'I told your dad.'

I practically choke on a shard of poppadum. 'You talked to him?'

She shakes her head. 'Email.'

'What did he say?'

'Not much. He wants to speak to you himself, when he can get on Skype.'

The curry in my stomach threatens to make a reappearance. It's been months since me and Dad managed to have a conversation. It was mostly about money, or how little of it I've been sending him.

The kid would at least be a change of subject.

A part of me wonders if he might even be proud of me. I've finally done something with my life. I have a family now. I'm on track.

Keisha's words echo in my head. *You know there's something wrong with the Children, right?*

'When's he going to be free?' I ask.

But the adverts are over, and Mum waves me away. I ditch the remains of my dinner in the kitchen and go to my room. The package is hidden under the bed, which isn't the most original spot, but I'm not expecting Mum to come looking. I fish it out. Its weight sits in my palm. A gun. It has to be.

If I deliver it for Tyrone tonight, I could probably be holding a package full of cash by the time I speak to Dad. I could show him the notes and shut him up.

There'd be no going back. I do this for Tyrone once, I'm his for good. No way out.

I pick up my phone and open the text conversation with Keisha. It's been two days since the last message.

I look at the keypad for a long time. Then I close it, and shove the package back under the bed.

## Keisha

*Richard Jacobs.*

I type the name from the newspaper article into Google. Siltoe, the village in Cornwall, might hold the answers.

The search results are useless. It would help if it wasn't such a common name. My eyes itch from looking at the screen. Two nights have passed with barely any sleep. It's felt so strange to be in this room by myself. It should feel great to have some space, but without the baby, without the connection, I can't shake the feeling that I'm missing something, like I've forgotten to put on underwear.

I open up YouTube and find some music to chase away the silence. Then I search again. *Richard Jacobs Siltoe.*

The results are still a jumble. The news article appears again. I scroll past it until something catches my eye and I get a little jolt through my nerves. There's a link to a directory, with the name – and a phone number. I check the area code. It's Cornwall.

My phone is in my hand before I even realise it. I turn off the music and dial the number. I have no idea what I'm going to say but I know it's important to reach this person. I need to find out what happened to them all. I want to know how he coped. Maybe he can tell me how to deal with all of this.

It only rings twice before someone picks up. They don't say anything, but I know they're on the line.

'Hello?'

Nothing. Nerves scurry through my belly.

'I'm looking for Richard Jacobs.'

There's a short rasp, like a woman's muffled gasp, then the call cuts off. The silence seems to roar in my ear. I end the call and stare at my phone. It takes me a long time to work up the guts to dial again. No answer. I don't leave a message.

I go to close Google but before I do I try one more link – a news story from the same local paper that reported on the Children. I have to will myself to click the headline.

LOCAL MAN DIES IN UNEXPLAINED FIRE.

I know it's him before I've even read the story. Richard Jacobs died in a blaze at the Siltoe doctor's surgery. The local fire service weren't sure how it started. The story mentions the wife he left behind, but not his son.

Was it her who answered?

I close the window, grab my phone, and send a quick tweet: Going to stream in five minutes, come hang out with me!

It doesn't matter that it feels like my brain's about to melt. Right now I can't bear to be alone.

I plug in the microphone. The game takes an irritating couple of minutes while it downloads an update. When I log in to Twitch, a few people are already waiting on my channel. Some names are familiar, and seeing them makes me smile; there's even a few I don't recognise. I type a greeting, then turn on my webcam and blow them all a kiss.

'Hi everyone, thanks for joining me,' I say, keeping

my voice low because my parents are in bed. 'Let's get going, shall we?'

Usually I would ask them to donate if they enjoy the stream. Every penny was going to my university fund. There's not much point in asking anymore.

I search for a game but after a few seconds a message pops up to tell me the servers are unavailable. The same happens when I try again.

'Anyone know what's going on?' I ask.

The answer comes from 'AnonChild', a username I don't recognise: Servers are down for maintenance.

'Shit. Well that's just typical.'

A couple of viewers leave right away. Another search comes up empty.

I sigh into the microphone. 'Sorry, everyone.'

AnonChild types back: Don't worry. I'm sure I'll see you soon.

I lean towards the camera. 'Have you watched before?'

The chat has emptied out entirely now. It's just me and AnonChild.

First time, they type back. I wanted to check you out.

'Sorry there wasn't much to see.'

I slide off my headphones and start coiling up the wires. It must be a minute or so before I look back at the chat window.

Where's the Child?

I freeze. Somewhere in the world this person is staring back at me through the webcam. The silence in my room suddenly feels dangerous.

'How do you know about that?'

My heartbeat judders inside me for what feels like minutes.

There are answers in Cornwall.

I start typing back, begging them to tell me more, but before I can finish they post a link and leave the chat.

'Wait!' I say, to dead space.

I switch the camera off and end the stream. Go into options and make sure it won't be archived.

Then I click the link AnonChild sent.

A new window opens.

It's a YouTube video. I don't recognise the username, but the title says it all.

*The Alien Truth.*

The video starts and Siobhan's face appears on screen.

*'People have been chatting a lot of shit about us. So now I'm going to tell you the truth.'*

And she does. She spills all of it.

# Chapter Twenty-six

**Keisha**

The video is all over Facebook. It's been shared and liked and quoted by people I don't even know. It's been on YouTube for a couple of hours and already has over 1,000 views.

It's all out there: the Nightout, the record-time pregnancies, the connection between us, the awesome power of the Children.

I knew it! Louise Krawczyk has written, linking back to her conspiracy blog.

At the end of the video, a static picture fills the screen. The family portrait Siobhan took in the flat. Morris grinning with his arm around me like we're a happy family. It makes me want to punch the computer.

I slam the front door behind me, not caring who hears or what they might think. I'm so hot with rage, the cold seems to sizzle on my skin. I reach the stairs and practically run up the block.

Someone appears on the stairs above me. It's Maida, peering over the railing.

'You're out late.'

I don't stop moving. 'You shouldn't be out here. It's not safe.'

'I needed some air. They're with Olivia.' When I hurry past her she attaches herself to my heels. 'Safety in numbers.'

My feet boom around the stairwell like a heartbeat, pounding through the block. We reach Siobhan's floor and I turn into the hallway. The orange lights buzz overhead.

'Tell me what happened,' says Maida.

I hammer on the door to Siobhan's flat. The noise doesn't matter. She's made our situation public enough.

Siobhan's voice pushes through the door, like she's been expecting this. 'Please stop.'

'Open the door.'

'Let me explain.'

'Then *open the door*.'

The lock clicks back. As soon as the door moves I push it with all my strength. It flies inward, nearly hitting Siobhan in the face. She staggers away and catches herself against the wall. Her parents appear behind her.

'Hang on,' says Siobhan.

I storm inside, fists clenched. My vision blurs red at the edges. The only thing stopping me from punching Siobhan is her parents, watching, too scared to come any closer.

'I can't believe you did this to us,' I say.

'It's not like that.'

'Then why are our faces on the internet?'

Maida taps me on the shoulder. 'Sorry to interrupt, but does anyone fancy telling me what's happened?'

'She made a video about everything,' I say, keeping my eyes on Siobhan. 'It's online now. On fucking YouTube!'

'Cool,' says Maida.

'Did you actually watch the video?' says Siobhan.

'Of course I watched it!'

'I told the truth! People should know what happened to you.'

'It's easy for you!' I shout. 'You don't have to deal with this anymore!'

'Is that what you think?' says Siobhan, her voice growing sharper. 'You said it yourself at the hospital – it's not like it just goes away. Nobody will talk to me. They still act like I'm a freak. And the Children won't leave me alone. The last two nights the boy's been hanging around outside the flat.'

I look to Maida. It's obviously news to her. 'Must be when I'm asleep,' she says.

'I thought when I lost my baby I was free,' says Siobhan. 'But I'm not. I never will be. It's like I'm tainted. And you want nothing to do with me because of what I did. I've lost everything.'

My fists stay clenched. I can't let myself feel sorry for her. 'That doesn't give you the right to expose us.'

Behind one of the other doors along the corridor somebody clears their throat. They'll all be snooping through their peepholes, ears pressed to the door to enjoy the drama.

I lower my voice. 'Everybody already thinks we're sluts. Now they're going to think we're crazy, or just idiots desperate for more attention.'

241

Siobhan shakes her head. 'I thought if they knew the truth . . .'

Before I can stop myself I grab her by the shoulders and shove her back against the wall. I want to break her. Shut her mouth forever. In this moment, it feels like I could do it and never look back.

## Maida

Violence sizzles in the air. It's terrifying. Also kind of exciting.

'Hey!' shouts Siobhan's dad, but he doesn't dare make any move.

'Hit me,' says Siobhan. 'I dare you.'

It occurs to me that it might be my job to intervene and break them up. There's several reasons why I don't. Firstly, in movies, breaking up fights never works, and you usually get punched for your trouble. I am but a tiny little Muslim girl. Secondly, Siobhan killed one of the Children, and even though it was inside her body I still don't believe she had the right. The least she deserves to lose is a few teeth.

Keisha leans forward and hisses into her face. 'You made your choice.'

She thuds Siobhan's head against the wall, then lets go and steps off. It's a bit disappointing, really.

Some of the tension simmers away, but something else replaces it. A familiar *hum* riding toward us along the hallway.

The Children turn out of the stairwell. Their golden eyes reflect and shimmer in the gloom. They are walking, as if they've been doing it forever. The boy heads them up, Marvel and Helena a few steps behind, holding hands.

'I can't stop them!' shouts Olivia, trailing behind. She tries to catch up to them, but when she gets too close her feet seem to tangle over themselves to trip her up. The Children are holding her back. To be honest, it's a bit like something out of a nightmare, but my chest expands with pride. They approach the open door as if we're not even standing here.

The energy flares and white light flashes inside my skull, stronger than I've ever felt it. My feet shuffle backwards, out of their path. The same happens to Keisha.

'It's all right, it's me,' I say.

Marvel glances at me. My beautiful daughter. I smile at her, but the boy grabs her arm and she instantly seems to forget all about me. I don't know what it is, but something inside me wrenches.

The Children line up in front of the door, facing Siobhan like a firing squad. 'The boy whispered to them,' says Olivia, trapped on the other side of the door from us. 'They just stood up and walked out.'

He spoke to them *out loud*? I didn't think they needed to do that.

'What are you doing?' Siobhan shouts at them.

A low throb holds us in place while their energy begins to grow. It feels like the moment before a thunderstorm breaks. Their faces stay calm. Eyes fixed on Siobhan.

I try and push back against them. They don't need to hold me like this, they should know I would never try to stop them.

243

'Don't!' shouts Keisha.

Perhaps they're holding me because they know they need to keep her back. Keisha is too weak to let them do this.

'Help me!' screeches Siobhan.

*Click.* A door opens behind me. Stan, pyjamas stretched over his belly, steps into the corridor, wielding a long umbrella like a sword.

'Get back inside,' I hiss at him.

Another door, right next to Olivia, opens up. Tito and Devin emerge, nervously brandishing frying pans.

The boy glances at the new arrivals and falters, for just a moment. The low thrum is interrupted by the clicks of locks being turned, doors opening, more residents stepping out with makeshift weapons. More appear from the stairwell, led by the Hag. Of course it would be her.

This is probably what you'd call a showdown.

They heard the noise, or perhaps they got a phone call. They must feel the energy in the air and know that something spectacular is going to happen.

A few of the residents risk an approach. Nostrils looks like she's going to wet herself. The boy prickles, strong enough to keep everybody back. It forces all three of the Children to tear their attention from Siobhan. Their faces crease with the effort.

'Show them what we can do,' I say.

But they're not strong enough yet to take on this many people. This isn't the right time. The girls are the first to back down, glancing at each other and unlinking their hands. The boy sags, and then turns to glare at Siobhan one final time.

'We'll be back,' he says.

The first words I've ever heard him say, and they're full of menace. Unemotional. Calculated. Forceful. Grown-up. Keisha makes a noise somewhere between a gasp and a choke.

They turn away from the door. The energy sinks to a defensive rumble, holding the residents back as the Children head for the stairwell. The neighbours watch, clinging to their weapons and glancing at the Hag, like she might issue the order to attack.

Only the Hag is brave enough to bar their way for as long as she can before she is pushed away. I have to respect her for that.

'We don't want you here,' Devin shouts after them.

'Not now,' the Hag says.

Siobhan slides down the wall like she's dissolving.

'We can't stay here,' says Keisha. We scurry off, following behind the Children. Marvel would protect me if anybody made a move. I know she would.

'We'll defend ourselves,' says the Hag as Keisha passes her.

They're going to need a lot more than umbrellas and frying pans.

Once we're safely up the stairs I slide in front of Keisha and block her way, letting the Children continue on to the empty flat.

'What would you have done if they'd attacked?' I say.

Keisha doesn't back down. 'There would have been nothing any of us could do.'

'You don't care about the Children,' I say. 'You only care about yourself.'

245

Keisha laughs coldly. 'Siobhan's video doesn't bother you?'

'Why should I be ashamed? Everything she said was true.'

'And now everybody knows about it.'

'We don't need to care what they think! The Children are special.'

'They're also dangerous.' Keisha's voice drops to a whisper as the voices below us grow louder. 'We don't know what they are.'

'I love them,' I say. A truth I've known since the moment they were born. 'And you wish they had never existed. You have no right to come with us. No right to expect them to defend you. So why don't you just turn around and leave us alone?'

She opens her mouth, but I'm finished with her. My Children are waiting for me.

I haven't said the last prayer of the day. *Salat al-'isha*. Instead of finding a fresh piece of paper, I settle onto the blankets between the Children and close my eyes, reaching out with my mind in hope of finding them.

# Chapter Twenty-seven

**Keisha**

When you barely leave your room for days, when you hardly sleep, time begins to stretch. The Children don't obey its rules, so nor can we. Days feel like weeks. Nobody tries to reach me. My phone stays silent. Not even Morris tries to get in touch. They've cut themselves out of my life, just like I always wanted.

I used to be proud that I was different from them all. It shouldn't make me feel this lonely now.

Is this how Siobhan felt? Maybe this was why she made that video.

A livestream doesn't feel safe anymore because there's no way of knowing who's watching. My Twitter mentions have been clogged with abuse. It's the same on Facebook. People talking about me as if I'm not going to see the conversation.

Slut.
I told you she hadn't changed.
Enjoy them benefits!

'Where's our boy?' asks Mum.

'Morris has him.' I lose count of how many times I say it.

From my window I see the Children appear outside by themselves, sometimes sitting on the green and watching people come and go, or walking around like they're scoping the place out. Mum's key fob for the door has gone missing and it's no mystery who has it.

After the other night, seeing the Children walk and talk, I can't think of him as an 'it' anymore. That worries me more than it should.

Maida is with them sometimes, getting as close as they'll let her, and once or twice I see Morris trying to play it cool, like he doesn't really care.

It must be killing him.

They're growing up fast. It's like they're in a race to adulthood, and they're ready to leave us all behind. They'll get more powerful as they grow, and they want to tap that potential as quickly as possible.

Often, they return to the block carrying armfuls of junk. I can't make it out properly from the window but it looks like mostly wires and broken pieces of machinery. They must be roaming the estate looking for it.

Whatever their plan is, it doesn't seem to include us anymore. We've served our purpose.

One afternoon I sneak out into the hall to see where they go. I follow them up the stairs, and they keep going past the empty flat. I lose my nerve when I hear people on the landing below me. Creeping down to see what's going on, I find a group of residents, Louise Krawczyk and Frank among them, gathered around the Hag.

'Tell everyone else what I've said,' she whispers.

Everyone nods and they part ways. I wait a long time until I hurry home.

After that the Hag seems to pop up everywhere. She was always sticking her nose into people's business, but now I see her watching the Children when they're on the green, talking to residents on the path, looking up at my window. She's the ringleader in this campaign against us. The sight of her makes my skin crawl.

I want to tell Morris but can't pluck up the courage to text him.

Instead I busy myself obsessively searching online for any more information about the Other Children in Siltoe. It turns out not much news comes out of a tiny Cornish village. I manage to dig up a few more stories about the fire, though. It seems like Richard Jacobs was the only fatality. One story has a quote from a tourist who swears she heard multiple voices inside, screaming for help. She also claimed the locals were pagans but honestly, there's certainly nothing to back it up and she comes off sounding nutso.

The one thing I'm sure of is that they existed.

So they can't have just disappeared.

I search for a list of missing children from the area. The first result looks official, but it covers the whole of Cornwall, a seemingly endless stream of faces. How can so many children go missing? I have no idea what the ones I need look like. All I have is a name. I hit CTRL + F and search *Robert Jacobs*.

One result.

No photo, just the name. Someone cared enough to report him missing, but no one ever took a photograph.

The bottom of the page is taken up with nondescript silhouettes, the default template for the children without a picture. There are so many. I have no idea what the other Children are called. They could be any of these or none at all.

I spend hours wondering what it means – if it means anything at all. They could have run away. They could have grown into adults so quickly that they had to run away and take new identities to protect themselves. The missing person reports could just be for show.

Or something bad might have happened to them.

The answers are in Siltoe. They might as well be in Siberia.

The days continue to trickle away. About a week after the argument I get a visit from Olivia. She perches on the edge of my bed.

'They won't let us near them,' she says. 'It's like there's a barrier around them. Even when they're at home in the flat.'

I stifle a smile. That must really piss on Morris's idea of happy families.

'Their bodies keep growing faster, but it's their minds . . .' she says. 'They look like they should just be starting school, but they're talking and reading far beyond that. They're so *self-aware*; nothing like children.'

'That just makes them even more dangerous.'

'It's the boy,' she says, nervously, glancing at me like I might take offense. 'He's trying to turn the girls against us. I can see it.'

A flicker of anger in my chest. It's like she's saying I'm to blame.

'Did you know I was a foster kid?' says Olivia.

Now I look at her. 'No.'

'I was in and out of children's homes, different families – it didn't always work out.' She says it so matter-of-factly it's somehow sadder than if she was crying. 'For a long time I didn't have anybody to guide me. And that was fine, for a while. Sometimes it's okay to let kids make their own mistakes, and maybe some are . . . not inherently *bad*, but more likely to make bad choices. There were times I could so easily have lost everything. My life would be very different if I hadn't found a family that really cared about me.'

'I get it, all right?' I say. 'This is different, and you know it. There's nothing I could have done to change who the boy is.'

'If you say so,' says Olivia, standing to leave. 'I've wanted to be a mother for so long, but I never wanted this. It feels like I've failed.'

When she leaves I look out over the estate. Some of the houses surrounding the block have fairy lights strung up in their windows. I'd barely even realised it's nearly Christmas.

The Children at twelve weeks look equivalent to five year olds. It's impossible. But I've come to expect that.


It's the next day when Mum shouts for me from the other room. It sounds urgent, but I feel incapable of hurrying.

A woman I don't recognise is standing with Mum.

251

She wears a thick jumper and chunky glasses, and she clutches a tablet to her chest like I might try to steal it.

'My name is Angela,' she says, extending a hand. 'I'm from social services.'

There's ID around her neck. I stay where I am. After a moment she retracts her hand and glances at Mum.

'I'm sorry it's taken so long for us to pay a visit,' says Angela. 'It's a busy time of year for us.'

That might be the most depressing thing I've ever heard.

'Why are you here?' I say.

'Keisha!' hisses Mum.

Angela points to the kitchen table. 'Can we sit?'

We take our seats around the table, like the most uncomfortable dinner time ever. Mum shifting her chair to be close to me. Angela sets her tablet down and swipes at the screen. Notes appear.

'I've been assigned to your case.'

'I have a case?'

'The school made us aware of your situation,' says Angela. 'Plus we've had several calls from other residents in your building.'

I choke back a laugh. No surprise there. I suppose it's better than getting my head caved in by a cricket bat.

'This is just a preliminary visit,' says Angela. 'There's nothing to worry about.'

'You realise when you say that it just makes people worry, right?'

Mum kicks me under the table. Angela tries to smile. 'That's the last thing I want.'

*This* was the last thing *I* wanted. There's no way I

can explain anything about this situation without them referring me for mental evaluation.

Angela presses on. 'You were expelled from school following a violent incident?'

The smell of coffee. Power flexing in my stomach. The sizzle of boiling liquid on bare skin.

His hand on my body.

Mum answers for me. 'That's right.'

'And you were pregnant at the time?'

I meet her eye. There's no way she could have put the two things together. 'Yes, I was.'

Angela flicks at her tablet screen. 'You had a little boy. Congratulations.'

I think about slapping the insincere smile off her face.

'How old is he now?'

I try to think. I have no idea what they're supposed to be.

'About twelve weeks,' says Mum, with a sideways glance at me.

'Have you decided on a name yet?'

I shake my head.

She waits for me to talk. When I don't she says, 'Is he here?'

'He's with the father.'

'So you know the father?' She taps out another note.

There it is again. The urge to break the tablet over her head. I know what she thinks of me. To her I'm just like every pregnant teen on a council estate she's ever met.

'It's normal, you know, to feel overwhelmed,' says Angela.

'You have no idea.'

Angela frowns. 'I've seen it before. But Keisha, you do understand it's illegal not to register a birth?'

Mum looks at me sharply. There's something else I never told her. I didn't think she would understand. Not only would registering him have made it official, it would have made it real.

'It's not a big deal, nothing's going to happen,' says Angela. 'I'm more curious to know why.'

The tabletop is cool against my palms. I tense my fingers and dig at the wood. There's nothing I can say that will make her understand, no version of this story that she'll believe. I'm not 'just another' teenage mother too frightened to take responsibility for their baby. It's more than that.

Angela looks around the flat, like she's scoping the place for potential weapons or torture devices, any sign that I'm obviously an unfit parent. If she stuck around the block for a day she'd get a lot more than she bargained for.

'Can you tell me what happened at school?' she says.

I stare at the table and remember Mr Arnopp's hand on my body. Just one hand, so casual. That man made me feel like I could build a future, then he knocked it out from underneath me. With just one hand. I hate him.

They look at me like they know I have something to confess. It seems pointless to talk about it now. The damage is done.

I shake my head.

'Are you okay?'

'I haven't been getting much sleep.'

Angela leans back in her chair and sighs. 'Like I said,

254

this is just a preliminary visit so we can get to know each other. It's my job to check that everything is okay. I'm here to help. But we do need to arrange a time for me to meet your son.'

She produces a card from her pocket and slides it across the table.

'It's a lot easier if you cooperate,' she says.

It sounds like a threat. She reaches for a handshake again and I ignore her.

Mum shows her out. Before she can close the door I hurry across and creep into the corridor just in time to see Angela turn into the stairwell. I pad along and listen to her footsteps. She's going up instead of down to the exit.

'What the hell is going on?' says Mum as soon as I'm back.

'She must have been assigned to Maida, too.'

'So, what?'

'We can't let her see the Children.'

I try heading for my room but she blocks me off.

'You think I don't see something's going on?' she says. 'I see your baby boy growing like he's on steroids. Everyone sees it. I've kept quiet this long because I'm scared, child. The whole block is terrified. But I can't help you if you won't tell me anything.'

'We can't let her get too suspicious,' I say, talking over her, moving to the front window.

I press my forehead against the cool glass. If the Children are outside Angela might walk straight into their path. A part of me wishes she could help, but she could never understand what happened to us. If she knew the truth – if the authorities discovered what the Children are – it could only go badly for us. No, I can only rely on myself now.

The green is quiet, nobody around, not a parakeet to be heard, but something catches my eye over in the fenced bin enclosure. A head pokes over the lip of one of the bins. It's the boy, rooting through the rubbish, throwing bin bags out, tearing some of them open like he's searching for treasure. I can't even think how he could have climbed in there.

'He isn't mine,' I whisper to myself, my breath making condensation run down the glass.

I can't be to blame for how he turns out. It can't be my responsibility. I was born in the block, and it trapped me into this life. My attempts to escape were futile. The social worker knew it. She must have known hundreds of girls just like me. Hopeless. Resigned.

The boy totters back toward the block, arms laden with junk, pausing to let a delivery van pass. A tin can falls and clatters against the pavement, startling Mr Hillier's cat into a streak across the car park. It looks certain to go under the wheels of the van, but at the last second the driver veers onto the opposite kerb, missing the cat by inches.

The van screeches to a halt before it hits the tree, and the boy watches the animal scurry away into a garden. From here I can see the driver, arms rigid, head pressed back into his seat. Only when the boy shifts his attention and walks away does the driver shake his head and peer confusedly out of the window.

Did the boy use his power to *save* the cat?

I can't change what he was born to become. Can I?

Mum puts her warm hand on the small of my back. 'Talk to me,' she says. 'Please.'

I wipe my fingers across the window, leaving dripping tracks in the glass. I shrug her off and retreat to my room without a word.

# Chapter Twenty-eight

**Morris**

I wonder if Tyrone keeps a logbook of threatening texts to refer to every day. They're getting worse. It started with a sort of countdown. Three weeks. 17 days. Nothing too original. Now it's more like, I don't want to hurt you and Deliver the package and I won't have to use it on you.

Still not very original. But a lot more terrifying.

Today's text has just arrived. 7 days. The countdown is back. I should change my phone number.

Seven days until Christmas. Seven days to work out what the hell I'm going to do.

Something catches the corner of my eye. I jump to my feet and run to the window. 'Holy crap, it's snowing.'

It's coming down heavy. Flakes as thick as Tubs's dandruff. A layer of it is already resting on car roofs and filling the gaps between the grass on the green. It's almost dark and the streetlights have taken over. A bunch of local kids are already pelting snowballs at each other's heads.

'Kids, on your feet,' I say, turning back to hustle

the girls off the floor. They've been here reading old magazines for a few hours, wrapped in their security blanket. I don't even know when they learned to read, but they're obsessed with wildlife, fashion, cars – any magazine we can get for them. My boy couldn't care less, and there's no sign of him now. 'You're about to get a lesson in fun.'

They look at me like I'm mad. But they also see the snow tumbling past the window, and curiosity gets the better of them. They follow me to the door.

Maida comes out of the bathroom and sees us leaving. 'We evacuating?'

I point to the window. 'Snow.'

Her face lights up. We head downstairs together. It almost feels like we're a family, except that the boy isn't here. Every day he goes off on his own and no matter how hard I try to follow him, he always manages to stop me. I've got no idea where he goes. Sometimes that scares me more than Tyrone's texts.

Snow blows through the main door. I crunch out onto the path. The girls stop in the doorway, freaked out, like the tumbling flakes might melt their skin.

'What is it?' Marvel asks.

I put out a hand and watch fat flakes melt on my palm. 'Scourge of trains, granny hip smasher, snowboard lubricant.'

They wear identical expressions of bafflement. Sometimes I forget they don't really know anything about the world.

'It's snow, all right?'

Maida shoves past them and bounds into the powder

like a dog let off its lead. She scrapes a lump off a low wall, scrunches it into a ball, and lobs it at my face. Little does she know I'm a ninja when it comes to snowball fights; I catch it like a total pro, but it breaks apart in my fist.

'Now you've done it!'

She laughs and runs into the car park. I see her glance up at her parents' flat but she doesn't stop. I beckon the girls after me and they follow, watching their feet as they stomp holes in the snow. By now most of the kids from the area are out, laughing and shouting. A few of them are kicking a football around. The snow's falling even harder now. We're covered in it.

'Snow is new,' says Helena, looking up at me with wide eyes. 'How do you make a snowball?'

It's still weird that they've taught themselves to speak, especially as the girls never seem to actually talk to each other. They sound like they should be halfway through primary school already. Still, I grin and scoop up a good load of snow. I pack it into a tight ball, the kind that really stings if it whacks you in the ear. The last time it snowed at school they let us out to lunch early. It took me less than two minutes to get a detention for slamming the perfect shot into a dinner lady.

I pass the snowball to Helena and it feels like I'm imparting knowledge. That's what parents are supposed to do, right? I turn back around and straight away the snowball smacks into the back of my neck.

When I look at her she flashes me a tentative smile, fingers flexing against the cold.

'I should've seen that coming, shouldn't I?'

I dart towards a deep patch on a nearby wall. The girls

peel away to get their own ammo. By the time I've made a couple of snowballs there are ten raining down on my head. I make a break for the green but Maida cuts me off and smashes one into my mouth.

'This is an ambush!' I splutter.

Three more snowballs hit my face. My feet slip and I go down on my arse. They all three stand over me and cock their arms. I put my hands up in surrender.

'I wish your brother was here for this,' I say.

The girls speak at the same time. 'He's close.'

'How do you know?'

They shrug like it's a stupid question. 'We can feel him.'

Before I can even think what that means they drop their snowballs on my face and set off running around the edge of the green. Maida pulls me up and we set off after them.

### Keisha

The world feels like a different place under a snowfall. It almost feels new, all the hard edges smoothed away, everything illuminated with artificial brightness. For a moment I stand out on the balcony and watch them all playing . . . but the snow makes me want to be part of the world. It makes me miss them. I grab my jacket and head for the stairs.

Once I'm outside I lean back against the cold wall of the block and watch. Nobody notices me. The girls hurl their lumps of snow and roll across the ground as Morris gives chase. The other children glance at them, uncertain about their presence, but the snow seems to make them equals. People hang out of windows, smoking cigarettes and watching the fun. It all looks so normal, so festive. The only thing missing is the boy.

The door swings open, and for a second I expect it to be him. Instead Siobhan steps out, immediately wrapping her arms around herself. The girls' laughter snatches her attention and she moves like she's going to join them. Then she catches sight of me.

There's nothing between us but clouds of our breath. It feels like I should extend a hand, ask her to lean beside me like we always used to. Snow makes things even. Maybe we could start again.

She reaches into her pocket and pulls out a roll of money. 'It's from my savings,' she says. 'I want you to have it. I want *them* to have it.'

'I didn't want anything from you before. I don't want anything now.'

She sighs and shoves the money back into her pocket, hugs her arms across her chest. 'I need to ask you something.'

I don't answer, and she decides to take it as permission.

'Have you had your period?' she says. 'Since you gave birth?'

I open my mouth to tell her it's none of her business. But then I realise I'm not sure. There's been so much happening I hadn't even thought about it.

'No,' I say. 'I haven't.'

Siobhan lets out a long, cloudy breath. 'Me neither. I mean, sometimes it takes a while to come back. But what if after all this we can't—'

I put my hands up to stop her saying more. I can't think about it right now.

'Don't push me away,' Siobhan says.

We look at each other for a long moment. 'It's too late.'

She turns her gaze across to where the girls are still playing. A tear rolls down her cheek, snowflakes melting in its trail.

'That used to be us.'

When I don't reply she turns and goes back inside the tower, the door slamming behind her.

A minute later, Maida comes panting around the edge of the green. She spots me and comes to join me against the wall.

'I'm getting old,' she breathes.

'You're fifteen.'

'These days I feel way older.'

A football lands soundlessly in the middle of the grass and stalls in the snow, instantly forgotten by whoever kicked it. At the far end of the green the parakeets are bustling in the trees, disturbed by all the noise.

'There's something else we need to talk about,' I say.

'Angela?'

'I thought she must have paid you a visit. She's trouble.'

'Yeah, she wasn't too happy about me bunking off school.'

'Have you been going at all?'

She nods. 'A couple of times, just to see. I don't feel like I need it anymore.'

Snow has piled up on our feet and shoulders. I twist my body to shake it loose.

'I know what you're going to say,' says Maida. 'You had a serious love affair with school, but it never meant anything to me. I was an outsider there, too. I only kept going because my dad said I had no choice.'

There's a burst of laughter as the girls shake free of Morris's grasp as he tries to deposit them into the powder.

'You can be anything you want, Maida.'

She glances up at the block toward her parents' window. 'No, I can't. I never could.'

I want to grab her by the shoulders and scream in her face. Maybe her parents made it difficult to see a future that belonged to her. Maybe growing up in the block meant she was as doomed as I was. That doesn't mean she can piggyback on the future of the Children. We still don't know why they're here. They're dangerous, and nurturing that capacity for destruction is asking for trouble.

I force myself to stay calm. There's something else I need to know.

'When you last went into school, did you see Mr Arnopp?'

She gives me a sideways glance. 'Yeah, I walked past him in the science block.'

The thought of him still walking around like nothing happened . . .

'His face is still pretty messed up, if that makes you feel any better.'

I never told her what happened with Mr Arnopp, but she must have some idea. She knows the Children don't attack for no reason.

'We need to keep the Children hidden from the social worker,' I say, changing the subject. 'She'll interfere and make things worse.'

'That might be easier said than done. Look . . .'

Through the snow I realise that everyone has fallen still and silent. In the centre of the green is the boy, clothes caked in white. It's like he appeared from nowhere. Something about him spooks the other kids in a way that the girls don't. The boy leans to pick up the abandoned football.

'Hey!' shouts one of the other kids.

Fear plummets into my stomach.

Two boys I recognise from around the block approach him, one with shaggy brown hair and the other with the sides of his head shaved. They're a lot bigger, and they don't realise it won't make a shred of difference.

'That's our football,' says shaggy hair.

The boy looks at the football in his hands, tests its weight, like it's a mysterious artefact. 'I wanted to play,' he says.

'We don't play with freaks,' says shaved head.

Before anyone can react the boy pelts the football at the second kid's face. It hits his nose with a sickening smack. The kid staggers away while shaggy hair lurches forward to attack.

He barely manages a step before the air buzzes. His legs stop obeying his will and root him to the spot. Shaved head wheels around, blood dripping down his face, and swings a punch, but his arm stops midway.

Everyone else begins to back away. Faces watch from the block windows. I see Morris near the tower entrance, holding onto the girls who are staring uncertainly at their brother.

'I wanted to play, so I'll play with you,' says the boy

to his two new toys. Olivia was right; he sounds like someone twice his physical age, or even older than that. 'I wonder what I could do. Could I make you peel the skin from your friend's bones?'

Shaggy hair turns sharply and kicks his mate in the stomach. A gasp goes around the crowd, echoed by the people leaning from their windows. Shaved head collapses, takes a punch to the face on the way down and slumps sideways into the snow.

'Maybe you would bite off his fingers,' says the boy. 'Squeeze his eyeballs out with your thumbs. I don't think you could do anything to stop me.'

Shaved head whimpers, and his friend kicks him again, snapping his head back. Shaggy hair cries as his limbs launch attack after attack, and he starts to shout, 'It's not me! I'm not doing it! I'm not doing it!'

There's a heartbreaking scream from one of the block windows and I know it must be one of their mother's noticing what's happening.

'Is this what you want?' I say to Maida.

Before I know it I'm climbing over the fence, pushing through the crowd and striding toward the boy. Morris sneaks through the gate, shepherding the girls with him, like I might need back up.

'Stop it,' I say.

The boy glances at me. A talon of energy ripples across my skin, but for now he stays out of my mind. 'What do you want?'

'Everyone is watching.'

'I know.'

I don't dare step any closer. The shaved head kid is

writhing in the snow, shaggy hair still standing over him, poised to strike again.

'You think you want to do this, but you don't.'

The energy feels like it's forming a ball around him, pooling together for one final assault. The killing blow. The boy turns to face me. 'You think you can tell me what to do?'

I almost laugh. 'So you've skipped straight to being a teenager.'

He doesn't get the joke, but I see the doubt in his eyes. 'I don't know how to be one of you. I can't pretend like my sisters.'

The girls watch him with their golden eyes, clinging tight to each other. Morris lays a hand on their shoulders and they sink back into him.

Shaved head spits blood onto the snow.

'This is what I am,' says the boy.

'I thought that too,' I say. 'Now I'm not so sure. So many bad things have happened to you, and you've only been alive a few months.'

He grits his teeth, like he has to prove me wrong, and turns back to his captives. The energy feels like a bomb, ready to detonate.

A *clang* of metal, and the tower entrance flies open. One of their mothers comes running outside, screaming for her son. The Hag follows.

The boy sees her and the energy bursts. It's not aimed at his captives. It seems to shatter in every direction, fizzing scattershot through the air, and the boy cries out like it's a last ditch abort sequence. All the other children make a run for it, like a spell has been broken.

267

The trees at the bottom of the green start to shake, though there's no wind. Dark shapes emerge from the branches and swoop down like a volley of arrows. As they come low to the ground the snow's reflected light catches them. It's the parakeets. They swirl around the boy like a shoal of fish as the last of the energy fizzles away on the air.

Shaved head is scooped up by his mother and hauled away. Shaggy hair regains control and runs after the others. Panicked bodies jam the door of the block, fighting to get to safety. Only the Hag stays behind to watch.

Laughter pours from the boy as the birds whip around him. 'I'm not controlling them!' he shouts.

The girls look on, their faces darkening with what might be jealousy. Maida is at my side, laughing along like this is the greatest thing she's ever seen. I can't move. I look to Morris for help but his mouth is just hanging open.

'They don't belong here either!' shouts the boy as the luminescent birds begin to sweep back to the trees. 'They understand!'

I watch the boy. It's the first time I've seen him smile. After the nightmare of his conception, the violation of him growing inside me, I wanted to stay away from him. I thought I could be free of any blame for bringing him into this world. But by staying away I might have pushed him down a path he didn't have to take.

Maybe he needed me to be a parent.

The tower door slams shut, and we're left almost alone on the green. Snow continues to fall, blurring the edges of the world. Faces stare down from the tower. They'll never understand.

'We all saw it!' shouts the Hag, her voice ringing around the front of the block. Snow clogs her perm. 'We're under attack. I don't know what you are, but you're not welcome here!'

The boy smirks, and lets fly the smallest of flares, just enough to make her take a step back. She gasps like he's slapped her.

'What are *you* going to do about it?' says the boy. 'I've been under attack my whole life.'

'I know what you could do to me,' says the Hag. Then she waves a hand up at the block. 'But what happens if we all come for you at once? Can you do it to all of us?'

She retreats like she's frightened to turn her back on him. Only when she's a good distance away does she run for the door.

'I don't need you,' says the boy, like he's read my mind.

'I don't think that's true.'

After a long pause the boy turns away from us and onto the path. We start to follow, but he stalls us in our tracks – of course he does. All we can do is stand there, watching as he slips away into the estate.

The windows of Midwich Tower slam shut all at once, a chorus of thuds like a battle cry, deadened by the fast falling snow.

# Chapter Twenty-nine

**Maida**

A gust blows through the hatch in the roof, raising rattles from the door knockers all along the hallway. The snow has stopped – *boo!* – but it feels like we're slipping deeper into proper winter. There's no way the Children are warm in their charity shop clothes, but still they climb up onto the roof as if they don't even notice.

'Where did they get the ladder?' asks Olivia, somewhat baffled and a little impressed.

'I'm guessing someone in the building is missing a ladder,' I say. They've become quite the little kleptomaniacs.

They completely ignore us as they pass equipment up through the ceiling. There's an old, boxy TV with a wire aerial – a real relic, properly *Antiques Roadshow*. It's joined by a bag full of cables, a jumble of computer parts, and a toolbox that jangles and clatters something chronic on its way up. They mean business out there.

'What are they up to?' says Keisha. 'I mean, I've been watching them gather this shit together and I thought it was weird and stuff, but they're scaring me now.'

'Don't worry, Keish. It's just junk,' I say.

'Seriously,' adds Morris.

'No. I'm telling you, there's no such thing as "just" anything with them. They have some purpose in mind. Like, I think they're building something,' says Keisha. 'Something they don't want us to know about.'

Annoyingly, she's right. The Children aren't going to be wasting time checking out the view. They could have asked me to help. They know I would have.

I want to know what's at the top of the ladder so much it literally hurts – my legs strain to climb, my muscles aching against the effort, but they won't let me do it.

If this is part of a big plan, they better finish it up quickly. Angela called this morning, basically demanding to meet my daughter. I know it's her job, but it's *really* annoying. It's tempting to lock Angela in a room with Marvel for an hour just to see what happens.

A door slams at the other end of the hallway. Keisha and Olivia jump about a mile in the air. After last night they're expecting some kind of attack from the residents. Retaliation. The thing is, after seeing what the Children can do when provoked, you'd have to be an idiot to come after them. Honestly, I'd kind of like to see them try. Pity the fool.

They finish passing the stuff through the hatch. The boy is already up there. Marvel starts climbing the ladder without looking at us. While she waits her turn, Helena glances back at Olivia – but the boy barks her name, like a command, and she reluctantly starts to climb, their security blanket trailing from her waistband.

271

'Hey!' I say, a little desperately, but Marvel is already out of sight.

I step towards the ladder and a low hum vibrates in my ears, stopping me dead. I know better than to bother pushing against it.

Olivia forces a laugh. 'What's the worst they could be doing?'

If this was a movie, it would jump cut to the rooftop, a sweeping camera shot of *exactly* what's going on out there, something to make you feel dizzy and go 'shiiiiiit' and rummage deep into the popcorn tub. Annoyingly, this isn't a movie.

'For all we know they're building a super weapon or calling their mothership to start the invasion,' says Keish.

A tune drops into my head and I hum it low in my throat, unable to place it. Something from an old sci-fi TV show?

'You only want to think the worst of them,' says Olivia. But she's looking at the hatch like something might attack us any second.

'No,' says Keisha, turning on her. 'I want to stop them being the worst they can be.'

I step between them. 'You know it's your boy who's doing it. He's pulling our girls away from us.'

'You're saying it's our fault?' says Morris.

'I didn't say it was *your* fault,' I say, lifting the bitchiest eyebrow possible at Keisha. Before she can answer, the ladder rattles. A foot drops down from the hatch and the boy climbs into the hallway, our girls following behind him. Their skin looks grey from the cold. The boy walks past us to the stairs like we've all *poof!* ceased to exist.

Marvel and Helena follow suit.

'*Munni*, it's me,' I say.

For an instant, I think I've broken through to her – she glances over her shoulder, just a fraction, eyes full of an apology, enough to make me hope . . . but then it's gone. That's that. She doesn't stop.

Olivia stifles a sob.

I can't let them see how much it bothers me. I bite into my bottom lip until I taste blood.

The hallway is freezing. Keisha goes after the Children, and Morris dawdles a moment before deciding not to go with her. I march towards the ladder again and reach out a hand. It stalls in mid-air. The hairs on my arm stand to attention.

They may have gone downstairs – but their power remains, fierce as ever.

## Keisha

The Children vanish out of sight downstairs. Part of me wants to try and find them – if something serious is going on I need to know about it, for their own good as well as ours; but the other part of me, maybe the greater part, is scared to find out.

A crackle of radio static down the hall. When I peer round the corner I see two policemen standing outside my door, muttering to each other, obviously vexed that nobody's home. I stumble back into the stairwell, only to be met by Angela coming the other way.

'Keisha.'

Angela rights her glasses on her nose. As I step away from her she lets out a long breath like she was hoping I wouldn't show up.

'We have to deal with this,' she says. She makes it sound like she's on my side.

The policemen have twigged me now. And they don't look impressed at being kept waiting. 'This her?' says the one who's a little too fat for the equipment-heavy vest strapped tightly around his front.

'This is Keisha,' says Angela, her voice kinder than I expected.

The officer nods. 'I'm PC Dyer and this is PC Clark.' The other officer is a smaller man with a fluffy moustache that might not be deliberate. 'We're here following a number of reports from your neighbours about an incident on the playing green outside the building last night.'

There's no point pretending I don't know what they're talking about. What's important is playing this as smartly as possible.

'Allegedly your son was involved,' says PC Dyer.

'That's impossible,' I say.

'Her son is only a few months old,' Angela explains.

The officers frown at each other. The information obviously conflicts with whatever the neighbours have been feeding them.

'Can we do this inside?' I say, fumbling for my key. I can sense the ears pressed against doors, eyes at peepholes, spying on the drama. The corridor doesn't feel safe. I shove the door open.

'Where is your son now?' says Dyer.

Before I can think of an excuse a voice echoes along the corridor. 'I'm right here.'

My heart shrivels. The boy is coming along the corridor from the stairs, smiling broadly at the policemen.

'I don't understand,' says PC Clark.

'This is my cousin,' I say quickly.

'Your cousin,' Clark repeats.

'Maybe people mistook him for my son?'

The officers look doubtful. It's hardly the greatest excuse but the boy standing before us now definitely does not pass for mere months old. They have no choice but to take my word for it.

'Let's talk inside,' says Dyer.

I try to catch the boy's eye but he pushes ahead, a grim smile on his face. I follow, Angela resting a supportive hand on my back that makes my skin go cold.

We sit around the kitchen table. It's fast becoming my least favourite place in the world. There are only four chairs, so Angela has to perch on the edge of the counter. She looks relieved, like she didn't know which side of the table to choose anyway.

The boy shifts his chair so he's not sitting too close to me. I throw him a pleading look. It's one thing to beat up a couple of kids on the estate, but if anything happens to these feds we'll be all over the evening news.

'There's nothing to be frightened of,' I say, like I really am just reassuring a child. 'You're not under attack.'

'You're not in trouble,' adds Dyer, assuming possibly the most patronising voice I've ever heard.

'I know,' says the boy.

Dyer clears his throat. 'How old are you, son?'

The boy stares at him like he doesn't understand the question. Like age is meaningless to him. I find an answer, estimating the best I can.

'He's seven.'

'And he's staying with you?'

My mind races. 'His mother's ill.'

Angela's brow creases – she's sharp enough to sense something's off – but it seems to be a good enough answer for the restless officers. Clark takes out a small pen and pad and scribbles a note.

Dyer turns back to the boy. 'And what's your name?'

The boy looks at me, his eyes holding a question. I open my mouth but I can't find any words. I'm already several lies too deep for comfort and any name I blurt out on the spot might stick. After a few seconds the boy fixes his eyes on the officers.

'Zero,' he says. 'Call me Zero.'

He avoids my questioning look.

Dyer rubs the shadow of stubble on his jaw. It's not hard to tell he's already sick of us. 'Now, the calls about last night don't make a lot of sense.'

I look at the boy. Zero. He's smiling. It makes me feel sick.

'I wanted to play,' he says.

'One of the others boys is very hurt.'

Zero shrugs. 'I didn't touch them.'

'That's just the thing,' says Dyer, the patronising tone slowly slipping out of his voice. 'Everybody we've spoken to says that too. Nevertheless, they insist you were behind the attack. We spoke to the boys in question too, of course. They say the same thing.'

'That's ridiculous,' I say, remembering I need to behave like all of this is a shock. It's my job to defend him. Maybe that way I can actually protect the officers *from* him – win-win. 'They were bullies.'

'They attacked first,' says Zero, confused.

I feel his hackles begin to rise, just strong enough to make my ears pop. Angela shifts on her perch, but if she feels it there's no way she could know what it is.

'I'm sure you'll agree it's strange that everyone would place the blame on him,' says Dyer.

Clark's head twitches, and for a split-second his eyes go blank. The air pulses, that familiar low hum vibrating in my ears. I turn towards Zero – his eyes are fixed on the officer. There's no subtle way to get his attention.

'I don't think anybody around here likes me,' he says.

'Have you had a falling out with any of the locals?' asks Dyer.

If only he had the slightest idea.

Beside him PC Clark slowly lifts the biro he's been using to doodle in his notebook. He grips it tight in his fist, aiming the sharp point at Dyer's neck.

'You understand we have to investigate?' says Dyer.

Finally Zero looks at me, almost like he's seeking permission, and I shake my head. His puzzled look in response seems genuine.

'You can't,' I say, desperate.

Dyer frowns. 'I assure you, we—'

Clark jerks his hand. Instead of a stab, the pen flies from his grasp and bounces off Dyer's cheek, halting him mid-sentence. He turns slowly towards his colleague.

'Why did you do that?' he says, like a disappointed teacher.

Clark shakes his head like he's just woken up. 'I . . . er, don't know.'

Zero doubles over with laughter, his head whacking against the table. I squeeze his arm, hard enough that it must hurt. I wait for him to lash out, but Zero just sits back in his chair and looks at me like I've betrayed him. Was he merely showing off his power, proving he's not scared of policemen, of any kind of authority? Or did he think attacking the policemen would do us both a favour?

Sometimes I forget he's still a kid.

Dyer picks up the pen and tucks it into his pocket, like he's confiscating it from a naughty child. Clark shrugs apologetically.

'Look, there's no further action we're within our rights to take here,' Dyer says. 'No one saw him lay a finger on the other boys. But, Zero – we need you to stay out of trouble, or we'll be back.'

'I'm looking forward to it,' says Zero, recovering his bravado.

The policemen stand, their chairs scraping across the floor. Angela lingers behind them.

'I don't know what's going on here,' she says to me. 'But it seems clear you're not willing to cooperate.' She glances sideways at Zero. 'You realise I have no idea if your son is safe or not? I didn't want the police involved. Nor do you. But hear me now, Keisha, if I can't assess your son, I'm going to have to apply to a court for a child assessment order.'

It's a threat. She expects me to crack, but there's no way I can agree to an assessment. My son is sitting a few metres from her and she doesn't even realise it.

'Has Maida agreed?' I say.

'I can't discuss any other cases.'

I smile. 'So she hasn't. Which means I won't either.'

Angela lets out a long breath through her nose. 'I'll be in touch.'

The policemen are waiting for her in the corridor. 'Little shit,' I hear Dyer mutter as I'm shutting the door. Someone further along the hallway calls out to them – *They should be locked up!* – but I haven't got the energy to worry about that now.

When I turn back into the flat Zero isn't at the table.

'Where are you?' I call.

He appears from the hallway that leads to our bedroom, hands crammed deep into his pockets. He heads straight for the front door but I block his path.

'Why did you do that?'

He tries to step around me, but nothing but brute force would make me budge. We stare each other down, neither of us quite ready to make the next move.

'Everybody wants to hurt me. I can feel it,' he says. 'But I can hurt them much worse.'

'That doesn't mean you have to. You have a choice.'

Now I feel that petulant spike of power – I guess I knew it would come – and my feet pull me away from the door. He moves to leave, but there's still something I need to know.

'Why "Zero"?'

The last shred of defiance falls from his face.

'Remember when you used to call me "it"?' he says, and for once he sounds as young as he looks.

Before he can say anything more a series of knocks hammer against the door and his face hardens. He turns his golden eyes on me.

'The way they look at me, like I'm unnatural . . . it just makes me feel stronger,' he says. 'I'm something new. Maybe they're scared because I'm their future.'

A chill shudders through me as he opens the door and pushes his way out. Morris staggers aside to let him go.

'Everything all right?' says Morris, concerned. 'I saw the police leaving.'

'It's okay for now,' I say, leaning against the kitchen counter. I am utterly drained. I've barely slept in days.

'You should lie down,' Morris says.

He tries to put a hand on my shoulder. I shrug away.

'I will. Can you follow Zero?'

'Who?'

'Zero. The boy has chosen a name. Mo, I'm scared; the way he sees the world . . . even if he doesn't go looking for trouble, it might still find him.'

Morris looks at me uncertainly, then nods and turns back into the corridor. I listen to his footsteps slip away before I shut the front door and cross to my bedroom.

The door is open.

Zero was in here.

I stand in the middle of the room and try to work out what's different. My bed looks untouched from this morning. The computer is off. My abandoned school-work is stacked in a pile in the corner.

Then I spot it. A round, blank space on the surface of my desk, untouched by dust.

Zero was here. And now my microphone is missing.

## Morris

In the end it's not my boy I find – it's Tubs. He's standing on the landing with a cone of tin foil crumpled around his head.

'Is that really necessary?'

'I saw what that kid did last night, man. He's not getting inside my head.'

There's no sign of . . . *Zero*. He's probably up on the roof. I don't want to believe that he's doing something dangerous up there but for weeks he's been pulling away from us, and his powers are only getting stronger.

'There's something you need to see,' says Tubs.

'If you think your dog's been probed again, I'm not interested.'

'Nah, I'm serious. Follow me.'

I let him lead me down the stairs. We don't have many friends left in the block, so I'm mostly just glad he's talking to me.

'Everyone knew the police wouldn't do nothing,' Tubs says, his heavy footsteps echoing. 'So they're taking matters into their own hands.'

'That sounds bad.'

We go right down to the ground floor. Paint fumes claw at my nostrils.

A single word is sprayed in massive letters on the wall opposite the main entrance.

# WARZONE

'Everyone saw what happened last night,' says Tubs. 'They're scared.'

'You think we're not? They can't treat us – treat our *children* – like we're unwelcome, like we're dangerous, and then act like *we're* the ones starting a war.'

Tubs holds up his hands. 'Whoa, man, I'm not taking sides. I just thought you should know.'

Things are out of control. I just wanted to try and make a life for us here in the tower, as a family, but however hard I try to keep hold of Keish, keep hold of my boy, keep hold of the others . . . I keep losing them. It all keeps slipping away. I have to turn it around. Christmas is in a few days. It might be my last chance.

'There's something else I need to tell you,' says Tubs, adjusting his tin foil hat.

'I guess there's no point hoping it's good news?'

'I don't know, man. You know the Hag? She's been slagging off you lot and the kids.'

'That's not exactly a surprise.'

'Yeah, but people are listening to her,' he says. 'She's turning people against you. Louise is helping. They're starting to get organised. They say we need to deal with this problem ourselves.'

I swallow hard. 'You make it sound . . . violent. Like, what are we talking about here, Tubs? Pitchforks?'

'After last night . . .' He doesn't finish the sentence.

I think of the package underneath my bed, the weight

of it in my hand. The Children aren't blameless, but I still have to protect them.

'Help me clean this off, yeah?'

Tubs glances at the stairwell like there might be someone watching him. 'I better not. Sorry, man.'

A gust of wind bites through my clothes as he slips out through the main entrance. I head back upstairs to get some cleaning equipment, like it might make a difference.

# Chapter Thirty

**Keisha**

There's no better time than Christmas Day to make the most awkward phone call of your life.

The amount of sweat pouring off Morris makes me wonder if he's about to faint. He adjusts the camera and, reading from the scrap of paper in his hand, punches the phone number into Skype.

'You sure you want me here for this?' I say. I'm sitting just out of frame at the end of the bed.

Morris nods. 'Moral support, I guess.'

It takes a few seconds to connect. Morris picks up my spare microphone. It doesn't have a stand, so he has to hold it to his mouth like a sad bedroom pop star.

After a moment of silence a face appears on the screen, one I haven't seen in a long time. His dad looks much older than I remember. I always used to think he looked just like Morris if Morris was wise and rugged, but it's hard to see the resemblance now.

'Hey, Dad,' says Morris. 'Merry Christmas.'

Either there's a delay on the line or his dad takes a few seconds to decide not to return the greeting.

'How's Granddad?' says Morris.

'Not well.' The voice fuzzes through the speakers. 'The medication is expensive.'

Morris wipes his forehead. 'I visited Nan earlier. She loves Christmas.'

'Where is he?' says Morris's dad.

'Who?'

'Your son.'

Morris glances at me, then at the desk, anywhere but the screen where his dad waits for an answer. I've never seen him like this. I can't imagine being this nervous talking to your own dad.

'He's with Mum.'

'She should be at work.'

Morris swallows hard. 'She isn't in until later.'

That seems to satisfy him. The connection isn't great, and the picture on the screen jerks in a stilted kind of nod.

'Are you working?' says Morris's dad.

'You know the answer to that.'

'I hoped the answer would be different this time.'

I watch Morris's face. Sadness slips into anger before collapsing into shame.

'How are you paying for the child?' says Morris's dad.

'We're managing.'

'And in the meantime no money is coming to me.'

Morris's cheeks flex as he grits his teeth. 'I've been trying. I sent you something a few months ago.'

He did? I didn't know he had money to give away. I suppose we were hardly on speaking terms back then.

'And then you give us another mouth to feed.'

'I hoped you might be proud,' says Morris quietly.

'What was that?'

Morris lets out a long breath. 'Never mind. Merry Christmas, Dad.'

He cuts off the call and drops the microphone heavily onto the desk. Then he turns to me and tries to pull the trigger on his smile.

'I had no idea he was like that,' I say.

The smile doesn't fire. 'It got a lot worse when he moved away. It must be hard for him out there.'

'Still,' I say, taking his hand. 'That's no excuse to be such a dick.'

He laughs and squeezes my fingers. I like how it feels. 'Now you know why I can't just give up on my new family.'

I look at my hand tucked inside his. Feel his grip. I never understood the pressure he was under. He looks at me for a long moment, and I almost expect him to lean forward. Instead he lets go of my hand and stands.

'Come on, let's have a great Christmas. That would really piss him off.'

I laugh, and follow him out.


## Morris

When I was a kid, the fanciest thing we ever did for Christmas was the time we got a real tree. That was a special year. By the time Dad had wrestled it up the stairs and into the front room it was balder than he was. We stood it in front of the fake 'coal-effect' fireplace. The presents underneath it were the same as they were every year: socks, chocolate, those gift sets with cheap shower gel and deodorant. Nothing mind-blowing. But that was the first year we sat together and ate roast chicken and didn't end up yelling at each other. After that I always thought real Christmas trees were a little bit magic.

So this year I'm making a proper effort. I don't care what Dad thinks. It's the first Christmas with my new family, and I want to set the bar high.

'This is the worst Christmas tree I've ever seen,' says Maida, picking at the anorexic branches. It's only as tall as her knee and most of the needles are already on the floor. A single string of tinsel completely bloody strangles it.

'You don't even celebrate Christmas,' I say from the kitchen.

'Yeah, and I could do better than this.'

I slice up the chicken carefully. I cooked it in the oven at home so it looks all right.

Today is the day I have to decide: pay off my debt to Tyrone, deliver the package, or . . . well, I guess there's no third option that includes my heart still beating.

We all sit around the edge of the blanket like it's a proper dining table. Tea-light candles flicker in jars in a line down the middle. On one side there's Maida and the girls, with Keisha and Olivia facing them. I made place mats out of cardboard, brought cutlery from home, and picked up some Christmas crackers from the pound shop. I even cooked some vegetables.

It's going to be a proper Christmas.

'Here we go!' I say, presenting the chicken with a flourish, like it's a work of art.

I place it at the centre of the blanket. Somehow it looks

a lot smaller than two seconds ago. Small enough that we'll have to exercise some portion control.

'It's, uh, Halal and everything,' I say.

'What does that mean?' says Marvel.

'It means I can eat it,' says Maida.

'Why?'

'Because it was prepared properly.'

'How?'

Keisha sighs. 'They slit its throat and let it bleed to death.'

The girls go quiet and look at the chicken with wide eyes.

'There's a bit more to it than that,' says Maida.

I wish Zero was here. My boy. We don't know where he is. And to be honest I think the girls only came because the whole Christmas thing sounded so crazy to them.

'What's a chimney?' asked Helena, after I had tried to explain it all.

That's when I realised Christmas might be a tough sell.

'And the fat man delivers a baby down it?' said Marvel.

It was a long time before they understood that Mary and Joseph and the wise men and all that – you know, the reason Christmas exists – have nothing to do with a bearded bloke flying magic reindeer all over the world to deliver presents made by elves in some kind of Arctic sweatshop.

After the third explanation Helena still looked troubled. 'So no one really knew for sure where Jesus came from, but everybody just assumed he was good and celebrated him?'

I didn't know what to say, so I pulled them both into a hug.

Keisha sees me looking at the last place setting – empty, perfect for a Zero – and tries a reassuring smile.

I'm at the head of the blanket-table. They're all looking at me. This is the part where I should say grace or something but I don't really know any prayers or blessings and I'm too scared of offending anyone or breaking some unspoken rule and ruining everything. The line between a perfect Christmas and a terrible one is thin and fragile, and my boots have a history of overstepping.

'Help yourselves!' I blurt.

Nobody moves, so I lean over and dish some chicken onto the Children's plates, along with some roast potatoes and veg. Maida and Olivia start serving themselves and I help Keisha load up her plate. There's not much left when it comes to my turn, but it doesn't really matter.

There's a few seconds where the only noise is chewing. Then it stops. Nobody will look at me. Maida fights to keep a smile off her face.

'What's wrong?'

Nobody says a word. I fork a bit of chicken into my mouth. It's like chewing a shred of bloody bike tyre. My teeth actually bounce off it.

'Is it supposed to be like this?' says Helena.

Maida goes over the edge and starts giggling.

I try one of the potatoes next. I cooked them right beside the chicken, just like the cookbook said, but even so they're seriously undercooked. They could have just come out of the ground.

'How is that possible?' I say, my fork clattering onto my plate.

Maida's still laughing, Keisha stabbing at her food like she's trying to resuscitate it. Across from me Marvel takes a bite of chicken and tries to chew it with a smile on her face. It looks more like she's grimacing in pain.

'Not *so* bad,' she says.

'Aah, my first ever Christmas dinner,' says Maida.

That does it. Everyone collapses all at once into fits of laughter, sinking forwards or rocking back like they're struggling for breath. The girls join in, like they're practising something unfamiliar.

I wanted it to be perfect. Instead it's pretty much the exact opposite of perfect.

'I really messed it up,' I say. 'Pray you don't get food poisoning.'

'Shit, it's been a few days since I prayed,' says Maida, wiping her eyes.

'Honestly, Mo,' says Keisha. 'This may not be good. But it is sort of perfect.'

It's hard to know for sure, but it looks like she means it.

Olivia studies a limp green bean on her fork. 'This definitely isn't the worst Christmas I've ever had.'

Maida snorts. 'Jesus, what the hell happened? Did somebody actually die?'

'Not quite. My first foster family had a son of their own, a couple of years older than me. They made this huge Christmas lunch – turkey, potatoes, Yorkshire puddings, the lot – but they only set three places at the table.' She looks at the abandoned remains of the food.

'They didn't make me go hungry or anything, but I had to wait until they had all finished eating before I sat by myself with the leftovers and just cried.'

'Why did they do that?' asks Marvel.

'I don't know. I suppose they didn't see me as one of them.'

'Jesus, Olivia, way to kill the vibe,' says Maida.

'You can eat as much of this as you want,' I say. 'There's pudding, chocolate cake, from the shop.'

I go to the kitchen to slice it up, making sure I leave a bit for Zero, just in case.

I'm back at the blanket just in time to see the girls produce a present, shapeless and wrapped in crumpled magazine pages, and hold it out to Maida and Olivia.

'We got you something,' they say, voices full of pride.

'O. M. G.' Maida grabs the gift – Olivia never stood a chance – and rips it open. Bundled inside is the blanket the girls have carried around with them ever since they could walk.

'We didn't have anything else we could give you,' says Marvel.

Maida lifts the blanket up and it falls into two pieces.

'We cut it in half so you'd both get something,' adds Helena, before looking at Keisha and me sheepishly. 'Sorry there's nothing for you.'

All I can do is laugh, while Keisha just looks dazed. Maida clutches her half of the blanket to her chest.

'Thank you,' she says. 'I mean it.'

The girls look pleased with themselves, like they've passed an audition.

I pick up one of the crackers and hold it out to Helena.

She looks at it like it's one of the great mysteries of the universe.

'Grab your end and pull.'

She follows my instructions. I was planning to go easy on her, but she tugs it harder than I expected. The cracker pops (not very loud, also pound shop), and she flinches away with the bigger half. Both the girls stare at it in amazement.

Marvel grabs her cracker and holds it across the blanket to Maida. She wins hers, too. The contents drop out onto the blanket. Helena gets one of those plastic frogs you can flick around. Marvel gets some kind of puzzle, two tubes of metal twisted around each other that need separating.

Olivia grabs a paper hat and shoves it onto Helena's head. It's too big and slides straight down onto her nose. She pulls it around her neck and laughs.

The laughter is cut short when both girls turn to the door like they've sensed a predator. It's a few seconds before it opens and a small figure steps into the room. Zero.

**Keisha**

The room falls quiet. The delicate atmosphere of happiness threatens to break.

'What are you doing?' he says, approaching the blanket.

The girls both look at their laps like they've been caught doing something shameful.

'Join us!' says Morris. He'll do anything for this day to succeed. 'It's Christmas.'

Zero screws up his face like it's a dirty word, but there's something eager in his eyes, and he takes a seat at the other end of the blanket.

'There's food, but, um . . . you're better off without,' I say. Maybe this is our chance to show him he's welcome here.

'I saved you some cake!' says Morris, retrieving it from the kitchen.

Zero looks at it like it might be dirty.

Marvel moves away from the blanket, fiddling with the metal puzzle cracker toy, keeping her gaze away from her brother. Helena stays behind and peels the remains of her cracker like a banana.

'Why do you Christmas?' she says.

'I explained it the best I could,' Morris says.

'Yeah, but why do *you*?'

We all look at each other. It's not an easy question to answer. Usually I'd wait for Maida to offer a sarcastic response, but she's too busy watching Marvel work the puzzle.

'It's about getting together with your family and having a good time,' says Morris.

'Can't you do that any time?' she says.

He shoots a glance at Zero. 'For some reason it's never that easy.'

Olivia places her hand on her daughter's back. 'I've always wanted to have kids of my own at Christmas, so I could make it perfect for them. That's what they say, isn't it, Christmas is for kids? But this . . . Don't get me wrong, it's nice, but I couldn't ever have imagined it.'

'Why?'

'I guess I always imagined that when I was a mum, it would be like you see on supermarket adverts. Warm and full of hugs and, I don't know, animated, and in a proper house with a proper fireplace and, whatever, sherry trifle? I don't know what I mean. I just wish I could have given you that.'

'Oh, come on,' I say. 'This is easily as staged and farcical as those.'

Olivia frowns at me. 'All right, then. Why do *you* Christmas?'

'This year?' I look at Zero. 'I honestly thought it was important to make an effort.'

Morris smiles at me like I've made his day.

It makes me think. Christmas is just something that happens. Time off school. Bad TV. Arguments with your family. I smooth my hair with my fingers, forgetting I'm wearing a paper hat. It tears loose and drifts down onto my pudding plate.

'It's a good way to pretend everything is okay, isn't it?' I say.

'It's stupid,' says Zero.

He looks at us like we're idiots. For a few seconds the only sound is the metal of Marvel's puzzle clicking together as she struggles to solve it.

'It's not for us,' he says, glaring at the girls. '*We're* not like everybody else. At least the people out there wanting to hurt us aren't trying to pretend, like this so-called *family*. The best present you could give them is if you killed yourselves.'

The candles flicker. The girls don't look at him.

'That's not true,' says Helena, almost whispering.

'Everybody wants us gone, and they're no different.'

A good parent would discipline him. Morris is thinking about it, but I know what stops him. He doesn't want to ruin his precious Christmas by shouting. Everyone knows that shouting is the point, on every Christmas, where all bets are off, all semblance of harmony goes out the window. He also doesn't want to get *himself* thrown out of that window. That would definitely ruin his Christmas, not to mention his jaw line, his teeth, and the integrity of all his limbs.

'I like it,' says Helena, louder now. 'Christmas is . . . fun.'

Before Zero can say anything more Marvel returns to the blanket, holding the separated metal bars of her puzzle like a broken trophy.

'Nicely done,' says Maida, clearly glad for a distraction. 'Now put it back together so your sister can have a go.'

'No point,' says Marvel, handing the pieces over. Maida reassembles the puzzle and gives it to Helena.

It's just two lengths of metal, shaped a little like thick paper clips, joined together in a way that makes them seem impossible to separate. It took Marvel about ten minutes. Her sister looks at it once, twists one of the bands, and hands the separated pieces back to Maida. It took her three seconds.

Maida gawps. 'How did you do that?'

Helena points to her sister. 'She did it.'

Maida frowns quizzically, and then pulls Marvel close to whisper something in her ear. Then she turns to Helena. 'What did I just say to your sister?'

I look at Zero questioningly. He turns away, like the whole conversation makes him uncomfortable.

'You said "Christmas isn't usually this crappy",' says Helena. 'Then you made a fart noise.'

'Hey!' says Morris.

Maida lights up. 'I knew it! They're connected like we were, but even stronger – they're like freakin' superheroes!'

Zero flicks angrily at the edge of his cake plate.

'Try it again,' I say. 'But nobody say it out loud this time.'

Maida whispers into Marvel's ear. She looks at her sister and they share a nod, looking impressed with themselves.

I turn to Zero. 'Can you tell me what she said?'

He glares at the wall like it's his worst enemy and shakes his head. All at once his isolation, his sullen behaviour, the way he's been pushing us all away for the last month, makes sense.

'You're not connected to them,' I say. 'Not in the same way.'

Zero springs to his feet and marches for the front door, like any normal kid storming away from an argument. Both Morris and I move to follow, but someone blocks him as he opens the door. He staggers back like he's been hit.

Siobhan stands in the doorway.

Immediately Zero's rage begins to sing.

## Maida

A cute knot of purple tinsel holds her hair away from her

296

face. She's holding a – very small – present in hands that won't stop shaking.

'Merry Christmas,' she says, stepping into the flat. 'I brought something for—'

A rippling pulse makes her drop the flat box and it hits the floor with a *slap*. The strength of this power is new and fearsome. The air feels thick as milkshake.

Zero points at Siobhan. Her body jolts rigid. He turns to his sisters. 'This is why we'll never be accepted,' he says. 'People like her. They're scared of us. She murdered one of us, and they won't stop there!'

The girls climb to their feet, but this time they don't join their brother in attack mode.

Keisha hurries across to Siobhan. 'You shouldn't be here. Go, before anything happens.'

Siobhan takes an exaggerated step deeper into the room.

'I'm sorry,' she says. 'I thought . . .'

Zero glances back at his sisters. 'What she did was an attack on you, too,' he says, almost pleading.

Marvel and Helena shake their heads. 'We know . . . but it's time to move on.'

The candles stutter as Siobhan walks awkwardly over to the window. Clearly Zero is strong enough without their help. There might as well be puppet strings attached, making her step, step, step across the room. There's no way he's letting her go now.

'Help me!' she screams, tears already painting rivers of mascara down her cheeks.

Keisha makes a grab for Zero but a thrumming lash whips her away.

There's this feeling I get when I reach the season finale of a show I love. It's a mixture of dread and excitement all at the same time. Somebody might die but you can't stop watching. It's just too good.

'You killed my brother,' says Zero.

Siobhan is able to shake her head. 'It wasn't like that.'

Her head slams back against the window. *THUNG!* Siobhan screams. Her body wants to fall, but Zero doesn't let it.

'Stop this!' cries Keisha.

'None of this was my fault!' shouts Siobhan.

I had no choice!'

*THUNG!* The whole window shakes. Siobhan's eyes roll like she's going to pass out, but Zero only allows her a swoon before he catches her again.

I feel sick for a moment. I don't want to see this. I don't want to see this. I don't . . . but I have to keep looking. I have to know. It's – it's exciting.

*Apostasy.*

Keisha turns to the girls. 'Can you stop him?'

'No!' I answer for them. 'This is what they were born to do!'

Marvel and Helena look at me sharply. 'That's what our brother thinks.'

'And you don't? You could rule the world if you wanted to!'

'All we've ever wanted is to be safe,' they say, pity for me in their eyes.

It's too much for me to take. Maybe they need to *see* what they're really capable of doing.

'Hit her again!' I shout to Zero.

298

Zero takes another step closer. Everything is primed. The sickness in my stomach is still there, but exhilaration overrides it. It's almost tempting to start a countdown.

'You ended him,' says Zero. 'Like he was nothing. I felt it.'

There's blood in Siobhan's hair, blood running down the back of her neck. The purple tinsel doesn't look so festive now.

'It's *my* body,' she says. 'It was my decision to make.'

*SMASH!* This time the impact is hard enough for the glass to break. Siobhan screams as it shatters outwards and cold air gusts inside from the empty space behind her. Down below someone cries out as shards hail onto the pavement.

'Oh, shit,' says Morris next to me.

Now she's up against the windowsill, leaning back over the drop below. The air is a cyclone around us. It *feels* incredible, as if it's lifting me off the ground, but something nags at the back of my throat: *fear*.

'Please,' says Siobhan, her voice a whisper.

'Come on!' I shout, before I can lose my nerve. 'She deserves it.'

It's true. She does. I know she does.

Keisha turns on me and snarls my name. In front of the window, Siobhan's body convulses. Snot runs over her mouth and chin. Real messy crying. Her neck and shoulders glisten with blood that she can't even wipe away. The boy has complete control.

Keisha addresses him.

'You don't have to do this. You don't have to be a threat. People already think you are,' she says, 'and if you do

299

this, there's no way back, they'll have all the proof they need. They will know you deserve to be hated; they'll know you are to be feared. And they *will* kill you.'

Zero glances sideways at her. For a moment the force of his power dips.

'They never gave me a choice.'

Keisha shakes her head. 'I don't think that's true. You were attacked before you were even born and you've always thought that gave you no choice. Now you have a chance to take your destiny into your own hands. If you do this, you're following a path you think has been set for you, but ignoring the path you could make for yourself.'

I try to move closer, but the girls stop my feet.

'Their power is everything!' I say. 'We have to let them use it.'

Keisha steps towards him. Nothing holds her back, while the girls keep me away, after everything I've done for them.

'You have to decide if you deserve a future,' she says. Another step, no resistance. 'There's no future for you if you do this.'

Zero doesn't respond for a long time. Siobhan closes her eyes, like she has accepted her fate. I want to see, but I find myself hiding behind my hands.

The pressure in the room drops. Zero takes a breath, and Siobhan slumps into a heap against the wall. His power disperses, draining into the floorboards and escaping through the broken window.

'No,' I say, but I don't know if I'm disappointed or relieved.

The girls seem to uncoil as the tension leaves them and they smile at each other, like they've won a victory.

But Zero isn't finished. He takes a step towards Siobhan. Another. Each step as if his shoes are forged from cement. When he reaches her he crouches down in front of her crumpled, broken body and presses an ear to her stomach. She flinches, as if just his touch could destroy her.

Time stops.

There's nothing now but Zero, ear pressed to her skin, as if he's listening for the echo of a voice.

A tear escapes down his cheek.

Then all at once he withdraws, time snaps back, and Zero hurries for the door. He runs out of the flat, scooping up Siobhan's Christmas present on his way. Keisha chases after him, and we listen to their footsteps booming away down the corridor.

Morris dashes across to Siobhan. 'Olivia! She needs a nurse.'

Olivia, sheet-white against the wall, shakes herself together and hurries across to help.

I feel powerless. I'm nothing without the Children. If they have given up their power, I have lost everything.

'I have a first aid kit at home,' says Olivia. 'Maida, you and the girls come with me. It's too cold for anybody to stay here.'

Between us we manage to lift Siobhan up and get her to the door. Almost every door along the hallway is open.

'Look – it won't stop just because you want it to,' I say to the girls as the residents watch us pass. They see the blood in Siobhan's hair and on her clothes, and their faces screw up with anger and hate.

'You think we're going to let you keep doing this?' somebody shouts.

'What are you going to do about it?' I say back.

'You'll see,' they reply. 'Soon enough.'

We reach the stairs. 'Merry bloody Christmas to you, too,' Morris shouts over his shoulder.

# Chapter Thirty-one

**Keisha**

Zero is quick on his feet. I chase him the best I can, up the stairs and through the block. People are too shocked by our speed to try to stop us.

At the top he runs to the ladder under the hatch. It's freezing up here – the hatch has been open for days, off limits. It's like there's a hole in space.

Just like before, as soon as I come within a few steps of that ladder I lose control of my legs. They're already tight and burning from running up the stairs, and I end up dropping to the floor where the cold burns through my clothes.

'I just want to talk!' I shout as he slips out of sight onto the roof.

I'm not giving up that easily. I head back downstairs towards home.

'You get him?' says a guy standing in the stairwell.

When I ignore him, he calls me a bitch. 'You're not better than us, y'know, you lot! And we're going to show you, too.'

Back home I find my parents collapsed on the sofa

with a mostly empty bottle of sherry in front of them. *Die Hard* is on TV, but judging by how they jump away from each other when I open the door they haven't been watching it.

'Keisha!' says Mum. I didn't realise my name could be so badly slurred.

I head across in front of them to my room. Mum laughs at a burst of gunfire on the screen, but I feel Dad glare at me as I pass him.

Instead of going into my room I creep through to theirs. The key to Mr Hillier's flat is in Dad's bedside table. If I can't get up to the roof through the hatch, I'm just going to have to find another way.

I have a plan. God knows if it'll work, but it's my only hope of finding out what Zero is up to, what his endgame is. It might already be too late, but tonight I got through to him. I know I did. If I'm ever going to make a difference – this might be the only chance I have.

'Come and join us!' says Mum when I head back for the front door.

'Don't bother,' says Dad, sinking into the sofa like a sulky teenager. 'She has better things to worry about now.'

He sounds just like the guy who called me a bitch. I slam the door behind me.

I press my ear against the door to Mr Hillier's. There's a TV blaring somewhere, but it could be coming from any of the flats. It's getting late, and I know he doesn't have anyone to visit him.

The door doesn't make a sound when I push it open. The flat is nearly identical to mine, but everything is browner. It's like time has drained the place of colour. A standing lamp casts everything in a dull light: frayed sofa, stacks of books, unusual ornaments. There are no Christmas decorations. And luckily, there's no sign of Mr Hillier.

I hurry across to the window. I wonder if this is how Dad feels when he comes up here late at night to get another handout of cash. The thought makes me want to turn around.

The balcony door sticks, and I have to lean my weight against it to shove it open. The cold is – holy crap, it's cold. But there are worse things to worry about right now.

I put my back against the railing and peer up at the roof. Then I turn and lift myself up to stand on the metal rail. I catch a glimpse of the drop below. The roads cut through the snow like noughts and crosses grids. Thirteen floors. There wouldn't be much of me left.

Everything else is white, even the cars that edge cautiously along, their exhausts escaping in enormous plumes. Multicoloured Christmas lights flash here and there, windows illuminated with the blue glow of televisions. Normal families are slumped on the sofa by now, too stuffed to move. I get my feet on the railing and turn away from the view. I'm glad there wasn't the chance to eat much at the meal.

The roof isn't that far above me. I reach for the edge but my hands scrape against the wall. My best chance is a thin pipe that juts out from between the bricks. It's metal, but not sturdy enough – it droops when I put my weight on it. Nevertheless, holding that pipe allows me to wedge a foot against the top of the open patio doorframe to try to push myself higher.

There's a creak inside the flat, and I hear footsteps crossing the sitting room. At the same moment the pipe sags in my fist, brick dust hitting me in the face.

'Hello?' Mr Hillier's voice reaches me from inside. He sounds scared.

I try again, more desperately now, reaching for the lip of the roof. My fingers just come up short.

Footsteps advance to the window. I glance down to see Mr Hillier's shadow cast through the glass. The streetlights far below swirl across my vision and I force myself to keep looking up. The pipe sags further and further, and now my fingers are numb from the cold.

The shadow moves away. I wedge my feet in as hard as I can and kick upwards, letting go of the pipe. My fingers find the edge of the roof, the coarse bricks helping my grip. I heave myself up, shoulder and stomach muscles screaming. I manage to scrape a leg over the side and roll bodily over onto the roof.

There's a lot of lying there and panting before I even try to stand up. My hands are scraped raw and bleeding. Slowly I push myself to my wobbling feet.

I take in the scene. A red light mounted on top of the electricity hub casts a glow over everything. Somewhere nearby is the ominous heavy drone of a helicopter. The roof is iced over with frozen snow that crunches under my feet as I follow a regimented track of footprints skirting from the hatch around to the far side of the roof.

The view opens up below me. First I spot the helicopter, hovering over the far side of the estate, startlingly close because I'm so high up.

I turn around, looking for a massive satellite dish pointed at the moon or a giant laser weapon aimed at Downing Street, anything unusual. It's only when the uneven ground makes me stumble that I realise what I'm looking for is right under my feet.

Two words, carved into the snow, the letters big enough that I could lie down flat inside them.

# COME BACK

It's a message to the sky, to anyone or anything that might be up there and gazing down at the block.

'They won't come.'

His voice makes me slip over on the ice. I get back up and turn around to find Zero standing at the edge of the electricity hub.

The message isn't a call to arms.

It's not summoning an invasion.

It sounds like a desperate cry for help.

'You want to leave,' I say.

'Maybe.' Zero looks across the letters at me. He's wearing a coat I haven't seen before. 'I thought I was strong. It took me a long time to realise I was lonely. I thought if I could find out what I really am . . .'

He climbs up onto a concrete ledge that's been cleared of ice and reaches for something. It's a cluster of wires attached to what looks like an old motherboard. My gaming microphone is plugged into it. One end has been threaded into the electricity hub, the other rigged via a thick cable and the old television to a cluster of TV aerials.

'We tried to send them a message to come back for us, or to at least say something. But we didn't really know what we were doing.'

'I'm amazed you didn't electrocute yourselves.'

'Marvel did, a little bit.'

'Is this coat Siobhan's present?' I say, plucking at his sleeve.

The boy kicks snow off his shoes. 'It would have been my brother's.'

He was supposed to have someone. A brother who would be part of him, like the girls seem to be part of each other. Instead he had nobody.

Tears spring to my eyes.

The helicopter hovers nearby, red lights flashing on its belly. Sadness presses its thumb against my chest. 'I'm sorry. We've all made it so bad for you here.'

'Do you know why I called myself Zero?'

I shake my head.

'Because I don't know what I am. Maybe I'm nothing.'

The thumb presses harder, sinking right into my breastbone. Part of me wants to rest a hand on his shoulder, pull him into a hug. I move to reach out, but I can't quite bring myself to go through with it and I shove my hand back into my pocket.

Zero notices and his face hardens. 'What did you think I was doing up here?'

As soon as the Children started coming to the roof I assumed they were doing something that threatened us.

I automatically didn't trust them because of who they are.

'I thought the worst,' I say. 'But the way you've been behaving, can you really blame me?'

Zero spears the ice with the toe of his shoe. 'I don't know how else I'm supposed to behave. I can hurt people so easily and I'm getting stronger every day. Maybe *that's* who I am. Why should I deny my nature?'

I take a step closer to him and try to keep my voice calm. 'I know how you feel. I was lost for a long time. It made me angry . . . sad; until I basically gave up on myself. But then something happened and it made me realise – feeling like that doesn't have to mean you're trapped, and that's the end of it. It might be hard, but you can fight for something better.'

'You *don't* know what it feels like!'

A powerful wave rushes off him, but I force myself not to yield or run away. He needs someone to be there for him. It's time I made it my responsibility.

'Whatever it is you have inside you . . . it doesn't have to be evil.'

'No one will let me be anything different when I can do things like this!'

He turns away and looks up at the helicopter, hovering low over a tangle of streets toward the main road. The frozen air seems to tear open around us.

The helicopter sways, like its lost control, before straightening up again and beginning to climb. Its blades drone on the air. Another flare, and the helicopter drops, whining through the sky, the pilot surrendering to Zero's control.

'Stop it!' I shout.

Zero starts to pant with the effort but his power keeps flowing. 'I can kill them,' he rasps, eyes fixed on the struggling helicopter. 'I could crash it down into the houses and kill so many.'

'You don't want to do that,' I say. 'I know you don't.'

The helicopter begins to swing down to the ground like its being pulled on a lead, closer and closer to the homes below.

'It would be easier,' says Zero. 'It would be so much easier to be what everybody thinks I am.'

I take a breath and put a hand on his shoulder, my bones feeling the crackle and hum. 'What's easy isn't always right. I understand. I do,' I say. 'The girls are linked even more strongly than we realised. It must have been the same for you and your brother. So when he . . . I can't imagine what that was like. I know I haven't been there to help you, but let me now.'

Zero screams. Sweat is pouring down his face and soaking into his clothes. The helicopter keeps dropping, cutting the air apart as it goes.

'You saved Mr Hillier's cat,' I say, my mind racing. 'You didn't kill Siobhan, even though you wanted to. You're not evil. I know you're not.'

Punctured, Zero's fury collapses, and he falls back against me. The helicopter levels out, the pilot regaining control, and it begins to lift away from the houses. I catch Zero, and he turns into me, throwing his arms around my waist.

'What if it's too late for me?' he whimpers.

I hold him tight, and for the first time it feels like he's a part of me.

'Right now I think we both need to rest.'

We climb down through the hatch and I take him home. He's exhausted, barely able to walk, and when we reach my room I take off his sweaty T-shirt and tuck him into my bed.

I text Morris, just letting him know that Zero is here, that he's okay.

By the time I lie down beside him, my poor exhausted lost little boy, he's fast asleep.

# Chapter Thirty-two

**Morris**

This much washing up should be illegal. There's only so much I can carry back downstairs at once, and this first load barely makes a dent. We had to wait a while for the corridor to empty out before we could all leave the flat.

I edge my way indoors, bowls rattling and cutlery clinking.

Mum's sitting on the sofa. I know something's not right because the TV's not on.

'Mum?'

Tears swim in her eyes when she looks at me. Her whole body shudders with a sob.

Her lip is split in the middle and there's a massive scuff across one of her cheeks. Both of her hands are shaking, grazed and covered in grit and dirt.

I almost drop the plates. Instead I put them on the floor and hurry over to her. 'Who did this?'

When you've lived round here your entire life it's not long before you learn that injuries like this don't come from falling over. I sit beside her, place an arm around her shoulder as her trembling lips try to find the words.

'I got a lift home from work to the end of the road,' she says, her voice quivering like she's sitting on a washing machine. 'They jumped me.'

'Did you see them?'

'There were three of them, I think. They pushed me once and I fell into the road. They didn't take anything.' She wipes at the blood on her hands. Then her eyes come up to meet mine. 'They said they had a message for you.'

Her words drop like a coin sinking into a well. It's a few seconds before the ripples resonate, hit me square, make me curl both hands into fists.

Tyrone can mess with me. I deserve it. But he's gone too far this time. Way, way too far.

'What was it?'

'They're outside the block,' she says. 'They're waiting.'

I go over to the window and pull back the curtain. Three figures lean against the fence, looking up at the tower.

'Mo? What did you *do*, Mo?' says Mum.

The fear and disappointment in her voice makes me want to cry. I go across to the buzzer and press the talk button.

'There's an empty flat on the eighth floor,' I say into the speaker. 'Graffiti on the door. Meet me there.' I press the entry button to let them inside.

I march back into my room. The package is still stashed under my bed. I shove it into the front of my hoodie.

'Mo, please,' begs Mum. 'Please stop.'

'They want me to pay them back. So I'm going to pay them back better than they could ever guess.'

'*Please—*'

'No! I might've done nothing else for this family, but the least I can do is put an end to this!'

The slam of the front door booms along the empty hallway. The orange light overhead flickers and buzzes. I don't care that it's late, that it's Christmas, that I'm making a racket. I let my feet echo around the block as I hurry up the stairs. Every inch of my body is shaking, like I would need to peel my skin clean away to let the anger out.

There are footsteps below me on the stairs. When I reach Keisha's floor I slow up so my steps are quiet. I knock on her door. She won't understand.

Her mum answers the door, eyes heavy and tired. 'Oh, Morris.'

'Sorry, I know it's late,' I say, fighting with all I've got to keep my voice calm. 'My mum wants to say Merry Christmas to the boy.'

She nods and stands aside to let me through. 'They're in her room.'

Keisha's dad is asleep on the sofa. As I cross the living room her mum settles back next to him. A plastic Christmas tree flashes with light.

The bedroom door doesn't make a sound when I edge it open. The only light comes from the flickering internet router on her desk, just enough to help me see them together on the bed. Our boy is tucked into the crook of her body, her arm around his waist. It's easy to see she's proper asleep because her mouth is open and she's dribbling.

Maybe she won't ever need to know.

I wake Zero. That doesn't go down well. His eyes snap

open, practically glowing in the dark, and a tendril of influence pierces my fingers, forcing them away from him. I bring my hand quickly to my lips and he seems to understand. He slips out carefully from under Keisha's arm and grabs a jacket I haven't seen before.

Keisha doesn't stir. That's not surprising. She hasn't slept properly in weeks.

Keisha's parents are fast asleep on the sofa. We walk past them to the front door and I pull it closed behind us. He gazes up at me in the orange light, his hair messed up with sleep.

'You want to make the most of your powers, yeah?'

He doesn't answer.

'I want you to come with me,' I say, trying to get him on my side. 'This is your chance to show me everything you've got.'

The stairs are deserted. They must be ahead of me now. As we pass the floors I can hear some people talking, the noise of TVs.

I push into the empty flat. Tyrone turns away from the Christmas tree and smiles at me. I have to fight every urge in my body not to smack him right there.

'Merry Christmas, Morris. You're at the wrong address.' He notices the kid behind me. 'You shouldn't have brought him here.'

At first I think he's alone. Then the two other guys step out from either side of the door, blocking our exit.

'I want to settle this,' I say.

'I think the kid should wait outside.'

I grab Zero's hand and pull him further into the flat. A chill leaks in from the broken window. Most of the washing up from Christmas dinner is still spread across the kitchen counter.

'You shouldn't have done that to my mum.'

'Honestly, I'm sorry about that. We just meant to scare her, but it went too far.'

He slurs his words a little. It's late. They've probably been drinking the whole day.

I take the package out of my hoodie. 'I'm bringing this back.'

Tyrone nods. 'Do you have my money then?'

I shake my head.

'What are you doing to me, Mo?' says Tyrone. 'You know I have to do something about this.'

The other two guys take a step closer behind me, ready in case I try anything. They have no idea.

Tyrone points to the parcel in my hand. 'Open it.'

'I'm not messing around with this no more.'

'Pretend it's a Christmas present.'

Reluctantly I slip a finger under the tape. It's tattered from all the nights I've spent holding it. I tear it open and tip the contents into my hand.

It's jet black and cold and a lot heavier than it looks.

'I wanted to help you make something of yourself, Mo,' says Tyrone. 'Your life is going nowhere. You fucked it up.'

The gun seems to vibrate in my grip. My finger brushes the trigger. It's exciting and sickening and powerful. It makes me feel like I'm somebody else.

'Shoot it,' says Tyrone.

He's crazy. He smiles and nods to the plates and glasses on the counter top.

'Go on. You want to know how it feels, right?'

I do. More than anything. I want to feel that power. I grip the gun harder and bring it up. For a moment I imagine pointing it at Tyrone. One pull of the trigger . . . but that's not going to happen. Instead I point it at a glass and hold my breath.

I glance back at Zero. He's watching everything with his golden eyes.

The breath bursts through my lips and I lower the gun.

'I might be a nobody,' I say. 'But it's better than being like you.'

Tyrone snarls and snatches the gun out of my hand. Before I can react he points it at my face and pulls the trigger.

I flinch away, eyes clenched tight. All I hear is an empty *click click click*.

When I crack open an eye Tyrone clubs me round the head with the gun.

'You really think I gave you a loaded piece?'

There's movement behind me. The other guys shove Zero out of the way and grab my arms, pulling them tight behind my back. I try to fight them off but they're too strong. Or I'm too weak.

'Zero,' I say.

'I tried to give you a chance, Mo,' says Tyrone, lodging the gun in his waistband and reaching for the countertop. He picks up a knife, blade smeared with cake or something. 'We used to be friends. But I can't just let this slide.'

I flex my arms but they're pinned. Tyrone steps closer and lifts the knife.

'Zero,' I say, more urgently now.

The kid is somewhere behind me. I can feel the first prickle on the air. 'I don't want to do this,' he says.

Tyrone waves his free hand. 'Go and wait in the hall, okay, little man?'

'Come *on*, Zero,' I say.

'Please,' he says, power rising to the surface, flickering on the air.

Tyrone brings the knife to my face and slowly presses the dirty blade against my cheek. Begins to push. At first there's no pain, just the electric anticipation of it, my skin resisting the assault. It gives up all at once. Pain flares through my jaw. Tyrone slowly slips the knife sideways, opening my flesh, and I know I let out a scream though somehow my ears don't hear it. Drops of my blood patter against the kitchen floor.

'I vouched for you,' says Tyrone, bringing the point of the knife to rest against my chest. 'I should have known better.'

He presses the blade so it pierces my hoodie, my T-shirt, and delves into my skin. The pain gnaws at my lungs. I struggle for breath.

'Zero!' I shout.

The pressure on the knife drops away. At the same moment my hands are released, and I slip quickly away from my captors. All three guys are frozen to the spot. Tyrone is staring at the knife in his outstretched hand, confused, scared. Suddenly, he lunges forwards and sticks the blade into his mate's chest.

I look over at Zero. His whole body shakes and tears glimmer in his eyes.

Blood trickles hot down my face. I think of my mum crying into her hands. 'It's okay,' I say. 'Just do what you're best at.'

The guy with the knife in his chest looks at it like it doesn't make sense. He shudders, but he still can't move. His T-shirt becomes more blood than fabric. Next to him the other guy starts to breathe hard in a panic but he can't move either.

Tyrone draws the blade out and, with his teeth gritted like he's trying to fight it, stabs again, this time in the throat.

The guy drops to the floor, gasping and spluttering like a fish.

A flash of energy, and Tyrone snaps into a frenzy. He turns to the remaining guy and slashes him across the chest, the mouth, the scalp. Something warm sprays over us. Beside me Zero breathes hard, like it's him making every cut.

Tyrone changes his grip and plunges the knife into the guy's shoulder. It seems to break the hold on him. The guy screams and lurches forward, tackling Tyrone and sending them both slipping over into the red puddle that's leaked across the floor. Tyrone is pinned and his mate starts throwing punches, slamming his fists again and again into Tyrone's face.

Tears are streaming down Zero's cheeks. I'm sorry, I think. I'm sorry. But I don't do anything to stop him.

The guy on top stops throwing punches like he's forgotten how, and Tyrone sticks the knife in his belly, kicking him away. He gets to his feet awkwardly, covered in blood, like a demon rising out of a grave.

'You don't come near me or my family again,' I say. 'It's over.'

Zero is breathing in short gasps, like the air's been sucked out of the room. Tyrone looks at me, his eyes wide and desperate, as the electric hum intensifies one last time. He turns on the spot and runs for the broken window.

'Wait!' I shout.

Tyrone dives head first into empty space. The energy sinks away and time seems to stop for a second. It's only a distant *thud* that gets me moving again.

I run to the window. Tyrone is laid out on the path, a dark shadow spreading out around him. Lights come on in the flats below me, windows pushing open, people peering outside. Somebody screams.

There isn't much time. I pick up the gun and wipe it as clean as I can on my hoodie, hoping it's enough to get rid of my fingerprints. I drop it down into the blood. Then I take Zero's hand and pull him out of the flat and into the hallway. I don't let go. His hand trembles in my grasp.

All around us phones begin to ring. The space behind every door comes alive with bells or a cheesy song or just a plain old ringtone.

There's no way they didn't hear what happened. The body on the street has been seen. The news is going to spread fast.

The phones cut off all at once as they're answered, muffled voices pushing through every door around us.

A door opens just ahead of us as we reach the stairs. A guy leans out, phone pressed to his ear. 'They're leaving now,' he says.

I keep my eyes down and head onto the stairs to Keisha's flat. I can't let my mum see us like this.

The whole building feels alive. The attack has snapped everyone into action, like they've been waiting for this moment to arrive for a long time. Going down the stairs feels like running headlong into an ambush. People on every floor, glaring at us with naked hatred or standing rigid with fear as we pass by. The air feels unnaturally still.

I don't even knock on the front door, just head inside. Keisha's parents are still asleep on the sofa. We go through to the bathroom, turn on the overhead light and stare into the mirror. The cut in my cheek isn't as bad as I thought. The cold has dried the blood into a thick scab. Zero has a spray of red across his face. I grab a cloth, wet it under the hot tap, and get to work cleaning him up.

He won't stop shaking. 'Why did you make me do that?'

'They were going to hurt me,' I say, rubbing the cloth gently over his cheek. 'They would of hurt us all.'

'I didn't want to do it,' he says. 'She said I didn't have to.'

'You . . . I didn't know what you could do.'

It's the truth. It has to be the truth. I didn't know Zero would go so far. Did I?

His eyes flood with tears, shimmering like flecks of gold. I don't know what to say. When I squeeze the cloth in the sink the water runs red.

'But you knew,' I say, and I realise the real horror of what I've done. 'You knew and you didn't want to do it.'

'I don't want it to be too late for me.' Zero breathes

in great, gasping sobs that shudder through his body. 'I don't.'

I had almost forgotten what he is: not a weapon, and not a monster – a child. My son. I wanted to give him the whole world and protect him from all the people in it who would hurt and abuse him – but I'm no better.

I failed.

I drop to my knees and pull him into a hug, wrapping him up tight in my arms. He tries to fight me off, using his fists rather than his powers, but I hold on like I might lose him forever if I let go.

'I'm sorry,' I say, my voice cracking. 'I'm so sorry.'

'What's going on?'

We turn around to find Keisha standing in the doorway.

## Maida

The bathroom door gives the full horror movie creak. The scene on the other side matches it. Two bodies, spilling blood onto the floorboards in heavy puddles, the Christmas tree lights reflecting strange colours in their surfaces.

They're blocking my way out. If I want to escape, I'll have to step over them.

I only came down here to collect some of our stuff. When they showed up, I hid in the bathroom.

But I saw it all.

A shudder wracks my body. It's the cold. Just the cold from the broken window. It's okay. I wanted their power to run unchecked, to see what they are capable of, and now I have it.

I force myself to move. Their bodies look so *heavy*, even though they've been drained. Their faces are pressed to the floor.

The gun, as empty as they are, lies between them.

I hear voices on the street below us. I cross to the window and peer outside. The body is sprawled across the pavement. People from the block have gathered around it. Every light is on, washing across the path, glowing on the hard-packed snow.

A sharp intake of breath behind me. I whip around, and see the boy furthest from me lift his head, his stuttering breath rippling the blood around his lips.

'Help,' he rasps.

I run.

Through the blood, jumping over the bodies. As I reach the door, people start pushing inside, residents coming to investigate.

I shove past them. My feet slip on the concrete as I run and run and run.

# Chapter Thirty-three

**Keisha**

I woke up and he was gone. It wouldn't normally be such a shock, but after our conversation on the roof I could feel that something was wrong.

And now I find him covered in blood. With Morris.

There's a nasty cut across Morris's cheek. I hurry over and check Zero for damage, but I can't find anything. The blood isn't his.

'I killed them.'

I drop to my knees and pull him away from Morris. His whole body shudders in my grasp and a tear runs down his cheek.

'Tell me what happened.'

'He knew they would attack him.' Zero looks up at Morris. 'He made me fight back.'

I'm desperate for it to be a lie. Some new kind of trick. But when I look at Morris I can tell straight away that it's true. He shakes his head, mouth opening and closing but not making any words. I squeeze Zero tight and he shrinks against me, sobbing gently.

'It was Tyrone and his crew. They attacked my mum,'

says Morris. 'They wanted what I owe them, money, big time. I gave them payback. They deserved it, Keish.'

'You took drug money?'

Morris holds out his hands like he had no other choice. 'I did it for you.'

'I knew you were stupid, but that's a whole new level.'

He tries to step towards us but Zero flickers and he stops dead. 'We needed money for Nan, to send away to my dad,' he says, his voice wobbling. 'All of you were expecting me to be earning by now. I wanted to show everyone . . . I wanted to show *you* I wasn't a waste of space.'

Zero's tears soak into my shoulder. 'So you took him to, what? Clean up your mess? Do your dirty work? You're no father figure. Happy families? Get away from us. I mean it. Go.'

'It was either that or work for Tyrone! I knew that would make you hate me. I didn't think . . .'

I gather Zero in my arms and lift, balance him on his feet. He wipes his nose on the sleeve of his jacket.

'Get out,' I say again. My voice is coming from some part of my chest I haven't felt before. I hardly sound like me. 'If you come anywhere near us I swear I'll break your legs myself.'

'Please. It was stupid. I know it was stupid.' He begins to cry. 'I didn't know what else to do. I shouldn't have made him . . . the things he did. I didn't know it would go so far, I swear!'

'After everything I told him. That he didn't have to be violent. That people didn't have to be scared of him.'

'I'm sorry,' Morris says.

325

He leaves my flat with his head down, looking at the blood sprayed across his hoodie. I get to work cleaning the rest of it from Zero's skin.

'What do I do now?' he says.

'You're going to move on.'

'I don't know if I can.'

I look at the anguish etched into his face. It seems impossible that he's only a few months old. He talks like he's been alive for centuries.

'How can I move on when I don't know why I'm here?'

'You're not the first,' I say.

Zero turns his golden eyes on me.

'It's happened before,' I tell him. 'In a village in Corn–wall. They had mysterious pregnancies, just like us.'

'How long have you known about this?'

I sigh. 'A while.'

'Why didn't you tell me?'

'I didn't know what it meant.' I grab a bag and start packing clothes into it. 'Those Children will have grown up by now. If we can find them, maybe we can find out what this was all about.'

Zero thinks about it for a long moment. Then he nods his head. 'But not without the others.'

There's no sign of Morris when we step into the corridor. I pull Zero by the hand, but shove us both against the wall before we reach the stairs. There are footsteps coming up. A *lot* of footsteps. People whispering to each other as they climb. When the last of them has passed I peek after them.

They all have weapons. Most of them aren't obvious. There are frying pans and cricket bats. Things that could be passed off as Christmas presents. The knives are less easy to ignore. There's only one reason you'd carry a knife around the block.

We follow as quietly as we can. They leave the stairs a few floors up. I peer into the corridor. They're all filing into the Hag's flat.

'They're going to come for us,' says Zero.

'Can you hold them all off?' I say. 'If they all attack at once?'

He watches the last of them slip into the Hag's flat, and then shakes his head. I take his hand again and we keep climbing.

We don't have much time.

## Maida

Keisha tells us about a village in Cornwall – Siltoe – and someone in her livestream who knew about our Children, how she tried to call them. She says they have answers to all of this.

I sit upright on Olivia's cream Ikea sofa, pick up my Ikea mug of tea from the Ikea coffee table. My hands are shaking. Siobhan is in the bedroom, where Olivia played nurse and patched her up. The girls are watching the shifting colours of the Christmas tree lights, while Zero stares bleakly out the window.

'We have to leave now,' says Keisha. 'We can take Olivia's car.'

'You don't know if there's anything there,' I say. 'From the sounds of it, it could be worse than here.'

'It's our only chance of finding answers.'

The girls are looking at me. God, I wish I could read

their minds, share their connection. I don't want them to shut me out.

Why should we run from the tower? If they don't want us here, that's their problem. We have the power, therefore we should stay.

Except . . . I can't stop thinking about what I saw in the flat. The blood I left trailing behind me on the stairs. Reality was worse than I ever could have imagined.

'Do we need answers?' I ask.

'Maybe you don't. But this isn't about you, or me, or any of us lot – this is about *them*,' Keisha says. 'There's nothing left for them here. Everybody in the block hates them, let alone *us*. Social services are breathing down our necks. There's a dead body on the street on Christmas day, Maida. Zero did that. There's no way back from this.'

'Yes, I know they're coming for us,' I say, trying to stop my hands from shaking. 'But we *can* come out on top.'

My daughter could do to the residents what Zero did in the empty flat.

'Oh, Maida. If you try and force them to use their power, you'll lose them,' says Keisha. 'But they need you *now*. If you really want to be part of their lives, you have to help them be more than weapons of attack.'

The girls are watching me. I reach out and stroke Marvel's cheek. I really thought their power made them special. I hoped their power made *me* special too but . . . maybe I got it wrong, blinded by what they could *do* and not seeing who they *are*. I see them now – little girls, months old. Powerful and beautiful and helpless. So helpless. So full of potential.

Oh, my girls. They're special not *because* of their power but *in spite* of it.

I pull both girls into my arms. 'I love you,' I say. 'I mean it, I always meant it.'

'I think that means she's coming with us,' says Keisha. She turns to Olivia. 'What about you?'

None of us has noticed that she's crying. 'This whole thing has been a disaster. I tried . . .' She wipes her eyes. 'I *tried*. I wanted to be a mother more than anything – but not like this, never like this. I can't pretend anymore.'

Before anybody can stop her she runs for the door and out into the hallway. Nobody goes after her. We have to try and stay together the best we can.

Noise pushes in from the corridor. Voices and footsteps thunder towards us.

'We don't want to fight,' say the girls, watching the door. 'We don't want to hurt them.'

I look at Zero, but his face is unreadable.

The door flies open. We're expecting an attack. If we want to get out, the girls might not have any choice. But it's only Siobhan's mum, eyes wide with panic.

'It's started,' she says. 'They're coming for you.'

We all get to our feet.

'Siobhan's in the bedroom,' says Keisha, and Siobhan's mum runs to find her. Keisha turns to the rest of us. 'It's time to go.'

The girls look at me, as if they need my approval. I nod. We have to leave.

But we might have to fight off the entire building to do it.

# Chapter Thirty-four

**Keisha**

The corridor is packed with people.

The residents have snapped, and they're going to try and end it tonight. The stairs are crammed. People block our way, faces etched with determination.

'Don't hurt them,' I say. 'Just get them out of our way.'

We push down the stairs like a miniature army. The first guy who attacks us is Frank, the guy who used to be my neighbour, who carried me home when I was hurt. He lunges at me with his fists. Midway through the move he twirls like a dancer and ends up slamming himself into the banister. Louise Krawczyk makes a grab for one of the Children but her hands stop before she can touch them. She bellows in frustration.

Down on the next floor a couple of guys bar our way. One of them is the shaggy-haired kid Zero attacked on the green, gripping a kitchen knife. He grins, glad for a chance at revenge, but as he advances there's a flare and both of them throw themselves down the stairs. It's almost comical, like it was choreographed.

Screams come from the corridor. A voice I recognise straight away.

'It's Olivia!'

We find her surrounded by a group of residents, swiping at her and aiming blows so that she slumps against the wall, blood running from her eyebrow.

The girls screech and the lights overhead burst in a flash of light. Broken glass rains down on us. The attackers fling themselves apart like a grenade has exploded between them. I rush forward and pull Olivia to her feet. She's shivering violently but I force her to run.

We hurry down the stairs, over the collapsed body of the shaggy-haired kid. The way down is packed with residents, maybe too many.

When we reach my floor the stairs further down are blocked by a crowd. The Hag is standing at the front. Facing them down is Morris.

## Morris

It's finally happening. Tyrone's body on the street was the spark, and now the block has ignited. I was coming to find Keisha and I ran right into the army.

'Why do you hate us so much?' I shout.

The Hag spits at my feet. 'I know what your children are.'

'No, you don't! They are what *you've* made them.'

'They're an abomination!'

The crowd glares at me, like security guards ready to jump into a fight if needed.

I press my fists against the cold wall, trying to squeeze

331

my anger out into the bricks, but it doesn't work. Maybe this place is already full to the brim.

'Nothing they did had to happen, if you hadn't turned the whole block against us. They didn't do anything wrong and you decided they were your enemy. *We* didn't do anything wrong – but we're young, we're not like you, so we couldn't be trusted. You had to try and crush us before we found a place in the world.'

The Hag's lip quivers, maybe with fear, maybe with anger. 'If you do anything to me – to *any* of us – you won't get away with it. Not anymore.'

I step away from her. 'I'm doing nothing to you. I've already made enough mistakes.'

The Hag looks past me, and I risk a glance over my shoulder. Keisha, Maida, Olivia, and the Children are all there, looking down on us from the stairs.

Straight away I push the Hag back, knocking her off balance.

'Go on!' I shout.

They run through onto Keisha's floor. I hang back, make sure nobody makes a move, and then follow after them.

'How much of that did you hear?' I say to Keisha as we reach her front door.

'Most of it,' she says. Zero clings to her leg and doesn't look at me. 'You did a terrible thing.'

'I know. I swear, I know. Maybe it's impossible, but I'd do anything to make it better. You know I would.'

'Good,' she says, pushing open the door. 'Because we're going to need all the help we can get.'

## Keisha

People are waiting for us inside. I almost turn and run
before I realise it's our families. All of them. My mum
and dad, Maida's parents and brother, and Morris's
mum. I slam the door shut and we end up falling into a
sort of messy group hug.

'What the hell's going on?'

'We have to get out of here,' I say.

Maida's dad looks like he's going to vomit. 'Why is
this happening?'

'We're not going to be able to come back,' I say. 'So
there's no reason not to show you the truth.' I can't leave
without them knowing what all of this was about.

Everyone crowds into my room. I don't know how
much time we have left. My computer is already on. I
log in to my Twitch account and find the archived video
from the Nightout.

'Just watch it,' I say. There's no time for questions, and
I can't bear to see it again. I skip ahead to a few minutes
before it happens and leave the room. The others join
me. The Children have collapsed onto the sofa, like
they're trying to regain their energy for what's to come.

'Do you think we can make it?'

Morris wipes sweat from his forehead. 'Nobody can
stand in the way of our future.' We all watch the Children
breathing, so quiet at rest.

'Do you think things can be different for them?' I say.

Morris's hand goes to the slice in his cheek. 'I hope it
can be different for all of us.' There's no way of knowing
what's waiting for us out there in the world. God only
knows what we'll find in Siltoe, if it will give us any

answers, but it can't be any worse than what we're leaving behind.

'It's weird,' says Maida. 'I actually got what I always wanted – to be far away from my parents, free to do whatever . . . and with you, even! I've got superhero kids who'll protect me. I should be happy.' She turns to look at her family, their faces bleached in the glow of the computer screen. 'So why aren't I?'

The sound on the video changes. It's the moment I drop into unconsciousness. The game goes silent. My mum begins to cry, while everyone else stands motionless until it's over.

I stand in the doorway. 'You don't want to believe it,' I say, 'but it happened, and not just to me.'

'But what—'

'There's no time. You have to help us get out of the block so we can get far away from here.'

They look one last time at my sleeping face on the video. Then they all turn back to us and nod.

## Maida

Beside me, Keisha's parents pull her into a hug. I hear her Dad whispering *I'm sorry I'm sorry I'm sorry* over and over again into her ear.

Things are a bit more awkward with my family. Mum looks about ready to faint, and Dad looks like his head might explode trying to come up with any words that might make all of this better.

Eventually he just says, 'We will help you.'

It doesn't fix anything. It's too late for that. But right now it's enough.

I crouch in front of Azraf so our eyes are level. 'You can be anything you want to be,' I tell him. 'It won't be easy. People will try and say you can't. But don't listen to them, okay?'

He nods shyly. He probably thinks I'm talking rubbish. I kiss him on top of his head. 'Now go wait in the bedroom, okay?'

He hurries away, past Olivia, who's standing as far away from everyone as possible, like maybe everybody will get a sudden case of amnesia and forget she ever existed.

I turn to Mum. 'You have to stay with him.'

She shakes her head, but I push her towards the bedroom. 'Take him away from here. Give him a chance.'

My parents hold hands, communicating without words, before she slips away to the bedroom.

'Mum, I need the car,' says Morris. 'I'm probably not going to bring it back.'

She looks too stunned to really understand. 'Of course.'

'Good, because I already took the keys,' he says, jangling them in her face. 'Tell Dad I went off to see about a future.'

There's a thud against the door, someone kicking it hard enough to make the floor shudder. Something else hits the door, something sharper than a foot; the wood splinters.

We stand as a group in the middle of the sitting room. Keisha's dad goes to the kitchen and reaches into a high cupboard. He comes back with a golden syrup tub. At first I think it's a strange choice of travel snack,

335

but then he prises off the lid and pulls out a thick wad of money.

'I know you don't like how I got it, but it was always for your future,' he says to his daughter. 'You're going to need it now more than ever.'

'That's a lot of cash,' says Morris.

Keisha pockets the money as another *thud* splits the door open right next to the lock. If horror movies have taught me anything, it's that it won't take much more punishment.

'We go straight for the main door,' says Keisha. 'We don't stop for anything.'

Our families form a circle around us, the Children right at its centre.

'Finally,' I say, nerves jangling in my chest. 'Squad goals achieved.'

'We're going to have a life away from here,' says Keisha. 'Believe in that.'

A final blow sends the door slamming into the wall. The first of the attackers lunges over the threshold, swinging an axe.

## Morris

He freezes in mid-swing, others behind him running into his back like cartoon characters. A wave surges from the Children, making them moan with the effort, and the mob stops in its tracks.

'Come on,' I say.

I push past the guy with the axe (where did he get an *axe*?) and into the hallway. It's crammed with people, clutching blades and hammers and cricket bats, anything that can hurt. Nobody speaks. Their bodies are rigid, posed like cowboys in the final second before a duel.

The others follow me, shuffling awkwardly through the door. The Children hold hands, their faces screwed up with the strain of holding everyone in place. There's no choice but to squeeze through the gaps between the statues.

'At least I'll never have to take you to Madam Tussauds,' I mutter as I lead the way.

I slip between bodies, pushing knives out of the way like bramble branches to clear a path. My heart smashes into my ribs. Our attackers twitch and shudder as they try and fight back against their invisible bonds. At the stairs, Stan's bulk blocks the way and I suck in my stomach to make myself as small as possible. His warm skin brushes mine as I edge past, his breath making my hair stand on end. All these people I used to know, who we've lived with for years, doing everything they can to make us dead.

I'm not really feeling too sad about leaving the tower behind.

'We can't hold them much longer,' says Zero through gritted teeth.

I wait for everyone to make it to the stairs, ushering them through the door like a skydive instructor. The mob is beginning to move. The Children are weakening.

The first set of stairs is clear and we run for it, but as soon as we turn the corner we stumble into more people. One of them shouts an alarm and they stand their ground. They've got dustbin lids and frying pans and knives. We don't stop. Keisha's parents throw their weight forward and close the distance quickly enough to avoid any serious blows. They start to grapple, but more people are coming up the stairs to join the battle.

The space is too narrow for us to help. There's no choice but for the Children to take action. Their hands come apart and the energy seems to blast at the walls like shrapnel, sending bodies flying down the stairs. Above us voices are mounting again.

'They're coming!' I shout.

We stumble down the stairs. Keisha's dad catches a punch to the temple and he flops onto the banister, but Maida's mum is there to pull him clear of the follow-up blow. My mum swings a fist that sends the guy staggering away.

'Nice one, Mum.'

For a split-second she looks pretty pleased with herself.

Footsteps thunder behind us, filling the block with noise. The descent becomes a blur of limbs and bodies, the tight space ringing with shouts and strikes. I lose track of the floors. The Children are still fighting, but only enough to push people back for a second.

Before I know it we've reached the ground floor. There are more people here than anywhere else. Some of them cry and whimper when they see us, like we're monsters, but a lot more of them mean business. They form a barrier to block our escape. Louise Krawczyk is here. The Hag stands at the front of them like a general, playing with something hidden in her grip.

'We just want to get away from here!' shouts Keisha.

'You're a threat wherever you go!'

It feels like we're two armies facing off on a battlefield, only the smallest of spaces between us. The wall is still scrawled with the graffiti – WARZONE. Maybe it always had to be this way.

Behind us the rest of the mob catches up, but stops when they see the stand-off. Now we're pinned between them.

**Keisha**

Zero pushes his way to the front of our group.

'We don't know why we were sent here,' he says. 'We're children without a home. *You* decided we were evil. *You* never gave us a chance. *You* never gave our parents a chance. But *we've* decided we can be more than what you expect of us.'

The Hag snarls, bearing her teeth like a wild thing, but the others around her don't look quite so sure. He's grown quickly, but his wide golden eyes tell a different story. He is still a child.

Zero stands his ground, holding out his palms to try and calm them. Something flares up in my chest and descends through my body, burning hot like an ember. At first I think it's hatred. Hatred for these people, for Midwich Tower, for Mr Arnopp, for everything that has happened to us.

It's only when I look at Zero that I realise it isn't hatred at all. It's love. I have never loved him until this moment.

'You don't have to do this,' he says. 'Just let us leave. Let us live.'

The people begin to mutter to each other, like his words are actually being heard. Some even begin to lower their weapons. The Hag casts her eyes around, growing feral with rage.

Zero, seeing the effect he's having, takes the opportunity to turn and beckon us forward.

The Hag moves quicker than seems possible. She clears the space between them and something glints in her hand. I cry out, but it's too late.

Blood blossoms under Zero's jacket where the knife blade sinks. A fizzing spear hisses past me from the girls and the Hag throws herself backwards like something has actually struck her. The *crack* of her skull hitting the floor brings the mob back to life. They charge for us.

I drop down beside Zero and press my hands into his side. A battle swirls around us. His blood stains the floor. It's hard to tell, but the wound doesn't look too big. That doesn't stop blood from trickling through the gaps in my fingers.

'It's all right,' I say. His whole body trembles.

His eyes meet mine and he smiles weakly. 'Thanks, Mum.'

I look up to see Olivia shoving Nostrils against the wall, my parents dodging swings from a rolling pin, the girls summoning the last of their strength to send attackers wheeling away. The exit is so close.

'Go!' shouts Maida's dad, grappling with a man twice his size.

There's no time to say goodbye to my parents. They catch my eye and throw their heads toward the door, before grabbing someone who's making a lunge for Maida. It might be the last time I ever see them.

We form a rough huddle, the girls bristling as I lift

340

Zero up onto his feet, not for the first time this terrible night. He hisses in pain, but he can walk. Hands grab and snatch at us as we hurry for the door. Louise Krawczyk springs up and claws at me, and I swing an elbow, catching her nose with a sickening crunch. She doesn't come back at me after that.

Someone catches Morris's foot and he trips, the car keys flying out of his hand and sliding across the floor. He scrabbles after them, but someone else grabs them first.

It's Tubs. He looks at the mob, half of them paralysed by the Children's waning influence and half of them trying to kill our families. He doesn't know what will happen to him if he chooses the wrong side. But he throws the keys to Morris and hustles us out the door.

A small crowd is too busy gathered around Tyrone's body on the ground to notice us stagger into the freezing night. Sirens are nearing the tower.

Zero is oozing blood but I force him to run. When Morris reaches the car he jumps inside and starts the engine, a belch of exhaust pouring into the night. I can just see the police and ambulance lights in the distance. Olivia, Maida, and the girls pile in and slam the doors shut. The suspension groans. I jump into the front seat, pulling Zero into my lap, and look across at Morris.

'Ready?' he says.

I nod. 'Ready.'

A pair of police cars skids into the car park. Morris accelerates and wrenches the wheel to take us over the kerb. The police manoeuvre to follow. Zero sits up to peer behind us, and I feel the inexorable energy well up

341

inside him. I can't help but smile. Whatever else he is or isn't, he *is* a fighter – but that's not a bad thing to be in this life. The police cars lose control, one of them hitting a garden wall and blocking the other, giving us a chance to pull away.

'Look,' says Zero dreamily.

There are parakeets swooping alongside the car, rising and dipping, an honour guard to see us on our way.

'Next stop: Cornwall,' says Morris.

We have no idea what we'll find there. The future is uncertain. But it's all we have to live for.

I rest my fingers on Morris's hand and squeeze. He glances at me with a smile, both our hands shifting the gear, and then he puts his foot down.

The engine growls and we speed away from Midwich Tower.

# Epilogue

The spark in his mind lifts him out of a dream.

When he opens his eyes he can hardly focus. Faces hover above him, swaying sleepily with the movement of the car. He is spread across their laps. Pain throbs in his side, his clothes wet, the smell of copper strong in his nostrils. It makes him remember the things he has done, and the power inside him stirs. He grits his teeth and swallows it down.

A hand strokes his hair. 'It's okay.'

'We're nearly there now,' says somebody from the front.

The sun is rising. He closes his eyes.

The spark flares, as if catching on kindling. It isn't his own power. It feels like a loose circuit inside his brain has finally been connected, a part of him that was missing flickering into life.

There is somebody else inside his mind.

'Do you feel that?' he says.

'We feel it.'

He gathers his energy and tries to send a message, a question, hoping the strain won't break the fragile

343

connection. No answer comes, but the feeling grows stronger as they drive.

'I'm going to need a new name,' says Zero.

# Acknowledgements

There are *a lot* of people without whom I'd have made a complete mess of this book.

First of all, I have to thank all the amazing women who have worked with me on this project, as well as the women I have met in the 'real world' and on Twitter who, through their kindness, bravery, and patience have opened my eyes about the world, and inspired me to write this book.

Thanks to Ella, my agent, whose constant support and shrewd editorial eye never fails to push my writing to the next level. She's the best.

Thanks to Sarah, my editor, who once again didn't think twice about taking on such a difficult book and instantly *got it*. This book is immeasurably better for her work on it.

Thanks to Jack, for a cover design and concept that's not only perfect, but also completely bonkers, and emblematic of the belief and support of the amazing Atom Books team. Thank you, Olivia, Stephie, Sam and everyone.

Thanks to Hannah, my girlfriend, for reading an early draft, for supporting my writing even when it makes me an unbearable grump, and for making my life better.

Thanks to Junaid for his guidance on Islamic practice, and thanks to Sam for her invaluable advice about all grisly things pregnancy and child birth.

Thanks to Dickens, for being fluffy.

Thanks to all the amazing book people in the YA community and beyond who have accepted me and put up with my relentless moaning on Twitter. I'm reluctant to name anybody individually as there are simply too many, but particular thanks must go to Michelle Toy, a fiercely loyal advocate of my debut book.

Thanks to all my incredible friends and family, except for two unnamed people who are so desperate to make it into my acknowledgements I feel like I'm doing them a favour merely by specifically excluding them.

And thanks, of course, to John Wyndham.